Family Secrets

KEIKO PALMER

FAMILY SECRETS
Copyright © 2019 **Keiko Palmer**

All rights reserved. No part of this book may be used or reproduced by any means, graphic, electronic, or mechanical, including photocopying, recording, taping or by information storage and retrieval system without the written permission of the author except in the case of brief quotations embodied in critical articles and reviews.

Stratton Press Publishing
831 N Tatnall Street Suite M #188,
Wilmington, DE 19801
www.stratton-press.com
1-888-323-7009

Because of the dynamic nature of the Internet, any web addresses or links contained in this book may have changed since publication and may no longer be valid. The views expressed in the work are solely those of the author and do not necessarily reflect the views of the publisher, and the publisher hereby disclaims any responsibility for them.

ISBN (Paperback): 978-1-64345-645-4
ISBN (Ebook): 978-1-64345-800-7

Printed in the United States of America

Acknowledgments

My dear friends, who eagerly await my novel each time, who often encourage me to write more, and do not mind critiquing:

Beverley Hescock, Liliane Arens,
Kay Dalton, Amy Brock (helped with Hawaiian language),
Etsuko Crissey (journalist), Michiko Lewis,
Jane Theodore, Etsuko Norman,
my family, and dear friends in Japan.

Contents

Prologue 7
Chapter 1: Manzanar 11
Chapter 2: John Richardson 21
Chapter 3: Unforgivable Acts 31
Chapter 4: Susanna Mendosa 40
Chapter 5: My Hobby 53
Chapter 6: Carbon Dioxide 60
Chapter 7: Disownment 65
Chapter 8: Bruce Hudson 74
Chapter 9: Betrayal 85
Chapter 10: A Secret 93
Chapter 11: Paris 103
Chapter 12: Alice and Nina 114
Chapter 13: Eric Johnson 124
Chapter 14: Grandmother 135

Chapter 15: Masao Okuma and Yoshiko Shō 144

Chapter 16: Okinawa 155

Chapter 17: General Palmer 164

Chapter 18: Confession 173

Chapter 19: Love at First Sight 182

Chapter 20: Mark Nakaya 192

Chapter 21: A Mysterious Fire 203

Chapter 22: Suspicion 214

Chapter 23: Investigation 225

Chapter 24: Reconciliation..235

Chapter 25: Confrontation 244

Chapter 26: Class Reunion..253

Chapter 27: The Last Secret..264

Epilogue...275

Prologue

When the aircraft was still at thirty-five thousand feet in the air, the control tower in Honolulu relayed an urgent message to the cockpit, no other details, but Captain Richardson must return to Honolulu as soon as possible. The message did not mean that I must turn the aircraft around and fly back to Honolulu.

I promised my new copilot and navigator who were assigned to my flight today to demonstrate my smooth landing. They were both eager to witness it because they heard about the soft landing of Captain Richardson.

Boasting is not my cup of tea, but I can land a giant aircraft without any landing commotion. It could be a feathery touchdown, so to speak. The passengers would not even know that they were already on the ground.

When I was young, my father made me practice for hours and hours on his Cessna, and I eventually mastered the skills. I could demonstrate it, but I could not teach others how to do it. I used my instinct.

My touchdown is always meticulously smooth because I calculate the speed and the length of landing space. After touching down, I gradually pull the brake gear, and then the aircraft comes to gradual halt without any commotion.

Five or six years ago, I was promoted to captain, with an accredited certificate…fulfilling the requirement of two thousand flying hours, making Category One on my physical examination, and passing the nonchemical dependency test.

The job requirement is similar with my previous job as first officer or copilot. However, the commander of aircraft has the upmost responsibility on delivering the lives of the passengers. Therefore, I faithfully follow the air traffic regulations and the traffic controller's live instructions.

The flight manual and checklist of the flight instruments are well recorded in my head, but I still reread whenever I have time. The checklist report from the maintenance department on my assigned aircraft is trustworthy, but I still go under the aircraft to check the fuel tank knob, cargo doors, engines, and other minute areas to be safe, so I always arrive much earlier than the other crew.

The descending mode is now registered on the flight instruments. The landing gear is shifted to the direction toward the Los Angeles International Airport, known as Tom Bradley Airport. In 1984, during the Summer Olympic Games in Los Angeles, the terminal was named in honor of Tom Bradley, who was the first African American and the longest-serving (1973–1993) mayor of Los Angeles.

An immediate landing order came from the control tower. It was at noon in the Pacific Time Zone. The copilot made an announcement for landing over the intercom.

After my usual smooth landing of the B767-400, I glanced at both copilot and navigator, and gave them a smile. Their eyes were wide-open, as though they just had an unbelievable experience. They both nodded several times to affirm their approval of my skills.

After I gathered up my belongings in a hurry and signed the necessary arrival papers, I asked both copilot and navigator to complete the rest—recording the last reading on the flight instruments and tidying up the cockpit.

Some passengers in front of me praised how smooth the landing was. With my satisfying smile, I followed them to the arrival gate. The concourse was crowded, but everybody seemed to be sailing smoothly, as though they were in a silent movie.

After several unsuccessful calls to my mother, I walked toward the operation center with my overnight crew bag. I tried to call my father on his cell, but no answer.

My coded key opened the door to the operation center. This large facility houses the aviation technicians, troubleshooters, programmers, dispatchers, and trainers.

Some were watching a wide screen on the wall that showed arrival or departure of fleet. Some were talking on the phone. Some were typing on the keyboard with headphones on. Some uniformed crew were discussing something with technicians.

I am to see Mr. Minoru Nakaya, who oversees dispatching pilots. I need my replacement for tomorrow's flight and want to find an earliest flight back to Honolulu.

As soon as he saw me, he stood up and walked toward the counter where I stood. He looked pale but wore a familiar smile.

His large and tall frame reminds me of a Hawaiian native rather than of a Japanese descent. He knows all the pilots who are based in Los Angeles, as well as many other pilots like me who fly the regular scheduled flights to Los Angeles.

Mr. Nakaya is one of the top-notch dispatchers in the airline industry. His scheduling is so thorough that the FAA requirement such as the eighty-five-hour flying time per month for each pilot is meticulously calculated into the monthly schedule. Moreover, in an emergency case like mine, he always has some standby pilots who are within his reach on a short notice. I have known him since I started flying between Honolulu and Los Angeles as a first officer and now as a captain.

"I gave your father the same message you got. He will be here soon and fly back with you."

"Thank you. I am glad he is coming with me. You look pale. Are you all right?"

"I had a touch of cold and sore throat, but I am getting much better."

"Take care."

He nodded and went back to his desk and brought some papers for me to sign. "I already found a sub for you. This is just a permission form for the sub to fly your scheduled flight tomorrow."

I signed several papers and gave them back to him.

"Now, I must find a flight back to Honolulu for you and your father. John is on the way. You can sit there and wait." He gestured to the sofa at the corner of the office. I knew it would take at least one hour for my father to be here, so I decided to sit on the sofa to wait.

Tonight, I was supposed to stay overnight at my father's condominium here in Los Angeles and take him out to celebrate his upcoming retirement.

Nevertheless, my ulterior motive was to tell him my recent discovery—about the secrets of my mother and her family that were sealed for the longest time since she was born.

After Mr. Okuma unveiled my mother's birth secret to me during my visit to Okinawa, he strongly suggested that my mother must know her birth secret before something would happen to her mother. Most importantly, they must reconcile since they have not seen each other for almost forty years.

However, I lost the courage when I came home and saw her. I needed my father's help. He might be shocked to learn her birth secret just as I was. Nevertheless, as he is a great husband to my mother, I was certain that he could help me unveil the secret.

Now, because of this urgent message, I do not know how to get my father's help. I could unveil my mother's family secrets to him during this long flight back to Honolulu, but they are so personal that I do not want any passenger to eavesdrop on us. So I decided not to think about it now. Instead, I closed my eyes and started thinking about my deceased grandparents who used to live in Gardena.

Chapter 1

MANZANAR

Mr. Minoru Nakaya was my father's high school classmate from Gardena, one of the cities surrounding Los Angeles. He and my father were born in the same year as next-door neighbors and grew up together like brothers until the age of eighteen.

My grandparents, Tom and Patricia Richardson, came from New York right after college. They started their teaching careers in Gardena years before WWII. My grandfather taught history in high school and grandmother taught in elementary school.

They taught at the neighborhood schools where many Japanese Nisei (American-born) children enrolled. They really liked the way Japanese children were disciplined or taught by their parents—behave well, be studious, and mind the elders and teachers. The children were eager to learn, and the parents were deeply interested in their education, hoping that the education could guarantee their children a promising future.

The teachers, especially the Richardsons, were respected and trusted by the Japanese parents and students in their neighborhood. The Richardsons fell utterly in love with the Japanese students who minded them so well. They did not want to move anywhere else, so they remained in Gardena to teach.

Historically, Gardena had many strawberry farms so that it was known as Berryland. Japanese immigrants were a key part of Gardena's farm community during the early years. The Japanese strawberry pickers worked and settled in the Gardena's farmland.

When the population of Metro Los Angeles started growing outward, the farm owners sold their farmlands to the housing developers and moved farther away to the countryside, but many Japanese farm workers remained in Gardena and made Gardena their hometown.

The Japanese immigrants in Gardena worked very hard, and their various businesses, including dry cleaners, managing small farms of fresh vegetables, grocery stores, and restaurants, thrived successfully before World War II.

Some worked as domestic helpers and gardeners. Whatever their occupations were, the Japanese, being immigrants to America, took them very seriously and worked very hard. They nurtured their American-born children and provided the foundation of their future.

The Japanese who immigrated to America were called Issei (Japanese-born) immigrants. They did not know much English, so they spoke Japanese in their Gardena community. Naturally, their Nisei (American-born) children had to speak Japanese with the Issei parents at home.

My grandparents insisted that their Nisei neighbors speak proper English because they were American citizens. In other words, they did not allow them to speak pidgin English at school or in the neighborhood. As a result, the Nisei children in the neighborhood spoke proper English. The Richardsons were respected for that.

Living in Gardena made the Japanese families continuously comfortable until their properties and privileges were taken away unlawfully by the US government during World War II.

When Pearl Harbor was attacked on December 7, 1941, President Franklin D. Roosevelt signed Executive Order 9066, which caused the forceful relocation of over 120,000 Japanese Issei and American-born Nisei to ten internment camps throughout the United States. Two thirds of the internees were recorded as American-born citizens.

Family Secrets

My grandparents were outraged when they saw soldiers rounding up innocent Japanese neighbors, including their students, and packing them like cattle into the covered military trucks.

Before the Nakayas' departure, the Richardsons promised that they would protect their house until their return. Mr. and Mrs. Nakaya and their son—Minoru's older brother—were forcibly shoved into a covered truck. The three of them had only one suitcase among them, and their destination was unknown.

Later, the Richardsons learned the Nakayas were sent to the internment camp called Manzanar, known as Apple Orchard in English, which was located 230 miles northeast of Los Angeles. They left in the summer of 1942 and came back in the fall of 1945. Almost 90 percent of Japanese descendants in Los Angeles were uprooted and sent to Manzanar, California. In June 1942, the record showed the Manzanar camp housed over 10,000 Japanese Issei and Nisei.

The weather at Manzanar was extreme. In the summer, the heat was unbearable on the desert floor of Owens Valley. Sometimes the temperature reached over one hundred degrees. In the winter, the cold wind blew so hard that rocks and sand were tossed around the tar paper–covered barracks; there were occasional snows, and the cold weather was so severe that the inadequate heating system was useless. The Nakayas lost their son (Minoru's brother) to pneumonia during the extremely cold winter.

The forcible huddling of the Japanese neighbors saddened the Richardsons, so they wrote several protesting letters to the president. Their letters were forwarded to the FBI instead. Consequently, they were listed as Japanese sympathizers.

I have seen some faded pictures of my grandparents. They dressed simple. With my grandmother's gentle eyes, she resembled somewhat my father. Her hair was long and lighter. She was rather short. My grandfather was tall and slender. Their eyes were gentle, and smiles were warm.

The mistreatment of Japanese descendants was much like Hitler's persecution of the Jews in Europe. The Japanese were not slaughtered like the Jews, but they lost their homes, properties, and businesses, just as the Jews lost everything before they were sent to the concentration camps. The emotional turmoil of Jews and Japanese were utterly similar.

The Nisei internees' resentments toward their birth country and psychological damages during the internment might be irreparable, even though some compensatory payments by the US government were made to the surviving internees in the 1980s.

The unhappy, detestable memories of the internment would probably remain as scars on their hearts to the end. Many nonfiction books or novels were written about their unforgivable and unforgettable experiences. Some movies were made based on their internment experiences as well.

According to the Manzanar document, about 150 internees died in Manzanar. Some were cremated and some were buried in the desert between 1942 and 1945. After twenty years, the surviving internees had Manzanar registered as a national historic site. It was approved in the 1970s.

Now visitors can see a replica of the camp, including the barracks, communal kitchens, toilets, and small living units for families. The watchtower had also been reconstructed.

Over the years, many surviving internees visited Manzanar with their descendants to reminisce about their past, but now there were very few internees left.

Immediately after the war, some Japanese Issei were enticed to leave the US soil to live in Japan. It was believed to be a form of deportation. The law at that time prohibited all Japanese Issei immigrants from becoming American citizens. Some young Nisei children who were American citizens did not have any choice but to leave their birth country to live with their parents in Japan. Later, those children faced citizenship problems in Japan. They, therefore, voluntarily came back to the United States as Kibei (reentering the USA as American citizens).

During World War II, some Nisei, such as Tokyo Roses, were stranded in Japan after the Pearl Harbor attack. An executive order lasting from 1941 through 1945 declared that no Japanese or Japanese descendants permitted to enter US soil. About twenty Tokyo Roses were stranded and forced to broadcast Japanese propaganda to undermine US troops' morale: the propaganda messages said that their wives were cheating on them at home while they were fighting, or they were losing the war badly, so go home and be with their families. The messages were followed by some nostalgic or familiar tune of American music.

After the war, Tokyo Roses and other Niseis who worked for the Japanese government were afraid of being convicted of treason by their birth country. They, therefore, renounced their American citizenships and remained in Japan.

However, one Tokyo Rose refused to renounce her US citizenship. She was brought to the USA to be convicted of treason. She was imprisoned for years until President Gerald Ford pardoned her in 1977.

When the Nakayas came home from Manzanar in 1945, they could not believe how the Richardsons had kept their house intact. They were so thankful that they could hardly voice their gratitude; instead, they embraced the Richardsons and cried openly.

The Nakayas remembered how their laundry business was sold for so little money to a bargain hunter before the internment. Therefore, they were pessimistic about their own home, but the Richardsons somehow protected the house from the law, looters, and bargain hunters during their internment. The Nakayas could not speak English very well to thank them, but the Richardsons understood how grateful they were.

When the internment camps were closed in 1945, some internees wanted to remain in the camps because they had no place to go. They had lost all their belongings when they were uprooted. They had nothing including their legal rights. They had nowhere to go. Therefore, they wanted to remain in the camps that they had called home for the past several years. No one, however, could remain in the camps. They were officially closed. Some internees used their only assets—the wages they earned during the internment—to start their new lives. Some internees went back to the place where they used to live, hoping to recoup some of their remaining properties or something.

The Nakayas said in tears in their broken English, "We lucky. You our neighbors, friends. Never forget your kindness until we die."

"I am sorry that the United States mistreated you and disappointed you. We, Americans, especially, the government should make an official apology to each one of you. At the same time, the government should make some monetary compensation for your sufferings and for the unlawful loss of your properties. It may not be now, but later American citizens and the government should realize we violated your human rights. In the meantime, we personally apologize to you on behalf of this country," said Mr. Richardson who taught history in high school.

"You no need to apologize. Japanese attack the Pearl Harbor first. Japanese were no good to America. You no need to apologize. We very thank you for what you did for us," said Mr. Nakaya.

During the first month of their return, the Richardsons invited the Nakayas to eat with them. Mrs. Nakaya and Mrs. Richardson cooked together. At the dinner table, they talked nonstop in broken English, describing what kind of living conditions they had in Manzanar. In tears, they explained how they lost their son during the cold winter.

The Richardsons helped the Nakayas reestablish their dry-cleaning business in the neighborhood. However, a year later, when the government expanded the highway near their business, they offered the Nakayas almost triple value on their property.

So Mr. Nakaya took that money to purchase a corner lot in Beverly Hills and built a dry-cleaning business. Minoru and John were born a year after the business opened.

Since his business was the only dry-cleaning business in Beverley Hills, it became almost an overnight success. He was able to hire some workers. Whenever the store became busy, Mr. Nakaya slept in the store to keep up with the demand, instead of commuting the long way home to Gardena.

Mrs. Nakaya did not think she could have any more children after the death of her first child, but she became pregnant and bore Minoru.

For years, the Richardsons gave up on having a child, but Mrs. Richardson became pregnant as well. She bore John at the age of forty-one. John was born four months after Minoru was born.

The new mother, Mrs. Richardson, always consulted with Mrs. Nakaya…how to feed a baby, how to change diapers, and some other issues about babies in general. She valued Mrs. Nakaya's experience.

As Mrs. Nakaya had to stay home with her baby instead of helping her husband at the store, she volunteered to keep John with Minoru so that Mrs. Richardson could return to her teaching. Mrs. Richardson was very grateful.

John and Minoru learned Japanese from Mrs. Nakaya while they were under her care. They spoke Japanese to each other while growing up.

John felt as if he belonged to both the Nakayas and the Richardsons. Minoru probably felt the same. They visited each other's houses without knocking on the doors and did science projects or homework assignments at each other's house.

On the weekends, they invited friends to spend a night at Minoru's house or John's house. Playing Japanese Go was very popular among boys in the neighborhood. There were no electronic games, just board games at that time.

Minoru spoke English with the Richardsons, and John spoke Japanese with the Nakayas. John's Japanese was as good as Minoru's. Even now, they feel comfortable speaking Japanese whenever they are together. Japanese is rather John's native tongue because of Mrs. Nakaya's care.

One day in early January, the Richter scale 6.5 earthquake damaged many homes in the Los Angeles area. It happened in the middle of the night when John was spending a night in Minoru's house. The Nakayas' house was intact, but John and the Nakayas heard a loud crashing sound nearby. The noise was so loud that neighbors came out to see where the noise came from. Someone called the police.

They saw the Richardsons' roof caved into the middle of the master bedroom upstairs where Tom and Patricia Richardson were sleeping. The entire house was in shambles. When the rescue team pulled them out of the wreckage, they both were already dead.

John cried so loudly that the neighbors kept hugging him and crying with him. John kept saying that his parents were the best kind of parents. How in the world could God kill them like that! His face was flooded with tears. Mrs. Nakaya embraced him and let him cry on her shoulder as though he was still a toddler. He was sixteen years old.

At the funeral of Tom and Patricia Richardson, hundreds of neighbors, friends, and students packed the funeral home; in addition, more neighbors were standing outside until the funeral service was over. John looked distraught, and it seemed his tears were dried out, but his puffy eyes drew everybody's sympathy.

During the funeral service, Mrs. Nakaya held John's hand and kept wiping her eyes with her handkerchief. Minoru and Mr. Nakaya sat beside them with their heads down.

John did not have any relatives in the Los Angeles area. His father's cousin, the only known relative, lived in New York. The lawyer called the cousin to see if John could live with him, but the cousin refused to take him in. The lawyer did not know what to do with John's guardianship.

Minoru's parents, however, earnestly wanted to become John's guardians until John turned eighteen. The lawyer knew if no one took him in, he had to hand John to the state since he was a minor. In other words, he would become a recipient of the state-operated foster care agency.

The lawyer opened a trust fund for John by putting the entire college fund that was saved by John's parents, the life insurance money, and later the money from the sale of the property would be added.

For the guardians, the monthly living expense for John including his monthly allowance was calculated. Mr. and Mrs. Nakaya did not want the money, but the lawyer said in Japanese, "It is a legal procedure that I have to follow until John becomes eighteen. A monthly check will be sent to you from my office. Thank you for being John's guardians. If you have any questions, don't hesitate to call me."

He gave them his business card with the signed contract paper for the guardianship. Then he turned to John and said, "John, whenever you want to know anything about your trust fund, you can contact me in my office. Remember when you become eighteen and are ready to go to college, I will set up your bank account so you can transfer your trust fund yourself. I am glad your father had me as his lawyer before this tragedy. You may not know it, but your father was my best high school teacher ever, and I really admired him. Because of him, I am becoming somebody."

After John signed several pages of his trust fund account, the lawyer gave him a thick booklet with his business card attached. He shook John's hand firmly as though he was expressing his condolences for his parents' deaths.

When John moved into the Nakayas' home, everybody tried to speak English for John so he should feel at home. However, John told them that he rather felt comfortable conversing in Japanese. Minoru liked the idea of having his friend, John in his house. He acted as though he gained a younger brother for life.

A month later, John saw his house being demolished by a wrecker company. Watching from the window of the Nakayas' two-story house, his heart actually ached with a harsh reality that made him realize his parents were no longer alive to protect him. He wiped his tears several times and stared obliviously at the crane and bulldozer for the longest time.

Now everything was gone: his parents, the house, and his fond memories of his childhood. He regretted that he did not tell his parents often enough how much he loved them.

All the memories of his parents were happy ones. Every time John glanced at the bare land from the window, he could picture the house, and his parents who were working in the yard, standing at the front door, and cooking in the kitchen. As he wished to see them again, his face was flooded with tears.

Chapter 2

JOHN RICHARDSON

While living with the Nakayas, John and Minoru did many things together just as brothers would do. Minoru's father taught them judo (martial arts) and practiced with the teenagers in the yard whenever he had the time.

He also played the game of Go with them. As the teenagers had already learned Go while they were growing up, they became skillful. The father was defeated from time to time.

Go is a strategic board game for two players that originated in China 2,500 years ago. The Japanese later mastered the game. It became a courtyard game for the warriors in the twelfth century, and the game became known in Japanese as Igo or Go.

It is noted in a written record: an elaborate wooden block table used by two warriors sitting on the floor in the Japanese manner. The tabletop is engraved with horizontal and vertical lines, black and white polished stones are used to play the game. The strategy is to expand one's own territories by conquering the opponent's territories, just as the feudal warriors did in real life. The strategy is somewhat similar to chess. Go, however, is much more complex and a mind-stimulating game.

Currently, Go is synonymous with Japan. It is also known as a male chauvinistic board game in Japanese society. Japanese women are prohibited from playing Go. In most Japanese newspapers, strategy plans of Go are described in daily column, just as word puzzles appear in daily column of American newspapers.

Minoru's father also taught the boys how to manage the dry-cleaning business. On the weekends and during the summer breaks, they both were hired to deliver the dry-cleaned clothes to the Beverly Hills customers on a bicycle. At the same time, they collected clothes that needed to be dry-cleaned.

Occasionally, Minoru's parents took the teenagers to the nearby beaches or mountains. The teenagers enjoyed each other's company wherever they went.

Minoru always protected John just as an older brother should do for a younger brother. Mostly he protected John from those bully Japanese boys who thought John was in the wrong school because of his race. When they called John a derogatory name for White, Minoru quickly blasted them off verbally to scare them. If they insisted on insulting John, Minoru was ready to use judo. Because of Minoru's protection, John truly felt a kinship.

Minoru and John mastered judo with the help of the father. They both acquired a black belt by competing in tournaments. Mr. Nakaya was an expert on judo, but he emphasized that judo is to defend or protect oneself from physical harm. While John was living with them, he learned some basic Japanese values as well: to be humble, to be compassionate, to be honest, and to be respectful.

The teenagers shared a large basement that was used as a playroom or storage room before. John's bed was brought in, so was Minoru's. A long rectangular table with four chairs was placed in the middle of the room between the beds. One big bookshelf was placed against the corner wall next to the closet.

The boys often stayed in the room to study, play games, or talk a lot about their future, education, political issues, and girls. When their friends came to play Go or other board games, they stayed up late without making noises. Mrs. Nakaya made plenty of cookies and a gallon of iced tea for the teenagers. She often reminded them in English—no alcohol, no drugs, and no cigarettes. Everybody nodded.

Family Secrets

From time to time, however, Minoru and John became curious about the anatomy of girls. They explored human anatomy through some erotic magazines that were acquired from their friends. They secretly shared them in their bedroom.

One day, when Mrs. Nakaya was cleaning up their room, she found some erotic magazines in the closet. She was shocked to see the girls' indecent nude pictures and lovemaking scenes in the magazines, so she quickly gave the magazines to Mr. Nakaya, hoping he should do something to stop it.

When Minoru and John came home from school, Mr. Nakaya made them sit at the dining table and spoke in Japanese. "Minoru and John, your mother wants you to take those filthy magazines from her house. Would you take them outside and tear them up and throw them in the trash bin in front of your mother?"

John and Minoru looked at each other. Minoru opened his mouth.

"Mom, those magazines don't belong to us. We borrowed them from a friend. Can we return them to the owner? We cannot throw them away. He will be very angry. We will return them tomorrow. We promise."

Mrs. Nakaya did not know what to say and turned to her husband.

"I just don't want to see this kind of dirty magazines in my house anymore. You should not allow them to bring them again."

"Honey, they will return them tomorrow. I will make sure they will not bring such filthy magazines to this house anymore. Right? Boys?"

"Yes, sir. We won't bring such magazines to this house anymore."

Mrs. Nakaya nodded in silence and disappeared into the kitchen.

After the mother left, Mr. Nakaya smiled and whispered, "Did you learn anything from the magazines?"

"Yes, sir. John and I learned a lot about girls."

"Good."

Those erotic magazines were returned, but some more magazines came into their possession. This time, they found a secret space between the bookshelf and the wall. There was enough space for several magazines at a time. No one could find them unless they happened to move the heavy bookshelf. Those contrabands were never discovered by Minoru's mother after that.

Whenever John and Minoru reminisce about the contrabands, even to this day, they could not stop laughing by saying how great time they had together as teenagers.

At the age of eighteen, Minoru and John both graduated from high school. John Richardson was accepted at MIT. The lawyer opened the bank accounts in Boston—deposited most of the trust fund to a savings account and enough money to a checking account so he can write checks for tuition, dorm fees, books, and get some spending money.

He learned how to write checks and balance the statement each month. He also learned how to transfer the money from savings account to checking account if he needed. The money in the savings account was substantial, more than enough for four years of tuition and dorm fees.

Minoru chose to attend a local college so he could help his parents with the family business. Their dry-cleaning business was prosperous and busy.

For John's departure to Boston, the Nakayas and Minoru were at the airport. They all looked somber and poignant, especially Minoru. He felt as though he was sending a helpless little brother to the unknown world and he could no longer protect him as an older brother.

John thanked them for what they had done for him for years. John really felt they were the only family he had in this world. "Don't catch a cold. I was told Boston is a cold place. Make sure to wear something warm to cover your shoulders before you go to bed. Bundle up in the winter. Come home whenever you can. I will send you your favorite sesame seed cookies often. Write us in English.

Minoru will read for us. Take care and study hard," Mrs. Nakaya said in Japanese with her teary eyes.

John nodded several times and embraced Mrs. Nakaya.

"Remember, if you need to use judo to protect yourself from any physical harm, use it. Eat well and take good care of yourself. Hope to see you soon. For the summer, I would like to hire you at the store. So come home."

Mr. Nakaya shook John's hand and embraced him at the same time. Minoru did not say anything but held John's hand tightly. His eyes were red and moist. Mrs. Nakaya was wiping her eyes with her handkerchief.

John's heart felt empty and sad leaving the only family he had and the only town he knew. He was born in Gardena and grew up in Gardena—never been out of state.

He started walking toward the departure gate, and they waved vigorously. When John turned and waved back, his tears blocked the view of his family.

After wiping off his tears with the back of his hand several times, he followed the passengers to his seat. It was his first airplane ride. He buckled the seat belt and looked out the window obliviously for a while. The tarmac outside looked so endless that he felt awfully lonely again, so he pulled the window shade down and closed his eyes to sleep.

When he woke up, a stewardess brought a tray of dinner with a cup of tea. The flight was half full. When he heard the propellers, he remembered the model airplane with the jet engines he assembled. That airplane model was the only one survived without any scratches in the earthquake. Minoru promised to keep it safely until John's graduation or his return. He knew that flying the modern airplanes with four engines was John's dream.

In the Boston Airport, he retrieved two bags and rode a taxi to the assigned dorm on MIT campus in Cambridge. The room had two beds, and each study desk was against the wall. His roommate seemed to be very nice, but John was somewhat quiet, so he left John alone.

John could speak Japanese but never learned how to write Japanese characters. Mr. and Mrs. Nakaya did not know how to write in English much, so Minoru wrote John for them in English. John wrote Minoru in English to let his parents know how he was adjusting in the unfamiliar place. He also wrote how much he missed them and especially missed Mrs. Nakaya's Japanese cooking. Mrs. Nakaya sent John's favorite sesame seed cookies almost every month.

On his first Christmas in Boston, John decided to stay in school. He just wanted to experience being alone without friends and family. Staying alone in the dorm was an awful mistake. He terribly missed Minoru and the Nakayas as well as his parents, who were no longer reachable. He thought he could combat the loneliness alone, but it was a mistake. He desperately wanted to talk to someone. John made a long-distance call by putting many dimes in the machine in the phone booth.

"Hello, Minoru. How is everything in Gardena? How are your parents?"

"Hello. John, are you all right? Where are you? We thought you were coming home for Christmas."

"I am sorry, but one of my classmates invited me to stay in Boston. I am having Christmas dinner with them. Say hello to your parents. Please thank your mom for the sesame seed cookies for Christmas. I just want to say Merry Christmas to everybody. I will write you soon."

"Okay, I'll tell Mom and Dad you called. Have a nice Christmas dinner with your friend. Merry Christmas, John."

"Merry Christmas, Minoru."

John's voice almost quivered, but he held his lips tightly. John sniffed and wiped his eyes after hanging up the phone. The hallway of the dorm was quiet. It was the loneliest and saddest Christmas he had ever spent in his entire life.

There were almost no students left, and the cafeteria was closed for the Christmas holiday. Some soft drinks and ready-to-eat food such as crackers, sesame seed cookies, and other junk foods were his Christmas dinner.

The campus security officer was surprised to see John in the dorm, but he smiled gently without asking any questions. During the two weeks of the Christmas break, John remained in his room most of the time and read tons of books.

He reminisced a lot about his parents—Christmas holidays with them—and wished to see them again. Remembering the very last Christmas with his parents before their passing made him wipe his eyes. It was almost three years ago, but it seemed like yesterday—being showered with many gifts such as nice trousers, casual shirts, dress shirts, tennis shoes, leather shoes, and a fashionable jacket teenager would proudly wear in the winter.

At the end, they gave him a box of the large model airplane kit that he had wanted for years. It was a model of a four-jet-engine aircraft, which Boeing manufactured in the 1960s. John completed the assembly with the help of his father after Christmas.

After inspecting his son's work, his father placed it on the metal pedestal in the living room. It looked awesome.

"Dad, I would like to fly the real airplane like that as a pilot in the future."

"Son, if you keep working hard toward your dream, yes, you could fly the jumbo airplane in the future. Some people just dream about it and do not do anything to reach the dream. You must work hard and study hard to reach your dream. I would like to live long enough to see your dream come true. I hope this model airplane will remind you of your dream in the future. Take good care of the model. You did a fantastic job putting it together."

It seemed the model airplane was the only thing that survived the earthquake. All the furniture and even pots and pans were destroyed. He thought it was a miracle that the model airplane was the only one spared, therefore, he had a mystical conclusion to keep the model airplane as long as he lived.

While John was in college and in military service, Minoru kept his model airplane in his parent house for John. When John bought a house in Honolulu, Minoru shipped it safely by UPS. He too knew how precious that model airplane was for John.

When my father bought a condo in Los Angeles, he left the model airplane with my mother. Its exterior color was faded, but it was one of his most important belongings. My father did not explain it, but my mother and I knew how precious and priceless it was for him.

On that Christmas Day, John thought he was the luckiest teenager in the entire neighborhood, who received such generous and numerous Christmas gifts from his parents. When he embraced his parents, he meant to say aloud that they were the best parents and he loved them very much, but he did not say it.

If John had said the words aloud, they could have known they were loved very much by their only son, but he just embraced them and said, "Thank you." For years after that, he was remorseful.

John thought about his parents' subconscious premonition—they thought subconsciously that it should be the last Christmas with their son. Therefore, they should be very generous and give him whatever he wanted.

As they had been very frugal when he was growing up, John did not expect being showered with so many gifts including the model airplane. Therefore, John concluded his parent must have had a premonition of having their son at Christmas for the last time.

John had a lot of thinking to do while being alone on the first Christmas in college. He assured himself that he was strong enough to combat his loneliness and was able to handle being an orphan.

However, he realized no one should ever live alone. Everybody must have someone—friends, children, relatives, spouses—with whom he or she could share the abundance of love and care.

Eventually, in his sophomore year, John acclimated himself and made many friends. Everybody liked him, especially the girls. He said he was approached by many girls, and his relationships were very active. As a child, I did not understand the word *relationships*, but I figured my father was very popular among girls.

John's roommate, Richard Palmer, became his best friend. John was invited to spend every Christmas at the house of Richard's grandparents in Maine.

Richard's mother died when he was young. Because of his father's station overseas as a fighter jet pilot in the US Air Force, Richard came to live with his grandparents. However, Richard spent most of his summers with his father overseas.

John and Richard had a lot in common. They wanted to fly airplanes. They took some aviation classes together and talked about being pilots in the future. Richard told him about his father being a fighter jet pilot for years. Now he's stationed at the US Air Force Base in Tachikawa, Japan, to oversee the base as General Palmer.

During all his college years, John never went back to Gardena. He knew that he had no home or no parents in Gardena waiting for him. Going back to his hometown, Gardena, would bring only sorrow. He did not want that; rather, he wanted to treasure the wonderful memories of his parents, in a faraway place, instead. Therefore, John stayed on campus during the summer and studied aviation.

The Nakayas and Minoru came to Boston for John's graduation. They came just as his own family would do. John took them around to show the city of Boston. They ate Maine lobsters, steamed black-neck clams, and New England clam chowder. After the graduation ceremony, they visited Cape Cod to see the Kennedy Compound on Hyannis Port.

At the airport, Mrs. Nakaya said in Japanese, "I wish your parents were still alive. They would be so proud to see the smart and handsome young man you have become."

Shortly after the graduation, John and his roommate, Richard Palmer enrolled in a flying school in California. Minoru graduated from a local college and married Kim, who went to the same high school with Minoru and John. She was working at Nakaya's Laundry at Beverly Hills. Since John was in California to be trained as a fighter jet pilot at that time, he attended Minoru's wedding as his best man.

Minoru's wife, Kim, moved into the Nakayas' house. As far as John remembers, Minoru had lived in the same house since he was born. As Kim managed the laundry business with Minoru's aged parents, he decided to work for an airline industry instead of taking over his family business.

Their only son, Mark, was born shortly after their marriage. By then my father was in military and stationed in Tachikawa Air Force Base. After he married my mother, they moved to Hawaii to finish his military duty. Yes, I was born in Hawaii.

After I became a full pilot, my father moved to Los Angeles and frequented Minoru's house to eat dinner. As far as Kim was concerned, John was always Minoru's brother. Whenever I overnighted at my father's high-rise condominium in Los Angeles, I was often invited to eat dinner with them too.

While I was with them, Minoru showed me the pictures of his deceased parents and old pictures of my father, when they were teenagers.

Kim used to ask me if I were engaged or if I had any prospects. As I shrugged my shoulders, she always smiled and said, "I have someone I want you to meet. I guarantee you will both like each other. I will introduce you to this charming person soon."

Kim acted as a matchmaker. However, "soon" never came. She suffered from a pancreatic cancer and passed away very fast.

Chapter 3

UNFORGIVABLE ACTS

Mr. Nakaya came to the sofa, handed me two tickets, and said by clearing his voice, "Two first-class seats are reserved for you and your father. The flight will be leaving in one hour. John knows the flight number, so he will meet you at the departure gate. Have a safe trip." His voice was raspy.

"By the way, do you know anything about this urgent message?"

"They said someone named Mr. Yamagata called. They could not understand his English, but he sounded upset and desperate, repeating your name and 'Come back to Honolulu' in broken English. It might be something to do with your mother."

He touched his throat and continued. "I met your mother several times in Honolulu. She is such a talented, beautiful person. I attended your mother's piano concert in the park one time. What a performance! Your father always brags about her cooking, piano playing, and concert performances. John really loves her and is crazy about her. I still do not understand why they live separately. Do you know they call each other every single day?"

I nodded and said, "I know."

"If something bad happened to her, John would be devastated."

I nodded again.

"Thank you very much for arranging the seats and my replacement for tomorrow. When we find out what is going on, I will have my father call you. My dad will meet me at gate 11 in this terminal, right?"

"Correct. Gate 11. Have a safe trip. Let me know as soon as possible."

"Thank you for everything."

I shook his hand and gestured to him to take good care of his throat. He nodded with a smile. I closed the door behind me and hurried down to the departure gate. Some of my colleagues greeted me on the way to the gate.

I tried my mother on the cell phone again but no answer. I tried my mother's neighbor, her best friend, Mrs. Kitano, but no answer either. Nevertheless, I left a message for Mrs. Kitano: "This is Mary. Please get in touch with Mr. Yamagata or his wife to find out my mother's whereabouts. She might be in the hospital unconscious. In case of emergency surgery, this message should be a family consent. My father and I will be in Honolulu around 4:00 p.m."

I scrolled down my cell to find the phone number of Mr. Yamagata, our gardener, but there was no number listed on my cell. I finally got my father on his cell.

"Dad, are you closer to the airport? I will be waiting at gate 11. The next flight is in forty-five minutes. Can you make it?"

"I just parked my car. I will be there as quickly as I can."

"Okay."

I was standing at the departure gate. They made the final boarding announcement. Captain John Richardson finally appeared, out of breath; probably he ran some part of the concourse.

"It took a little longer at the security point since I was not scheduled to fly and did not have a boarding pass. The security is getting tighter even to the flight crew."

We, two pilots in uniforms hurried into the aircraft.

Whenever I thought about the security point at the airport, I could not help but think about 9/11. I could never forget where I was, on Tuesday, September 11, 2001. I was in bed at my father's condo.

My return flight to Honolulu was in the afternoon on September 11. During the attacks, most of the West Coast people were still in bed because of the three-hour time difference between East and West.

My father knocked on the door and called me urgently to watch TV. I believe it was about 6:00 a.m., Pacific Standard Time. I was in pajamas. He had a cell phone in his hand talking to someone. I sat on the sofa in the living room and watched the news on the big TV. The small TV in the kitchen was also turned on. My father brought two cups of coffee and put them on the coffee table and sat with me.

The first sight I saw was the north tower of the World Trade Center spurting the black smoke as though it was a giant chimney. I brought in my laptop and opened CNN.com at the same time. My father's laptop was on MSN.com. The airplane crashing into the north tower was broadcasted repeatedly on TV.

I wiped my eyes with the back of my hands and watched TV unbelievably as though I was watching the plot of a science-fiction movie. TV again showed an airplane crashing into the north tower and exploding. Was it a pilot's error, flying too low and inevitably crashing into the building? Was it an accident?

While we were watching, within twenty minutes, the second airplane crashed into the south tower and exploded. Two accidents in a series? No, those are not accidents. No, it must be something else, intentional.

I was wide-awake. We were all ears and eyes. The CNN commentators immediately announced those airplanes were hijacked by terrorists who were affiliated members of Al-Qaeda. They were known as suicidal attackers. CNN spearheaded the worldwide broadcast.

The terrorist attacks on the World Trade Center seemed to be declaring war against the USA, just as Japan declared war by bombing Pearl Harbor. This time, the name of the attacking country was not announced. Which country was responsible?

The United States government and President George Bush were left defenseless without any visible enemies. The US military soldiers were ready to defend their country, but they did not know where the enemies were, or which country was behind these attacks.

All the attackers had already perished with the innocent onboard passengers. They left nothing but their calling cards, as suicidal terrorists affiliated with Al-Qaeda, known as Islamic extremists. That was all the world knew—no enemy country.

The world was overwhelmingly angry at the Al-Qaeda's unforgivable acts and cried for the USA. Their attacks were described as hateful, hideous, appalling, atrocious, vicious, despicable, and unforgivable.

I saw the confusion, agony, and tears on people's faces on the TV screen. The crowd tried to escape from the immediate danger area of the Twin Towers. They were running without looking back. Some people on the ground did not know what was going on high up in the giant buildings but intuitively figured out that the danger was coming their way, so they just ran and ran. We watched the chaotic scenes on TV—workers and residents were running with black ashes on their faces, and sirens from the fire trucks were heard throughout the broadcast. Debris and ashes were pouring down on the streets. Now flames were visible on the buildings high up, large chunks of debris were hitting nearby buildings, thousands of evacuees were using the high up Brooklyn Bridge to walk, and screams and cries were heard.

Everything looked chaotic in Manhattan. Firefighters were bravely going into the buildings to bring out some of the office workers. Now all the debris and ashes were pouring down to the foot of the Twin Towers. Debris mounted and covered the entrance of the buildings quickly. Some firefighters and workers were trapped, and debris continuously poured down. The situation seemed totally out of control. The fire trucks and firefighters had to evacuate urgently as well.

Shortly after the second crash, a third crash at the Pentagon was reported. It destroyed part of the Pentagon, and some workers were killed instantly. The fourth crash into a wooded area in Pennsylvania was reported.

We were utterly petrified as though we were watching a war movie. The third and fourth crashes were not shown on the screen, but reports were rushing in chaotically. The Twin Tower destruction scenes were broadcasted from helicopters because the streets in Manhattan were impassable and dangerous for the TV trucks. The evacuation of the residents and workers in the Twin Towers area were mandated.

Later, CNN announced that a total of nineteen Muslim suicidal terrorists had hijacked four airplanes almost simultaneously. Their whereabouts prior to the attacks were announced as well; some had lived in Portland, Maine, and some had lived in Florida as students in a flying school. Others came directly from Muslim countries to join them. All the nineteen suicidal terrorists chose scheduled flights from the East Coast to the West Coast.

It seemed their precise targets were executed in a series, except for the fourth crash. The fourth one was rerouted to a wooded area in Pennsylvania. It seemed the crew and some passengers overpowered the hijackers but could not prevent the crash. Their original target was the Capitol Building in Washington DC, or the White House.

All the hijacked airline flights were named. None of them were from the company that my father and I worked, but I empathized with the fate of the pilots onboard—it could be my own fate with flight, crew, and passengers. I was sure that my father was thinking the same.

Four attacks were executed within a little over an hour, 8:46 a.m.–10:03 a.m., EST. Later, I googled to find the facts on those unforgivable attacks.

The first crash by American Airlines Flight 11, a scheduled flight from Boston to Los Angeles, a Boeing 767-200 wide-body aircraft, crashed into the North Tower of the World Trade Center at 8:46 a.m., Eastern Standard Time.

The second crash by United Airlines Flight 175, a scheduled flight from Boston to Los Angeles, a Boeing 767-200 wide-body aircraft, crashed into the South Tower at 9:03 a.m., Eastern Standard Time.

The third crash by American Airlines Flight 77, a scheduled flight from Washington, DC, to Los Angeles, a Boeing 757-200, crashed into the Pentagon at 9:38 a.m., Eastern Standard Time.

The fourth crash by United Airlines Flight 93, a scheduled flight from Newark to San Francisco, a Boeing 757-200, crashed into a wooded area in southwest Pennsylvania just outside of Shanksville, about 150 miles northwest of Washington, DC, at 10:03 a.m., Eastern Standard Time.

These terrorist attacks (in 2001) were compared to the Pearl Harbor attacks (in 1941) that occurred sixty years ago. About 2,500 military soldiers lost their lives in the Pearl Harbor bombing attacks. About 3,000 innocent US citizens, including the airline crew and passengers, lost their lives in the 9/11 attacks.

There are some similarities between the two attacks in addition to their unexpected nature. The Japanese soldiers seemed to be brainwashed by Tojyo under nationalism like a religious belief. The suicidal terrorists were brainwashed by the masterminded Islamic extremist, Osama bin Laden, under Islamic religious beliefs.

If their horrendous acts were influenced by their religious beliefs, here we are again, killing the people in the name of religion or God. I am like my father: I believe in the human decency, not in God.

The difference between Pearl Harbor and 9/11 was that the US government knew the enemy was…the country of Japan in the Pearl Harbor attacks, so they fought back. In 9/11, the enemies were hiding all over the world, especially in the Muslim countries, as Islamic extremists. The US government were overwhelmingly frustrated because they could not pinpoint an enemy country and did not know Osama bin Laden's whereabouts.

The US military forces had not captured yet the masterminded commander of Al-Qaeda named Osama bin Laden. His whereabouts was still unknown to this date, even though a five-million-dollar "dead or alive" reward had been posted for many years.

Those suicidal terrorists, members of Al-Qaeda, and Islamic extremists had been trained by Osama bin Laden for many years. He had been known to target the people of Western countries, including the USA, England, and other European countries. Some US establishments such as embassies in Islamic countries had been attacked by the Al-Qaeda group numerous times in the past.

After the World Trade Center crumbled down to ground zero on September 11, 2001, the TSA immediately set up security points in airports throughout the USA. For a week, air travel was shut down. TSA was recruiting workforces to secure the security points at each airport. Hiring was done urgently.

In the meantime, thousands of cancellations, forfeiting, changing, and refunding took place in the airline industry. Air travel became unpopular instantly. People were afraid of air travel.

However, several months later, the airline industries began increasing their scheduled flights. The security lines were a mile long because of the insufficiently trained TSA employees. Many passengers missed their flights due to the time-consuming security checks.

At the end of 2001, scheduled flights increased, and airplane seats were gradually filled. In 2002, the euro currency was established among the European community. Everything was becoming "normal."

Although the airport screening machines have become increasingly sophisticated and upgraded every year, the security has not slacked off at all, especially in the United States. In fact, it is getting tighter and tighter. All the passengers seem to abide the security rules and go through the rituals at the airport without complaining. They must tolerate it for the sake of their own safety in their air travels.

As a pilot, I am thankful for the work of TSA to prevent hijacking. We have not heard of any hijacking incidents since the security points were set up in every airport after 9/11. Some passengers may be discouraged from flying due to the time-consuming rituals at the security points, but people know air travel is still the safest and fastest among all modern transportations.

The Islamic communities in the United States became scapegoats, just as Japanese communities once became the scapegoats because of the Pearl Harbor attacks. Some Muslim men were beaten to death, but no assailants were ever apprehended. Muslim American communities were afraid, but the human rights protection laws have assured the protection of Islamic American communities in the USA.

The World Trade Center, commonly known as the Twin Towers, ranked as the second tallest buildings in the world at that time. I can still picture the skyline of New York City with the Twin Towers. I was lucky enough to visit the Twin Towers with my parents when I was young.

I believe, however, that no younger generation who were born after 2001 could ever imagine having such tall buildings in Manhattan that crashed down to ground zero.

In the future, our descendants may be reading about the dinosaur-like existence of the Twin Towers in their history books. However, they are unlikely to understand the depth of the despair their ancestors witnessed in 2001.

I still vividly remember what kind of day it was. CNN was continuously broadcasting the scenes of the disaster from the helicopters on that day.

My father was not flying on that day, but I had a four o'clock scheduled flight back to Honolulu. I needed to call my boss, Captain Turner, at the hotel. I was his copilot.

"Are we flying today, Captain Turner?"

"So far, yes. All the flights to the East Coast were canceled, but I am sure we will be flying back to Honolulu today. The temporary security point will be very tight. No one will be allowed to the departure gate without a boarding pass."

I heard his coughing.

"They are waiting for more instructions from the FAA. Just come to the airport, and we need to stand by. I was told there are many cancellations. We may have an empty flight back."

He continued, "They said there are thousands of stranded passengers. I was told it is extremely chaotic at the airport. Ticket agents are instructing the passengers to make reservations with Amtrak, Greyhound, or rental car companies. I am very sure there will be no air travels for a while. In any rate, come early."

The FAA OK'd us to fly back to Honolulu that day. Surprisingly the flight was full. I concluded there were no other transportations other than airplanes to cross the ocean to reach Hawaii.

We were told to stay put at home until the FAA was ready to open the security points. Once the TSA security points set up in each airport, the scheduled flights would resume. Therefore, we were grounded for a week.

I remember that airline travel became unpopular overnight and we started losing daily revenue drastically. The scheduled flights started flying, but each flight was almost empty for several months. The stock market plummeted, and the world's economy was paralyzed.

The airline industry was so devastated that some major airlines reduced the employees and operations in order to cut back the company expenditures. Our airline company was one of them.

Some of our flight attendants were laid off. Some ground service workers, including ticket agents whom I knew, were laid off. Some pilots became standby part-time pilots. The company asked older employees to take an early retirement. Pilots' salaries were slashed, medical benefits were reduced, and travel benefits were limited. However, my father and I remained employed.

Airport security has continued to be tight. Due to the security screenings, all the passengers were required to arrive at least two hours prior to domestic departure and three hours prior to international departure.

To me, as a pilot, 9/11 should be the most unforgivable and unforgettable tragedy in the aviation history. Every person who witnessed the unforgivable acts of 9/11 believes the religious fanatic who masterminded should be found and punished without any delay.

Chapter 4

SUSANNA MENDOSA

Now the airline business has returned to normal and is rather prosperous. Although the security rituals at the airports continue, most of the passengers do not seem to mind going through the checkpoints anymore. All passengers, including the airline crew, rely on the security screening at the airport to feel safe—no more hijacking.

Today, the entire airplane seemed full of the vacationers to the paradise. The cabin seemed to be too cold, so I kept my uniform jacket on and sat at the window side. Our crew bags were stowed in the crew closet. My father kept on his uniform jacket as well.

The seats in the first-class cabin are wide, cushiony, and comfortable. Those seats are made to be luxurious for the passengers who can afford the fare difference. In contrast to that, the pilot's seat in the cockpit is padded and narrow. The upright sitting is required. I felt anomalous, sitting in this luxurious seat instead of the captain's seat in the cockpit.

My father was quiet unlike his normal disposition, but his eyes were gentle as usual. As soon as he sat down, he touched my left hand. He knows my hands are always cold, especially in distressed situations.

He figured I was distressed by the mysterious and urgent message I received. So he decided to warm them up just as he used to do when I was growing up. His hands were warm and comfortable. It has been so long since he held both of my hands with his warm ones.

When I was a toddler, I used to cry when my feelings were hurt. He used to lift me up and put my cold hands under his armpits to warm them up. At the same time, he used to tickle my sides and made me laugh. Then he asked me why I was crying. By then I could not remember why I was crying.

When I was probably in first grade, a girl named Susanna Mendosa in my class had been very competitive and hateful toward me. She looked so wicked with her thick black eyebrows. I used to see her face in my dreams and screamed in the middle of the night, which used to wake my parents up.

In my dream, she always looked old, like an evil stepmother of Cinderella, but the face was hers. As far as I was concerned, as a child, seeing her face in a dream was a nightmare. Because of Sue and her followers, my childhood memories at school were always of being threatened or bullied.

She was always jealous of me because I was probably making better grades or the best grades in class and I was very popular among our classmates. The teacher once said to my parents, "I wished all the children were like Mary, so I could have a nice class. She is such an ideal child."

Sue probably heard what the teacher said to my parents. She could not stand me because she probably thought I was more popular or much smarter than she was, or most importantly, I behaved well.

Everybody knew Sue was a daughter of the most important person in our private school. Her father was the chairman of the school board, and he practically owned the school. Because of it, she probably thought she should be as important as her father was; some people called such a person delusional.

An attitude of grandeur delusion was built in her at an early age because of her father's position in school. She troubled many classmates. I was her major target for years, as well as my dear friends, Alice and Nina, just because they were my friends.

Everything I did, she could not stand. She attempted so many times to trouble me. Later I learned her grandeur delusion was derived from an inferiority complex, along with an obsessive jealousy. I really did not know what part of me she was jealous of or hated. Her obsessive jealousy was always aiming at me with her watchful and envious eyes.

One day, after school, while I was waiting for my father, who was late picking me up, at the curbside in front of school, Sue and her followers who were also waiting for their ride saw me and yelled at me loudly in a chanting tune, "Mary is u-g-l-y Jap. She is u-g-l-y ha-pa ha-o-le. She is du-mb, du-mb. Mary is u-g-l-y Jap. She is u-g-l-y ha-pa ha-o-le. She is st-u-pi-do."

When I heard their chanting, I started crying instead of rebutting. When my father arrived, my cold hands were wet with my tears. He quickly lifted me up high and circled me around in the air. He finally pinned my wet cold hands under his armpits and tickled my sides as usual. I kept laughing and laughing. Later in his car, he asked me why I was crying, but I could not explain my emotional status at that time. I was too young to explain Sue's vicious chanting, calling me with names like ugly hapa haole and Jap. I therefore just shrugged my shoulders.

In the Hawaiian language, *hapa haole* means a mixed Caucasian breed with Japanese or Asian. It does not have any bad connotation, but rather has a good insinuation in the name—something like physically improved looks, or prettier looks. Only the indigenous Hawaiians know such words. In any rate, that is my identity in Hawaii.

Some people think I am a haole (Caucasian) because of my looks: light pinkish skin, big hazel eyes, facially no trace of Japanese descent, except for my hair color, which is shiny black, just like my mother's. Therefore, the people think I am a kamaaina Portuguese, a Hawaiian-born Portuguese.

Even though Susanna Mendosa had kamaaina Portuguese parents, her skin color was dark, just as a Hawaiian native's. Her long nose with thick black eyebrows made her rather ugly. If she had smiles on her face, instead of no smiles, her facial expression could be gentle; however, her looks revealed her to be unfriendly, obnoxious, cold, invidious, and additionally her long nose was always up in the air. Naturally, the teachers and adults would interpret that she could be a difficult child.

She had several followers, but their friendships were rather superficial and somewhat bribed, such as giving a ride home in her father's chauffeur-driven car after school and being invited to her pajama parties or pool parties.

When some of her followers had enough common sense not to trouble others or not to be a bully like her, they eventually withdrew from Sue's circle, but as a result, Sue would become revengeful and trouble those who left her. Sue was extremely hateful and jealous. Her behavior was psychotic.

In our private school, each grade level had two classes. For some reasons, the same students were put in the same class every year. I wished Sue were in another class so I could avoid seeing her, but it did not happen. Sue kept enjoying being the bully in my class.

I asked my parents to put me in the nearby public school, but they said my private school had the best academic record in Hawaii, so they wanted me to stay and study. As I did not tell them why I wanted to be transferred, they never knew that I was having a terrible school life when I was young.

Because of seeing Sue year after year, I felt as though she had lived in my body as a parasite during those years. That was how I invented a self-defense mechanism to shrivel or kill my parasite called Sue in my early age.

Writing became my self-defense mechanism to maintain my sanity. I probably started writing when I was in the second grade. All my ruthless and murderous thoughts against Sue were transformed to my story writing each day.

Some of my stories described: a wicked girl accidentally poisons herself and dies because of her greedy eating habits, a wicked girl wants to show off her sports car and drives too fast and kills herself, a wicked girl robs a bank because she wants some spending money and gets shot by a security guard and killed, etc.

In my stories, a wicked girl always acts like a criminal and dies without any remorse. My wild imagination helped me end the life of the wicked girl every night. That was how I dealt with Sue's intimidation and harassment.

If people had ever read my diary, they might have thought I had a dangerous and murderous mind. At that time, I did not have any choice but to write something like that to maintain my sanity, and I also needed it as my therapeutic relief as a child. While doing that, my writing skill had improved a lot, and I thought about being a writer in the future.

My diary books were accumulating, so I put them in a big box and hid under the bed and continuously wrote without worrying about anybody's access.

While watching the sunset, I wrote and finished before the sun went down. I stared at the orange glow over the ocean for a while until my mother called me to eat dinner. I remembered as a child, that gorgeous and beautiful sunset made me happy for some reason.

At school, Sue's intimidation and harassment continued. Once she removed somebody's purse and put it in my desk. Then she told the class I stole the purse.

However, an eyewitness told the class that he saw Sue remove it and put it in my desk during the recess. Therefore, she got in trouble with the teacher.

Her usual plot was to remove someone's belongings or her own belongings to a targeted child's desk. She stole someone's lunch money once and said she saw Mary steal it.

As the teachers praised my schoolwork and behavior quite often, Sue probably wished she were like me. In any rate, I was brought up to be humble, kind, generous, and so forth. She was probably brought up without any guidance from her parents. Her parents were too busy taking care of their business. Perhaps she was brought up by their housekeepers.

We were probably in the fifth grade. One day, my friend Alice was targeted by Sue just because she was my dear friend; there was no eyewitness, but the purse was found in Alice's desk. Sue loudly accused Alice for stealing her purse during the recess.

Our teacher Mrs. Thompson, who knew Sue well, said, "Sue, are you sure you did not put your purse in Alice's desk by mistake?"

"No. My purse was stolen during the recess. The fact is my purse was found in Alice's desk. It is not a mistake. She stole my purse. Aren't you going to punish Alice for stealing my purse? If you do not punish her, I will tell my father about you. So you will be fired."

"Sue, during the recess, Alice and Mary were with me at the storage room in the basement. We were organizing the bookshelves. Alice never went back to the classroom during the entire recess. It was impossible for Alice to steal your purse. Alice has an alibi and two witnesses, Mary and me. I refuse to punish her. If you want to tell your father about me, please do so. I will tell the principal how Alice is accused by you even though she has an alibi. If I take the matter to the principal, you may be suspended from school."

The teacher's face was red, and I felt her anger just as mine.

Sue shouted, "No one can suspend me from school. I am the most important student because my father is the chairman of this school board."

The teacher turned to the class and spoke, "Boys and girls, no one was supposed to be in the classroom during the recess. But if you think you saw someone came back to the classroom during the recess, raise your hand."

A friend of Sue raised her hand hesitantly.

"I saw Sue going into the room during the recess. I don't know what she was doing, but she was the only one who went in."

"Pamela, shut up! You liar! You are not riding home with me anymore. I will tell my father about that. You walk a long way home alone."

Sue glared at Pamela. The teacher took both to the principal's office. I forgot what happened to Sue in the principal's office, but I recall she came back to the class the next day. She was not suspended. The principal was probably afraid to face a complication with the chairman of the school board.

Another time in the classroom, a handsome hapa haole boy named Eric Johnson wrote me a love letter. It happened probably in the sixth grade. Everybody knew Sue was interested in Eric for some time. Eric was the smartest boy in class and very kind to everybody. Especially he was kind to me.

When she found about the love letter that was sent to me, Sue became extremely jealous. She stole the letter from my desk, erased the greeting, "Dear Mary" and changed to "Dear Sue." She showed it around to everybody. Eric was embarrassed and almost punched her in the stomach in front of the class.

Eric had to tell the class the letter was for Mary, not for Sue, then grabbed the letter from her, tore it up in many pieces, and threw in the trash can. Boy, Eric was angry.

"Sue, I hate you from the bottom of my heart. That letter was for Mary, not for you. Remember that!"

Sue put her head down on her desk. Nobody ever saw her cry, but on that moment, she was probably crying due to Eric's rejection or from a broken heart.

When the teacher entered the room, she lifted her head up as though nothing had happened to her. She started wearing the grandeur mighty attitude as usual by putting her nose up in the air.

One day, in the junior high, the science teacher told everybody in the class, "Mary Richardson made the perfect score on the midterm test. This never happened before in my teaching career."

I did not know why he had to make such an announcement in front of the class, but he did it. I thought he was happy because someone paid attention to his teaching and made the perfect score.

After the class, Sue's verbal comment reached me like a sharp knife. "Mary, you think you are smart, but you are not. I know you cheated on the test just as you were bribing everybody when you were voted for the most popular student in the class. I heard you gave Ann some money when she forgot to bring her lunch money, and then you told her to vote for you. You just watch your back. Next time, I will catch you right in your act."

I did not say anything, but I wished I had the guts to rip her clothes off right in front of my classmates, but I just walked away.

My writing was to cease a wicked girl's sly smirks, arrogance, delusional attitude, altogether by giving her a fatal moment each day, but during summers, holidays, vacations, and weekends, the writer had some time off from a murder series.

As the years went by, murderous and vindictive plots were running out; I made her homeless or put her in the jail or put her in the hospital or made her psychotic, crazy. As a result, she was put in the mental facility instead of being killed.

Without my self-defense mechanism and the inspiration from the perfect sunset, I did not think I could have survived to this date; probably my emotional state was unbalanced and developed a psychological problem. Who knows? I might have committed suicide because of Sue's relentless intimidation, threat, and bullying.

On the contrary, my childhood at home with my beloved parents was extraordinary: traveling, speaking three languages at home, having flying lessons with my father, receiving piano lessons from my mother, eating my mother's good cooking, having many inspirational conversations with my father, and planting flowers with Mr. Yamagata.

I had never mentioned to my parents about Sue, but one day, in junior high, I decided to tell my father about Sue, who had been intimidating me since the first grade. I also told him how I had been coping with the situation by writing some ruthless stories, giving her a fatal moment, and burying her or killing her each night.

He thought I was joking first and laughed loudly, but when he saw my serious face, he stopped laughing. "I did not know you have had such miserable school life."

I nodded several times and said, "Yes. She still intimidates me almost every day, but do not worry. I am handing my situation quite well by writing."

"Well, if writing could help you cope with the problems, keep writing. It would not harm anybody, but let me tell you something what happened to me when I was in high school."

He sat up straight and continued. "I had a classmate who picked on me every time if he had the chance because I am White. He often called me derogatory names of White. He was an obese Japanese boy who looked like a sumo wrestler. I was not afraid of him. When I could not stand him any longer, I challenged him to a judo match after school. Minoru's father taught us judo at home for years. Minoru and I had black belts, but the boy did not know that. One day, Minoru escorted me to the schoolyard. The boy was too fat, out of shape, and looked scared when I started using judo techniques. It did not take much time when I threw him hard on the ground. He was flat on his back, looked hurt, and wet his pants. When I pointed out his wet pants, he was embarrassed and disappeared behind the school building."

My father's index finger was waving in the air as though he was pointing out to the boy's wet pants, and he continued, "Minoru shouted, 'Come back, pee wee boy, come back!' but he never came back. After that incident, he avoided me in school. No more name callings. You can do the same thing by challenging her."

"Dad, I am not a boy. I cannot fight as you did with judo. My writing is good enough so far. I can easily get back at her with the power of writing."

He knew what I meant. He glanced at me with his proud look, but somewhat unsatisfied. "Mary, your writing would not stop her harassment. Next time that girl…what's her name?"

"Sue."

"When Sue talks to you in a hateful manner, you talk back to her in the same way. You seem to be too nice. Talk back to her and humiliate her by using your sharp tongue as sharp as hers, or sharper. This is just like a judo challenge, but you will be fighting with words instead of judo. Try it and see how it goes. Use the most humiliating words you can think of. You are too nice to everybody. Be mean or ugly in this case."

Well, my father could be right, but I did not think I had the courage. Whenever I saw her face in school, I imagined her in a coffin with her dead face just as I described in my story. That was how I was getting back at her on my mind.

In the reality, her humiliation and harassment continued. She usually humiliated me in front of her followers. I used to avoid her crowd and walked away before her tongue started rolling.

However, one day I finally followed my father's advice and talked hatefully, loudly in front of many classmates during the recess so everybody could hear me.

"Sue, do you know you are the ugliest haole in Hawaii? Have you seen yourself in the mirror lately? I don't know where your wicked looks come from, but I always think you are uglier than a frog."

I did not know why I was comparing her with a frog. It did not make any sense, but it seemed effective because Sue's mouth was wide open and speechless. Everybody was listening. They were all ears. I was nervous but continued with my sharp tongue.

"Just admit it. I am prettier and smarter than you are. That is why you are always jealous. You know you cannot catch up with me in schoolwork because you don't study, or you are not smart. Everybody knows it. Especially Eric knows it. I do not need to bribe anyone to get votes for the most popular person in the class. I am already popular unlike you. Everybody knows I am the nicest girl in the class and the smartest. That was the reason they voted for me. I gave Ann the lunch money because she was crying. I told her the money was my gift. I did not bribe her. Ask her. Another thing, I don't need to cheat on the test to make the perfect score. I study a lot more than you think. That is why I made the perfect score. Eric likes me because I am a good person. He hates you because you are not a good person. I know you like Eric very much, but he will never be your boyfriend."

I could not believe that my sharp tongue was rolling smoothly. I was not nervous anymore, but I felt as though I was becoming like Sue; I did not like it. I would rather challenge someone with judo just as my father did, if I knew how, instead of this verbal challenge. I felt hideous and wicked. However, I continued.

"If you want Eric, be pretty like me and be smart like me. Eric said you look like Cinderella's stepmother with a long nose. Next time you accuse me of stealing or talk to me in a nasty manner, remember this: I am no longer a nice person, especially to you. I can humiliate you better than you can humiliate me. Comprende?"

Everybody applauded as though the stage play was finished. Sue really looked startled and shaken, almost in tears. She ran to the classroom. Everybody wooed. I saw Sue's group followed her in a hurry.

In the past, I used to cry and walk away from her without saying anything. Today, Coward Mary was no longer a coward. Sweet Mary was no longer sweet. My father was correct—eye to eye or sword to sword. Alice and Nina looked astonished, but at the same time, they covered their mouths with laughter.

After that day, my diary writings were somewhat shorter without murderous episodes, thanks to my father. At school, Sue was avoiding me just as I had been avoiding her for many years. Her oomph and vigilant energy of rolling her frog tongue against me seemed temporarily hibernating. Her long nose, however, was still up in the air with the delusion of grandeur.

Later, I told my father about my sharp tongue incident with Sue.

He said, "Sue might be psychotic or have some mental disorder since she cannot help herself being that way. Her attitude might be derived from a severe inferiority complex disorder." My father reads many medical and psychology books. "We all need to have the courage to literally fight with the intimidating person in order to make our point. Such persons like Sue seem to enjoy harassing, humiliating, and just to cover up her inferiority complex. She could be a social climber when she becomes an adult since she acts under a grandeur delusion."

He sipped some coffee and continued. "A social climber usually displays all kinds of titles or glories to impress socially advanced or successful rich men or governmental officials just to place her on the same category in hoping to catch one of them to marry her. If she becomes a social climber, she might lie about her background or education in order to marry a wealthy person. There are many social climbers in this world, especially among women."

I did not know his statement came from a psychology book or a medical book, but as a teenager, I just nodded. He looked at me with watchful eyes and continued.

"When a social climber marries a well-to-do husband with lots of money, they start wearing a grandeur delusion or a mighty rich attitude to look down on those who did not marry well."

He was looking right in my eyes and continued. "Mom knows such a Japanese woman who lied about her past and education to marry a wealthy man and refused to reacquaint with the friends from her past. Anyway, her marriage did not last long. I heard she is in jail now because she secretly embezzled a lot of money from her husband's company. She also had several criminal records in the past that her husband did not know about."

He continued, "There is a verse, 'What goes around comes around.' It means, if you trouble someone by lying, cheating, and stealing, later in your life, those things will come back to haunt you as a punishment. If you are kind, honest, generous, and genuinely nice to other people, you will be respected, and good things would come to you in return."

After my humiliating speech against Sue, I thought Sue's behavior would change, but her delusion of grandeur act did not stop; rather it escalated.

Yes, she avoided me and did not bother me anymore, but she repeatedly bragged about her background in front of her new acquaintances or new students, including her followers.

She stated that her father had been the chairman of the school board for years, that they had been living in a mansion that contained ten thousand books, and that they were one of the richest families on Oahu Island.

Additionally, she told them that she was the only heir to their fortune. From her statement, Sue received a lot of admiration. Her delusional grandeur speech made her as though she was a celebrity in school.

One day, that celebrity stopped coming to school. Later, we learned Sue and her mother moved to Maui in a hurry because her father was indicted for embezzling millions of dollars from his own company as well as stock manipulation…or something like that. Their mansion, yes, with ten thousand books, was sold quickly. It was almost at the end of junior high.

Sue's brainwashed followers were perplexed because of Sue's sudden departure. They lost the ride home, no more pajama parties, and no more pool parties.

After Sue left for good, my diary entries became short and happy. In high school without Sue, I thoroughly enjoyed my school life with Alice, Nina, and my sweetheart, Eric. I also enjoyed traveling with my parents.

The long-lived parasite in my body was finally jettisoned, and I did not mind shouting at the beach, "No more parasite! No more parasite!" I was sure nobody would understand what I was shouting about. Anyway, my high school life without parasite was so memorable, peaceful, and romantic that I would never forget.

Before I went to college, I discarded all my diary books. I was somewhat ashamed of those murderous stories. Those could be interesting plots for novels, but I did not care to become a writer anymore. Instead, I decided to follow my father's footsteps.

Chapter 5

My Hobby

A flight attendant came to see if we needed some beverage before our departure. My father ordered a bottle of water for each of us by glancing at me. I nodded.

Many flight attendants and ticket agents have known us as father and daughter. They call my father Captain Richardson, but they call me Ms. Richardson or Little Captain Richardson or Captain Mary. I guess they wanted to distinguish two of us from calling differently, instead of calling both Captain Richardson.

"Your mom usually calls me in the morning, but she did not do it today, so I called her, but no answer. Later, I got an urgent message from Minoru."

"I got it when I was in the air."

"Minoru thinks something happened to Mom. Not knowing what happened to her is very worrisome." His blue eyes were somewhat moist with a faraway look.

"I left a message on Mrs. Kitano's phone to find out Mom's whereabouts by getting in touch with Mr. Yamagata or his wife."

Even though my parents lived in different places for many years, they both were very much committed to each other as husband and wife. The reasons they lived separately was not known to his friends, even to Minoru, but as their only child, I could guess some possible reasons.

Their separation was probably caused by my father's subconscious culpability, which he had felt for years. He had probably blamed himself for his wife's occasional *anxiety neuroses*, another name for hysteria attacks, toward him.

I had witnessed her violent attacks twice when I was growing up. My father had never mentioned to me anything about how my mother's attacks started, but he knew what it was. He kept it to himself. I could not ask him…it seemed to be too private. Therefore, I decided to keep my mother's violent attacks on him as my family secret forever.

The separation had made their relationship much better over the years. Whenever my father came back home to visit my mother, they acted like honeymooners, kissing, touching. Whenever I saw them act as a couple of lovebirds, I was not embarrassed, but rather felt relieved as their daughter.

Another reason my father decided to live in Los Angeles might be that he wanted to live in his birthplace or his hometown once more. He had the great memories of his parents and the place he grew up. He also wanted to bond with his high school friends, especially with Minoru, whom he considered the only kin or brother in this world.

My father was well connected with his high school friends since he moved to Los Angeles. They often got together in their favorite Japanese restaurant in Little Tokyo.

In the past, my father took me to meet up with them several times; they occasionally played Go in Minoru's house, and sometimes they played card games in my father's condo. His high school friends were all Japanese descendants who spoke Japanese among them most of the time.

Nevertheless, my father's favorite pastime was to fly his Cessna T-182 to Palm Springs or Las Vegas to play golf. He always shared a ride with Minoru. Sometimes, Minoru's son, Mark joined them. I was told Mark is a pilot and works for a different airline. His regular route was between Los Angeles and New York before he moved to San Diego.

Family Secrets

When Mark accompanied Minoru and John to play golf, my father made Mark the commander of Cessna T-182. I knew it was not my father's intention to exclude me, but I was quite annoyed. If I were a boy, I was sure he would invite me to play golf with them, and he would be happy to let me fly his airplane.

I have been jealous of Mark for some time. He has been somewhat a threat to my relationship with my father. I have never met him, but I heard a lot about him such as he was living with his girlfriend for a long time.

Whenever my father brags about Mark's flying skills, I become increasingly jealous. I am very sure that Mark is treating my father as his favorite or only uncle and getting together with him more often than I think.

The Honolulu International Airport has been my home base. Flying between Honolulu and Los Angeles has been my regular route for a long time. However, occasionally, I would be assigned to fly different routes as well.

Before I was hired by the current airline, I used to fly a charter flight for military groups and tour groups to different Hawaiian Islands.

Now I fly the wide-body aircraft as a captain. My safety record with Boeing 767 from 200 to 400 series has been excellent. My smooth landing skills as well as ascending skills have been admired by my colleagues. My father does not say much about my flying skills, but he knows about my excellent flying record.

My father is one of the top-notch senior pilots. His reputation is renowned among the colleagues in our company. He is a legend. He had flown Boeing 747 to foreign countries for years when he lived in Honolulu. Now he flies the new Airbus A380 to Mexico City or other Latin American cities from Los Angeles.

When I officially became a captain, I purchased a high-rise condominium unit with two bedrooms. The building was newly built by a close friend of my parents. The owner gave me the best choice unit on the top floor with an ocean view. I was proud of myself purchasing the unit with the money I saved.

My parents, especially my father, were very happy because my condominium is conveniently located—near my mother's house. He knew my mother and I would look after each other.

My mother gladly decorated my entire condo, especially the living room, with the help of her best friend, Mrs. Kitano, the widow who lived next door to my mother. My condo was in a mess for a month. Now, however, my place could be a showcase condo for a single person's luxurious living.

From my living room, I see the ocean; from my bedroom, I have the view of the Diamond Head. Whenever I am home, I often walk on the walkway along the beach to the Kapiolani Park. Occasionally, I walked to my mother's house for dinner. Her cooking and the view of the perfect sunset from her house on the hill often lured me.

The freedom of being alone could be rewarding, but at the same time, it could be lonely, but I was determined to make my single and independent life as happy as possible.

For years, I wanted to set up a language lab to study languages as my hobby, but I did not want to do it at my mother's house. When I moved to my own place, I splurged to build an elaborate language lab just for myself. A technician was hired to set it up in the second bedroom.

I remember, in college, I kept studying languages as my hobby that saved me from getting lonely. I had a difficult time when I lost contact with my high school sweetheart, Eric.

In high school, Eric and I became sweethearts. The bully, Sue, who was crazy about Eric in junior high, moved to Maui suddenly, so we were free of Sue.

Eric wrote me numerous love letters since junior high. We liked each other. I thought we were a perfect match. He was the smartest boy in the class. He came to my house to see my parents and helped my father with his airplane at the airfield, and we flew together quite often.

We used to do our homework while babysitting his sisters at his house. Yes, we were good friends and we were in love. I still think he was the best kind of high school sweetheart.

He did not express his love verbally much, but his love letters were so beautiful and romantic that melted my heart every time I read them. We kissed a lot at the beach, but never went beyond.

He was a good-looking hapa haole. His Caucasian father left his Chinese mother and three children when Eric was in junior high school. His mother was left without any monetary support from his father, but for some reason, Eric was able to remain in the expensive private high school and graduated.

His mother worked at a Chinese restaurant for long hours. Eric wanted to go to college, but his mother could not afford it, so Eric had to work to help his mother and his younger sisters instead.

When I was leaving for an aviation college in Florida, Eric and I embraced each other for the longest time and cried at the airport. That was the last time I saw him. We wrote to each other for a while, but later I learned he and his family moved to Seattle, where his mother's relatives lived. After that, I had never heard from him again.

If I did not have my hobby. I could be so sad and lonely that I could quit school and wanted to look for Eric. However, my hobby made me realize that it could help me open my horizons and communicate with the world in the languages I was learning. Of course, I studied a lot of my college subjects too.

I was determined to finish college and reach my dream as a pilot. I wanted to have a better future as a pilot, just as my father has achieved. Eric could be someone like my father who could love me unconditionally, but he could never have a future like my father's. It took a long time to recover from Eric, but I was glad that I finished college.

My college was a male-dominated school. Most of the time, they displayed an attitude of the male chauvinistic arrogance in front of me as though they tried to convey a message that I, as a female, should not have enrolled in this aviation college.

In fact, there were very few females in my school at the time. I lived in an apartment near college and studied a lot alone. Sometimes, some male students asked me to see movies—just to say they dated a girl who invaded their world.

On every date, I was asked why I enrolled in the aviation college. As I always said that I wanted to be a pilot in the future, I had never had a second date with the same student during college. My existence was very odd to the male chauvinistic society, but I was not discouraged.

In any rate, when it came to actual flying an airplane, I was the best in the class. They did not know that I had a flight instructor who taught me how to fly for many years in the past.

During my college years, whenever I was discouraged to pursue my goal or having some difficulties in my subjects, my father flew over to visit me, helped me with the subjects, and talked to me. At the same time, he listened to my problems. He was the only one who did not display male chauvinism around me. I respected him for that.

After finishing college, I went back home and got a job as a pilot in a charter company. I met some male employees in the same company and had some dates, but each relationship did not last long. They all seemed to be intimidated by my profession.

When I landed a job in the same company my father worked, I was very busy learning my job as a navigator, so no time to develop a personal relationship. When I became a full captain, I still did not have time to meet anybody desirable.

However, one day, I met a man at the pilot association and fell in love. He was tall and handsome, intelligent, respectful, had no display of male chauvinism, and was easygoing, just like my father. Most importantly, he was a pilot and respected me as a pilot too, so he was not intimidated by me.

I thought we were in love. Naturally, I thought he was it, my destiny, my Prince Charming, but our relationship only lasted for six months and then he was gone. I took a long time to recover from it. My mother found out about my love affair accidentally, but my father was not informed.

My father tried to get situated in his seat. He looked very much worried about my mother, so I tried to cheer him up.

"Dad, Mom will be all right. She is a strong and physically fit person. Remember she walks every morning and she is very healthy.

She will be all right." I was repeating as though I tried to convince myself.

"I wonder why she did not call me back. I left a message several times, but she did not do it. I hope she is all right." He repeated his thoughts without thinking.

Chapter 6

CARBON DIOXIDE

When we felt the ascending motion, we stopped talking. My father was looking at a magazine for a while, but put it back in the seat pocket without reading it and then rolled his pillow, put it behind his neck, and closed his eyes.

I closed my eyes when I saw dark clouds covering the window when ascending. As a pilot, I felt guilty because I know my aircraft can spew tons of carbon dioxide to form the dirty air pollution in the sky.

Whenever I descend toward the Los Angeles Airport, especially at sunset time, the layer of air pollution looked like an orange-colored blanket that was thrown over the city. It looked poisonous and ugly.

As the scientists started crying about global warming for several decades, I went to the neighborhood library to learn more about it including the carbon dioxide that is the culprit gas of the global warming.

On the surface of the globe has plenty of oxygen and carbon dioxide; humans and animals breathe in oxygen to stay alive and breathe out carbon dioxide. All greeneries such as trees, plants, flowers, vegetables, and grass take in the living creatures' wasted gas called carbon dioxide to thrive and then give out oxygen as their wasted gas. This is our planet earth's natural ecosystem.

Therefore, for millions of years, the ecosystem of the earth was balanced with plenty of carbon dioxide and oxygen. Living creatures and greeneries have coexisted by exchanging the air naturally, but the modern industrial revolution in the nineteenth century began disturbing our ecosystem.

Two hundred years ago, at the beginning of the industrial revolution, some scientists predicted that the fossil fuel combustion spews tons of carbon dioxide that might cause the temperature to rise five degrees and form the greenhouse effect, but their research and theory were forgotten for a very long time.

The industries, manufactures, automobiles, trains, ships, airplanes, and modern mechanical equipment that used the fossil fuel kept jettisoning carbon dioxide emissions into the air freely for many decades.

The air pollution problem got worse, especially in the cities, and humans started suffering, but the governments and the scientists did not know what to do.

In 1955, the first law on air pollution, the Air Pollution Control Act, was signed in California. However, many government officials still did not believe in global warming or did not care to control carbon dioxide. Therefore, again they slacked off on reducing or controlling carbon dioxide emissions.

In the 1980s, the scientists reported that the climate on earth significantly became warmer than any period since 1888. The theory of the greenhouse effect was again discussed.

Soon, the United Nations formed an organization (IPCC) with 2,500 science and technical experts from more than sixty countries to research the greenhouse effect around the globe.

The carbon dioxide concentration at the atmosphere was discovered. The yearly climate change and affects were reported—in the past two hundred years, the global temperature has increased by 30 percent and the sea level has risen as much as three feet across the globe. They concluded the carbon dioxide emissions are proven to be the culprit of the air pollution and global warming.

The atmosphere is like an invisible greenhouse roof. The lighter chemical gases and the warm temperature get trapped under the atmosphere just like the roof of a greenhouse. Those layers of gases are made of 60 percent carbon dioxide and 40 percent other lighter gases, according to scientific analysis.

Although the Global Warming Solution Act of 2006 was to reduce carbon dioxide emissions, scientists think it might be too late to reverse climate change.

The trapped warm air at the atmosphere circulates along with the earth's rotation. At the poles, the rotated warm air drastically melts the ice on the glacier lands. Some animals, especially the polar region animals, may become extinct soon.

Global warming causes the erratic climate change that dangers the environments according to scientists. Currently, the erratic disbursement of warm air brings violent storms such as hurricanes, cyclones, typhoons, tsunamis, tornados, as well as floods on coastal areas, along rivers and lakes.

In recent years, the strength of those storms has become increasingly stronger, causing catastrophic results. Many casualties and calamities around the world have been occurring unpredictably, thousands of human lives have been lost, and millions of dollars have been wasted every year.

Hurricane Katrina in New Orleans in 2005, Cyclone Nargis in Yangon, Myanmar, in 2008, Tsunami in Phuket, Thailand, in 2009 are known examples.

The people who are not informed about the global warming accurately or who don't care to know tend to ignore the cries of scientists.

However, because of the recent climate-related calamities and Nobel Prize winner Al Gore's educational film, the world began to pay attention to global warming or the greenhouse effect.

In order to eliminate the excess carbon dioxide, we must use alternative energy sources such as solar energy, wind energy, water energy, geothermal energy, and bioenergy that do not spew carbon dioxide emissions into the atmosphere.

We, as humans, can also neutralize carbon dioxide in our immediate surroundings. Grow more plants and trees around us so the greeneries would give out an abundance of oxygen for humans and animals. The trees and plants around us take in our wasted air called carbon dioxide to thrive.

Oxygen is heavier, so it remains on the surface of earth, but carbon dioxide is lighter so the excessive carbon dioxide forms air pollution in the sky and also becomes the global warming agent in the atmosphere.

The United States is known to be one of the worst air polluters (21 percent) in the world. Therefore, we, as Americans, must do something fast to eliminate the air pollution and global warming agents.

Every country now has some reduction plans of carbon dioxide emissions. They are long-range plans, but manufacturers, industries, transportation companies, including airlines, and individual car owners must comply with the deduction plans for our future generations, and our planet.

The airline industries are now taking steps to change the situation, pledging to plant millions of trees on earth, especially in the cities. The city of New York, as well, has pledged to plant a million of trees inside the city. Planting trees in the cities seems a small project compared to the size of the earth, but every effort counts in order to reduce global warming agents such as carbon dioxide.

As an individual, we should avoid unnecessary driving. We should walk, carpool, use the mass transit to minimize carbon dioxide emissions, stop burning trash in the backyard, and prevent forest fires. Burning anything outdoors always sends out air pollutants, which are mostly carbon dioxide or carbon monoxide.

Some people think the layer of global warming agents and the ozone layer coexist in the same atmosphere. No, their layers are in different levels: the global warming layer is in the lower atmosphere called the troposphere; the ozone layer is in the higher atmosphere called the stratosphere. The layers are invisible, but scientists can know where they are by looking through the special equipment.

The ozone layer is very thick. It is a natural phenomenon since the earth was formed, and it protects humans and other living things by repelling harmful ultraviolet rays of the sun.

In other words, because of the ozone layer's natural repellant forces against harmful ultraviolet rays, human and animal species were protected and thrived for millions of years.

Now global warming chemical agents such as carbon dioxide are believed to be making holes in the ozone layer. In recent years, the penetration of harmful ultraviolet rays through the holes worsened, causing skin cancers in humans as well as causing abnormalities in human genes.

If we can reduce global warming's culprit gas, carbon dioxide, significantly in the future, perhaps the holes in the ozone layer might be filled again, and the natural repellent of harmful rays might be restored. If there could be no more holes in the ozone layer, the human species would not suffer from skin cancers nor gene abnormalities.

If we push each of our governments in this world to make strict laws to reduce carbon dioxide emissions, it may not be too late to reverse global warming.

At the same time, the world must increase the use of solar, wind, water, and atomic energies that have no carbon dioxide emissions. We should also welcome newly developed battery-operated automobiles and golf carts because they, too, do not spew carbon dioxide emissions.

Nevertheless, scientists must figure out how to clean the carbon dioxide layers at the atmosphere. If we can clean that area in the future, we might reverse global warming—no more rotated warm air (carbon dioxide) to melt ice at the poles and no more warm air to disturb the climate violently, but the earth is too big…the atmosphere is endless.

Chapter 7

Disownment

Even though my father's eyes were closed, he was adjusting his pillow behind his neck from time to time. Most of the first-class passengers started searching for movies on their individual screens while placing elaborate earphones on their ears. Most of the window shades were pulled down.

I did not care to see movies, so I closed my eyes and continued reminiscing about anything and everything.

When I was growing up, I spent a lot of time with Alice, who lived a couple houses down. Her grandmother was the best cookie maker in the neighborhood, and she always waited on us with cookies, especially, when I spent the night at her house. I always envied Alice about having such a nice grandmother who could bake cookies as big as my palm.

One day, I asked my mother, who was peeling potatoes at the kitchen table. "Mom, is my Japanese grandmother as nice as Alice's grandmother? Alice's grandmother can bake cookies as big as my palm."

Without any hesitation, she answered, "Yes, your grandmother could bake cookies as big as your palm, or bigger. She was the best cook and baker in the neighborhood. She went to a French cooking school. She taught me how to cook and bake when I was your age. She was able to bake any kind of cookies. Yes, she can bake cookies bigger than your palm. When I was living in Paris, she used to send me tons of homemade cookies every Christmas and on my birthdays. I used to share those cookies with Liliane, my roommate. They were delicious. See, my father was the Japanese ambassador to France. I was born in Paris and grew up there. I came back to Japan to finish high school, but I was able to attend college in Paris. I studied music in Sorbonne University with Liliane."

She had a sip of Japanese tea and continued. "After graduation, we both were hired to play violin for a symphony in Paris. Additionally, I played piano at an exclusive hotel restaurant on weekend nights to earn extra money. Liliane did the same thing with violin."

She had another sip of Japanese tea and stopped peeling potatoes for a minute. She was counting how many potatoes she had peeled. Mrs. Kitano wanted her to make a bowl of potato salad for their luncheon meeting.

"See my mother was a musician before she married my father, so she was very happy about my being a musician in Paris. She taught me how to play the piano, starting when I was three years old. I really enjoyed being a pianist. Several years later, after I worked for the symphony in Paris, my father wanted me to come home to get married…to someone he arranged. Anyhow, going back to cookies, your grandmother was the best. I still could taste her cookies."

It was rare for my mother to talk about herself or her family. I knew she was the only child to her parents, but my grandparents had never visited us in Hawaii. My mother did not have any photos of them, so I had no idea how they looked like.

While sipping tea, my mother's eyes were sparkling as though she wish she could have some of her mother's cookies with her tea.

"Why can't she visit us and bake some cookies for us? Can you ask her to visit us? I am sure my grandfather wants to come along to see me too."

Suddenly, she stopped peeling potatoes and got quiet. "Mary, let's stop talking about my parents."

"Why, Mom?"

"It is a long story… My parents disowned me. I don't belong to them anymore. So let's stop talking about my parents."

Family Secrets

"What does *disown* mean?"

"That means I am no longer their child."

"Are you going to disown me too when I grow up?"

My mother suddenly embraced me and cried uncontrollably on my shoulder. "Oh, no, my dear. You will never be disowned by your dad or me. You are our precious, dearest child. Never! Never!" She kept crying.

"I am sorry, Mom. Don't cry."

I kissed her cheeks and wiped her tears with my small hands. After that, I would not dare ask my mother about her parents and never mention cookies again. However, the word *disown* got stuck in my head since that day. From time to time, I tried to figure out why she was disowned, but I had no clue. I just guessed something bad happened between my mother and her parents or they probably got in a big fight. I often wondered if my father knew why my mother was disowned. Was he involved in her disownment?

I understood my mother was no longer my grandparents' child, but could they reconcile if they wanted to? As a result, could I meet my grandparents? I thought Alice was a lucky girl because her grandmother did not disown any of her children, baked the biggest cookies for everybody, and waited on Alice after school. I wished I had a grandmother like hers. I did not tell my mother, but for years, I really wanted to meet my grandmother who could bake cookies as big as my palm, or bigger.

The only person who ever came to visit us from Japan was Mr. Masao Okuma. He was my mother's boss, the symphony conductor. I really liked him. Whenever he visited us, Mr. Okuma and I went to Ala Moana Shopping Center or Kalakaua Avenue at Waikiki Beach to shop. At the stores, whatever I wanted, he bought them, including fashionable school clothes, jeans, colorful T-shirts, blouses, my favorite Barbie dolls, and other toys. He always said that someone in Japan gave him some money to buy things I wanted or needed, so I should honor the request. He said it every time he took me out for shopping.

I thought to myself that he was just saying it because he did not want to get in trouble with my parents, who did not believe in spoiling their child with a shower of gifts. To my surprise, my parents acted as though they could not see all the shopping bags around the house. In any rate, I was happy because I really enjoyed being spoiled by Mr. Okuma as a child. I still have a Barbie doll collection somewhere in my mother's house. Alice and I used to play Barbies whenever she came to visit me. When I lost interest in playing Barbies, my mother stored the collection carefully in a wooden chest. She said, "I'll save these Barbies for my future granddaughters. I hope they would enjoy as much as their mother had enjoyed them." I did not realize that she was talking about my future.

Mr. Okuma came at least twice a year. He stayed with us every time he came. The house I grew up has three bedrooms, and he stayed in the guest room.

The three bedrooms, along with a kitchen and a living room, were built on the second floor on top of the oversized two-car garage, the storage room, and my father's study downstairs. The living room had a huge glassed window and a glass door to an overhanging terrace. My bedroom also overhung equally as the terrace. One side of my bedroom was a wall for the terrace. The terrace had stylish outdoor furniture under an adjustable awning cover.

My bedroom window had an awning cover matching that of the terrace to shade the window from the afternoon sun. An undisturbed view of the Pacific Ocean can be seen from the terrace as well as from my bedroom window. In other words, no trees or no buildings obstructed the view of the ocean from our house.

My bedroom was used as a guest room before, but when I was probably in the first grade, I moved into the guest room with my parents' permission. Even though I was young, I discovered the value of the room…with the beautiful sunset view. I was so mesmerized by the sunset that I spent a lot of time staring at it while sitting on the windowsill.

My bedroom window reminded me of a display windowsill with the wide space at a department store. My mother put a thick long cushion to cover the windowsill so I can sit against the side to read or write. The windowsill was spacious enough for a small child to take a nap. Occasionally, my parents found me sleeping on the windowsill when I was young.

Viewing such beautiful sunset each day made me feel as though I was rewarded with the greatest fortune because of my good behavior at school for the day. The sunset became my inspiration to my secret story writing when I was growing up.

The terrace and my room were partially supported by the humongous boulder underneath. Some rose bushes were planted in front of the terrace. When they bloom, our front yard looked gorgeous, but nobody could see them because beyond our front yard was a cliff. However, our family knew those roses were the work of our gardener, Mr. Yamagata.

The master bedroom faced the back of the house that had a long driveway. Both sides of the driveway had beautiful Japanese gardens, with several Japanese stone lanterns. Our garden had year-round blossoms of different flowers. We have had one of the best gardens in our neighborhood.

My mother's grand piano was in the corner of the living room. My mother used to teach children violin and piano in the living room. She taught a group of children, including me, every afternoon.

Whenever Mr. Okuma visited us, he and my mother played violin and piano to entertain my father and me after dinner. My mother was a solo concert pianist for the symphony under Mr. Okuma when she was in Tokyo. Now she plays as a guest pianist for the symphony in Honolulu.

After shopping with Mr. Okuma, we never failed to eat at a nice hotel restaurant. We put all the shopping bags under the table and ordered from the menu. Mr. Okuma could not read much of English, so I explained the menu in Japanese and ordered for him. A waitress once asked me in English, "It is nice to be out with your own grandfather, isn't it? You resemble your grandfather a lot. I had a grandfather once and we used to dine out just like you two do, but he passed away when I was in high school. I have a great memory of my grandfather. He is your grandfather, right?"

I nodded several times in a hurry and ordered for Mr. Okuma and me. She smiled at both of us as if she was recalling her own grandfather by looking at us. Mr. Okuma did not know what she was talking about and why I was nodding hastily. I did not mind lying about Mr. Okuma being my grandfather. He looked a little puzzled, but I did not interpret for him what the waitress said about him.

In fact, I looked a lot like Mr. Okuma, having the black shiny hair and cowlicks on top of my head. Mine was not as bad as Mr. Okuma's cowlicks, but I knew I had them. My mother had to use hairspray to press down those cowlicks every morning when I was going to school.

Whenever I saw him, I always wondered how my real grandfather looked, but seeing Mr. Okuma, I imagined my Japanese grandfather in general.

On the way home, we often sat on the beach near Kapiolani Park to watch the sunset. I told him we could see the perfect sunset from my room.

He nodded and said in Japanese, "You must see the sunset in Okinawa as well. It is equally beautiful. When I was growing up on the island of Okinawa, I often sat on a giant rock at the beach and saw the beautiful sunset. It was perfect every time. You must visit Okinawa to see what I am talking about." He smiled at me with the nicest smile.

Somehow, his smile reminded me of somebody, but I could not recall who at that time. Mr. Okuma was tall and slender just like my mother. If someone looked at my mother and Mr. Okuma, they might have thought they were father and daughter. Their eyes were gentle and big.

Mr. Okuma always wore a nice jacket and looked sophisticated. Because of his profession as a famous conductor, I thought he had to wear nicer clothes. My mother always dressed elegantly as a musician. Even though I was young, I judged Mr. Okuma as a handsome man for his age.

"When I retire, I am planning to go back to Okinawa so I can see the perfect sunset. I think I am going back there just to see the sunset every day. I have missed seeing it. I took it for granted for so many years. I used to get a tremendous inspiration from the sunset. I think I would work on music compositions as my retirement project in Okinawa." While speaking in Japanese, he smiled and winked at me.

I understood how he felt about the sunset. I would miss seeing it whenever I was away from home.

"When I visit you in Okinawa, can I see your sunset with you?"

"Of course. Come visit me when I retire. You will see my sunset. I promise."

"Is Okinawa as pretty as Hawaii?"

"Yes, probably prettier, but since the beaches are sporadically located, unlike Waikiki Beach, many tourists feel inconvenienced. Nevertheless, some tourists prefer the remoteness of beaches in Okinawa."

He had forgotten he was talking to a child. However, I pretended I understood what he meant. When we stood up to head toward the hill, he smoothed my cowlicks and his at the same time.

Every time we took Mr. Okuma to the airport, I remembered my eyes were always filled with tears. As far as I was concerned, Mr. Okuma fulfilled my unknown grandfather's place in my heart. I was glad I had him as a make-believe grandfather for the longest time.

He came to my graduation in Florida with my parents. I graduated from an aviation college with an AMS degree. After the ceremony, we went to Disney World. I have never forgotten how Mr. Okuma enjoyed all the rides with me. He visited us in Hawaii several times after my graduation, but he stopped coming to see us after my parents' separation.

I had worked for a charter flight company for several years before I was hired by one of the major airlines. Yes, the same airline which my father has been working for. My father did not have any influence on my being hired. I did it by proving myself as a good pilot.

When I started flying as a first officer to Los Angeles, I remained living in the same house with my parents. When my father moved to Los Angeles, he wanted me to remain living with my mother so that we could look after each other. Besides, they wanted me to save my salary while living with my mother so I could afford to purchase my own place later. That was how I was able to purchase the condominium with the money I saved.

After I moved into my own place, I often made excuses to visit my mother for dinner before the sunset and wound up spending a night in my bedroom. It seemed that I was addicted to the sunset and my mother's good cooking. She liked the way I visited her often.

Suddenly, I opened my eyes. I thought I saw my mother in person. I probably dozed off while I was reminiscing about her. A flight attendant came over to see if I needed lunch or something, but I declined. My father's eyes were closed, but he shook his head as well. I rolled my pillow behind my neck, rested my head again, and closed my eyes. Nevertheless, my thoughts were still on my mother.

Last night, I ate dinner with her at her house. We hugged each other at the door as usual before I left for my place. Her beautiful face was radiant. I did not suspect any premonition on her face. Nevertheless, I concluded this urgent return must be something to do with my mother.

I tried to analyze the message logically: Did she fall from the stairs? Was she involved in a car accident? If she were conscious, she could have given our cell phone numbers to Mr. Yamagata so he could contact us directly. She must have been unconscious.

If she fell from the stairs, Mr. Yamagata probably heard her scream. It must have happened while he was working in the yard. When he saw her being unconscious under the steps in the garage, he probably did not know what to do, so he went in the kitchen and dialed 911. In the meantime, he went to Mrs. Kitano's house to get her help, but she was not home. When an ambulance came, he probably rode with my mother to the hospital. However, he was asked to contact us immediately in order to have the family's consent for surgery.

On the other hand, was my mother driving to a garden shop with Mr. Yamagata to get some flowers or fertilizers? They did that together often in the past. Was she hit by another car from the driver's side and became unconscious? An ambulance must have taken her to the hospital immediately with Mr. Yamagata. Again, in the hospital, he was asked to contact us immediately.

My worst fear flashed back on my mind again…her death. It seems the time is passing too slowly on the airplane. I wished we were already there to find out what was going on with my mother.

As I felt my father's movement beside me, I glanced at him. His eyes were opened, with a faraway look, and he was quiet. He looked as though he was thinking about the same worst-case scenario about my mother…just as I was thinking.

"I hope nothing bad happened to your mom," he said with a sigh.

"Dad, I left a message on Mrs. Kitano's phone to get in touch with Mr. Yamagata or his wife so she could locate them or find out where Mom is and what happened to her. If the hospital needs my consent, she has my permission to give it to them. I also let her know our arrival time. I am very sure they are working hard with Mom in the hospital. Mrs. Kitano must be with Mom by now. She is her best friend. Anyhow, I will call Mr. Yamagata or his wife as soon as we get home. Mom has his home phone number posted on the kitchen wall. I wish we could be there faster."

He nodded several times without saying anything.

"Dad, Mr. Yamagata still comes on Wednesdays. Today is Wednesday. I am glad he was there with Mom. I am sure he is helping her as much as he can."

Chapter 8

BRUCE HUDSON

Mr. Yamagata has been our gardener since I was nine or ten. At the age of twenty-five, he came to Hawaii with his wife as an immigrant from Kumamoto, Japan.

He had worked for the Dole Company to pick pineapples, but later he decided to make a living as a gardener. His wife took a job as a domestic helper.

He has been contracted to do the yards for some affluent families here in Honolulu. He would mow the lawn, plant flowers, clean gutters, and other necessary yard work.

His wife would work inside the homes of those families. My mother hired his wife on many occasions when she had dinner parties for her friends. They both are hard workers. Even though they do not have any children, they seem happy together.

Mr. Yamagata has never learned much English. My parents wanted to speak English to him for his sake, but they wound up speaking in Japanese. He was probably too shy or felt intimidated. Nevertheless, he has never been shy with me when it came to speaking his broken English.

In Hawaii, Mr. Yamagata did not feel compelled to speak English because many Japanese Issei maintained their Japanese language without hindering their social life or communication in Hawaii.

Family Secrets

When I was young, I used to help Mr. Yamagata in the yard planting flowers. He and I talked a lot. I always spoke proper English to him, and he answered me in broken English. I never corrected his English because I did not want him to feel intimidated. He knew I could speak Japanese, but he spoke his broken English with me. We enjoyed speaking English together when we planted flowers.

I learned Japanese customs from Mr. Yamagata. One was about names such as Taro and Keiko. He said Taro and Keiko are textbook names in Japan. "Taro and Keiko went on a picnic with their parents on Sunday." The name of Taro is traditionally used for the firstborn boy in the family just as John would be in English.

The names of John and Mary are used in the textbook in the United States. "John and Mary went on a picnic with their parents on Sunday."

It could be coincidental, but I felt strange. My mother's name is Keiko. My father's name is John. My name is Mary. My family has three textbook names from two countries.

When I was young, I asked my parents where my name, Mary, came from. My father said my mother named me, but my mother never gave me any explanation. She just smiled mysteriously. So I had interpreted in the past she must have liked the sound of my name, Mary.

However, I got a different interpretation by listening to Mr. Yamagata's explanation. I thought I got the answer to my mother's mysterious smile. Perhaps she wanted to complete two countries' textbook names in her family. She must have planned to have a boy after me who could bear the name Taro, but she failed to do so.

If I had a brother, I was very sure she would name him Taro. So my family would be completed with four textbook names. I did not tell my mother about my findings on our names, but I told my father. He laughed aloud and praised my mother's cleverness.

In any rate, Mr. Yamagata taught me many Japanese customs. I taught him some American customs. Because of my understanding of his broken English, he treated me like his own daughter. Even though I was young, he brought some documents in English and asked me to help him. I forgot what they were, but I taught him how to form alphabets in cursive and showed him how to sign his name in cursive. I was too young to grasp all the legal contents in the documents, so I asked my parents to help him fill out the forms at the end. My parents were glad to help him without intimidating him. I remember what he said in his broken English. He said that my family was the kindest family he had ever worked with.

As I was growing up with Mr. Yamagata, I discovered my hidden talent in languages. Especially I have been good at understanding certain languages, including broken English, accented English, such as my mother's French-accented English, Mr. Yamagata's Japanese-accented broken English, Hawaiian's pidgin English, black people's Ebonics, or some foreigners' accented English. I can easily understand them once I identify the accent. That talent had motivated me to learn many more foreign languages as my hobby.

Now my hobby has become my silent companion or partner. Learning languages excites me a lot as though it is a joy of living or a purpose of my life. I know there are not many people who understand how I feel about languages. That is the reason I don't reveal my hobby to anyone.

When I am home, I devote myself to my hobby by following a strict schedule. No one knows how much language I study at home and how much I can comprehend the foreign languages. Nevertheless, the field practice in a foreign country would give me the most gratifying experience.

When I was growing up, I spoke three languages at home: English and Japanese with my father and French with my mother. At that time, my mother thought I was gifted in languages. She praised me and admired me a lot. She noted how well I spoke French to her. As I only speak English to them now, they think I forgot the languages.

I read novels in foreign languages. Language, in general, fascinates me a lot. I memorize tons of vocabulary and then I am off to my language mission—in other words, I am off to a foreign country.

When I decided to spend a week in Paris, my mother drove me to the airport. She asked me in her car inquisitively, "Mary, are you rendezvousing with someone in Paris?"

"I wish I were, but no. I am traveling alone. Why?"

"I thought you would be lonely when you travel alone."

"Well, not really. For me, I rather like to travel alone. I can plan my own schedule without compromising with my travel companion. I can eat lunch or dinner anytime and anywhere I desire. I visit a foreign country with a purpose. I learn their customs, languages, history, and other things by meeting nice local people. That is my way of communicating with the world. So don't think I am lonely."

"I am glad to hear that. I thought you are escaping from your personal problems."

"No. I don't have any more personal problems. So do not worry. I will be home in a week. When I return, I will take you out to eat dinner at your favorite French restaurant. Is it all right?"

She nodded gladly and said with a smile, "I don't mind if you import a French beau to Hawaii. I would cook French cuisine to keep him here for you. Anyhow, have a safe trip, and I hope you meet nice people on the trip, but be careful."

Two years ago, I had a personal problem and escaped from it by giving myself a trip. My mother knew it when she drove me to the airport. Yes, that trip was my way of recuperating from a broken heart. I could recall how miserably I felt at that time. The ending of my relationship with Bruce Hudson was so capricious that I was left perplexed with a broken heart.

Bruce Hudson and I met at the pilots' association conference in Honolulu. There were many good lectures to attend. Bruce and I were in the same session. The room was rather large with eight or ten rectangular tables. Each table was covered with a white tablecloth. Four folding chairs were provided for each table facing the podium.

I took a chair next to the wall. A man with salt-and-pepper hair sat at the aisle side of my table. An attendance roster was passed around. The man signed on the roster and slid it down to my direction.

When I looked at the roster, the line above me had no last name, no employee number, just first name. Therefore, I asked him if the name was his. He did not hear me, so he left his seat and came to check his name. He glanced at me with a smile and took a chair next to me.

When he was completing his name with his left hand, his right hand accidentally touched my left hand under the table. We both were startled first, but he courageously held my somewhat cold hand with his warm one. I was petrified, but his hand felt so warm that reminded me of my father's hand, so I let him hold it.

He seemed to be contemplating first, but his warm hand started caressing mine gently without saying anything. His handholding was so sexually arousing that my adrenalines rushed out to enjoy the feeling. I was not concentrating on the lecture—all my attention went to my left hand.

After the lecture, he finally released my hand. We both stood up at the same time. Now I could see his handsome face closely. His prematurely gray hair looked great. His height was comparable with mine.

"There is a great restaurant in this hotel. Would you like to eat lunch with me?"

"Well, I was going home and eat sandwiches. My place is only two blocks away from here. Would you like to come and eat sandwiches at my place instead?"

I was surprised at myself inviting a stranger to my place. His gentle eyes and facial expression were very favorable, and I thought I could trust him…he should not be a bad person because he came to the pilots' association conference. His background was already certified as a pilot. I had to convince myself it was all right to invite him. In any rate, I liked the way he held my hand under the table. I would not mind knowing him well and letting him hold my hand again.

"Are you sure it is all right?"

"Yes, if you don't mind walking."

"Oh, I forgot to introduce myself. My name is Bruce Hudson, Captain Bruce Hudson. I just started flying between San Francisco and Honolulu. I used to fly between San Francisco and Chicago or sometimes to Mexico."

"My name is Mary Richardson, Captain Mary Richardson. I fly between Honolulu and Los Angeles."

We walked together. No, we were not holding hands. When he walked into my house, he gasped at the sight from my living room—the ocean. He gazed at the sight while I was preparing ham sandwiches and iced tea. While eating sandwiches, he profusely apologized the way he held my hand without my permission.

"When I saw you, I was mesmerized by your beauty. I felt urged to get to know you. Touching your hand was accidental, but holding your hand was not. It was like a magnetic attraction. As I did not feel any resistance from you, I kept holding it. I am sorry for being impulsive."

"Well, I was startled first, but the way you held my hand was so gentle and comfortable…I enjoyed being held. You don't need to apologize. Let's blame it on the magnetic attraction." We both laughed aloud. I did not tell him his handholding was sexually arousing.

After the afternoon sessions, we chatted at the beach café for the longest time—about the flying experiences, flying schools we went, where we grew up. He was admiring my courage to become a pilot. He said less than 5 percent of pilots are females in this world. He had met several, but I was the most beautiful female pilot he ever met. I almost said that I was glad to be discovered by the most handsome pilot on earth, but I just smiled sensually instead.

Before we parted at the café, he gave me his flying schedule between San Francisco and Honolulu. I gave him mine as well. Therefore, we could meet for lunch or dinner whenever he was to overnight in Honolulu. Our cell phone numbers were exchanged.

Because of my profession, no male would willingly approach me. They would be intimidated if I said I was an airline pilot. However, Bruce Hudson seemed to be interested in me personally. I did not think he was intimidated by me.

The first impression of Bruce was so great that I did not mind going out for dinner and getting to know him. His mannerism was also so well-groomed that I would be glad to introduce Bruce to my parents or to some of my obnoxious colleagues who would ask me about my sexual preference bluntly since I have never been married.

Once, one of the senior pilots asked me, "Captain Richardson, it is not my concern, but are you homosexual?"

I was flabbergasted but answered, "No, I am not. Why do you ask?"

"If you are not, you should get married, have some kids, and stay home to look after your husband and kids before you get too old."

Sometimes, those male chauvinistic colleagues dumbfound me with questions like that. I often face their belittlements to discredit my being a pilot just because I am female. I get very frustrated with this kind of male chauvinistic mentality.

My colleagues who do not know my excellent record as a pilot would always bring me down to the level of their wives just because I am female.

"My wife entertained my friends at the party last night. You would not believe how great a homemaker she is. Everybody admired her. Captain Richardson, if you were married, would you cook and entertain your friends as good as my wife? Do you think you could handle being a wife and a pilot? Or you would rather have your husband be a wife?"

"I don't know. Since I don't have a husband, I should not worry about what I should do or what my husband should do, should I? Do you think your wife enjoys being your wife? Have you ever thought about becoming a female? I am sure your wife would like to see you take her place so you would understand how she feels."

My statement did not make any sense, but I did not care. Those male chauvinistic colleagues had aggravated me a lot in the past, but somehow, I learned to walk away from them just as I walked away from Sue when I was a child. As soon as my acquired sharp tongue dumbfounds them for a change, I purposely walk away in the middle of the conversation.

Once, my airplane's nose landing gear did not retract into the slot after ascending from Honolulu. I calmly notified the control tower of the nose gear malfunction. They told me to fly without retracting the nose gear. My copilot and I flew without relaying the news to the crew and passengers.

When we reached the vicinity of Los Angeles, the control tower was already notified and waiting for us to land. I had to fly around for a while to empty some of the remaining fuel and landed with the rear landing gears as smoothly as I could without using the nose gear. Then I slowly used the nose gear to touch the ground and stopped to support the aircraft just as before.

A fire truck was sent just in case. The nose gear certainly supported the aircraft up right, so we were told to taxi to the ramp. The control tower was very impressed by my smooth landing with the rear landing gears and praised me, by saying how professional and meticulous a landing I performed. I was happy to be recognized, especially by the control tower.

Those colleagues who had flown with me know how well I can land the jumbo aircraft without any commotions. They respected me a lot as a pilot. To them, I am not a female—I am a professional and skillful pilot. Those skills have nothing to do with my gender. They come with many hours of practice and many hours of flying experiences.

Bruce Hudson called me on my cell two weeks after we met. We arranged to meet at a Japanese restaurant to eat sushi. He said he used to live in Japan when his father worked for the American embassy. He spoke Japanese, but not as well as I spoke it, but I did not tell him about my Japanese. I pretended I was a non-Japanese speaker. I made him the star of the night in the restaurant. He enjoyed conversing with a chef in Japanese at the sushi bar. We ate various sushis, but *hamachi* was his favorite. He wanted to pay for the dinner, so I let him.

We got along so well that I felt as though I had known him for a long time. There was the chemistry between us; the same magnetic attraction was still there as well.

After dinner, the full moon was shining on Waikiki Beach. We decided to walk on the beach. We took off our shoes and walked on the warm sand. The moon and the sound of waves were just right for a romantic evening, I thought. Yes, we held our hands for the second time. It was so romantic with the full moon.

Eric and I used to walk on the beach quite often after seeing movies on the weekends. We walked holding hands just as Bruce and I were doing. I remember Eric caressed my hand gently when he wanted to kiss me. We kissed a lot on the beach. It had been too long since someone held my hand on the beach.

Bruce and I sat on the ledge of the beach to gaze at the moon above us. The moon seemed to be encouraging us to be more romantic. Bruce kissed me for the first time. His warm hands cupped my face and kissed me on my lips gently. His hands moved to my neck, caressing. His lips overwhelmingly covered my mouth. My whole body was aroused. Our tongues were tangled, and his soft lips were hot and moist. One of his hands started caressing my thigh through the slit of my long muumuu. There were not many walkers on the beach. It was quiet with the sound of the ocean waves. The moonlight was generously shining on us.

I could not recall how we wound up being in my condominium, but we were in my place. When I realized, we both were in bed, stark naked. Bruce's magical hands were caressing me gently as though he intended to arouse every cell of my body. He was taking the time to do it. He was not acting like a horny or sexually deprived person at all.

I noticed his overwhelmingly thick chest hair was sexually arousing my nipples as well. It reminded me of Alice's pet dog, a golden retriever that loved to sleep with girls, whenever we had a slumber party at Alice's house; he acted as though he was supervising the girls at the party. He was the first one to get into the large bed. I could not recall the dog's name, but he listened to the girls' chats in bed and cuddled with us. He did not mind being pillowed. His golden hair was short but had nice texture, just as Bruce's chest hair.

After Bruce's lengthy kissing and caressing, we finally merged. Bruce's excellent foreplay and vigorous lovemaking sent me instantly to heaven. After Bruce heard my moaning, he lay beside me by elbowing himself on his pillow, looking down on my flushed, satisfied face, said I looked beautiful.

Bruce and I became lovers. He came to my place to stay overnight at least once a week. We tried to match the flight schedule, but sometimes, we did not have any choice but to miss each other. However, whenever we got together, we ate dinner and walked on the beach. Our sex life was just perfect.

He was open to any subject. However, when I think about him now, he had never given me his home address or home phone number. The only contact I had was his cell phone number. I did the same, giving him my cell phone number for my only contact, even though he knew where I lived.

Eventually, I thought, we would exchange our addresses when our relationship would develop to the certain point. I convinced myself to wait for the next level of our relationship.

On the other hand, he had never asked me for my home address. So I thought he was thinking about the same thing, waiting for the next level of our relationship. However, from time to time, I thought it was not fair because he knew where I lived, but I did not know where he lived and had never been invited to his place in San Francisco.

I should have thought it was peculiar not knowing his home address or whereabouts in San Francisco, but I decided, rather, to value every moment we were together instead of worrying about not knowing his home address. I guess I was blinded by love and trusted him totally.

Once I asked him if he could take three or four days off to go to a resort, but he made excuses about not being able to change his flight schedule because some colleagues were taking some time off. Therefore, I had never traveled with him during our entire relationship.

Another time, I was flying a scheduled flight to San Francisco to stay overnight. I called Bruce on his cell to meet me somewhere in San Francisco to eat dinner if he was in town, but he told me he was scheduled to fly to Chicago that day.

As a result, I stayed at one of the designated hotels in San Francisco, and I decided to eat at Fisherman's Wharf alone. I chose a nice seafood restaurant on the second floor of a building with glassed-in windows so I could view the sunset on the bay and the street below. I took a table next to the window.

I enjoyed viewing the sunset and the crowd below during dinner. Out of the blue, I saw Bruce with a woman and two kids in the crowd. I recognized his gray hair, but I had to convince myself… he could not be Bruce because he flew to Chicago that day.

Chapter 9

BETRAYAL

My father was leafing through the magazine impatiently as though he wanted the time to pass quickly. However, he decided to put the magazine back in the seat pocket, put a pillow behind his neck, and closed his eyes again.

Around his eyes, some fine wrinkles revealed his age. When I was a toddler, I used to touch his eyes, compared them with mine, and learned some color words, *blue* and *hazel*. His were blue and mine were hazel.

I still could not recall what color of eyes Bruce had, brown or hazel, but his long eyelashes were what I remembered. I even told him that I wished I could have eyelashes like his.

One day, my mother left several messages on my cell for me to come and eat dinner when I come to pick up my mail. My mother received all my mail at her house because I kept my home address the same as before.

She did not mind it at all; in fact, she rather liked it so she could make some excuses to bring my mail to my place or she could invite me to eat dinner when I picked up my mail at her house.

Bruce was coming to stay overnight on that same day she called. I called her back and told her that I would be eating dinner with a friend. I did not tell her that the friend was my lover. I wanted to keep my relationship with Bruce secret for a while until I could be sure of each other.

In any rate, Bruce was never eager to meet my family or friends, never asked me about them either, so at the same time, I withheld all the information about my love affair from my parents and friends.

Since there was no mention of meeting each other's parents after six months, I thought Bruce was not ready for the next level of our relationship, nor to take our commitment further.

I was somewhat frustrated because I felt like I was hiding something, especially from my mother. I sensed Bruce did not want me to tell anybody we were lovers.

My mother and I always chatted, and she knew what was going on with me because I told her about the people I dated and how I felt about the dates, and so forth. However, the relationship with Bruce was different. I felt like I was having a secret love affair.

My mother came to my place the next morning. Even though I did not return the call, she assumed I got the message. She often came to clean up my place while I was at work. Sometimes she came early in the morning to make breakfast while I was out to a morning walk. However, she always called me before she came.

Bruce and I were still in bed. When I heard some noise in the kitchen, I woke up and went into the kitchen in my robe. I saw my mother. She was preparing coffee. When she saw me, she was startled.

"Hi, Mary. Good morning. I thought you were walking. Are you all right? I left a message last night to bring your mail this morning and make breakfast. Did you get my message?"

"Good morning, Mom. No, I forgot to turn on the cell. Mom, I have someone here with me."

I wanted to be clear with her about Bruce Hudson. I am a grown woman and should not be embarrassed being caught having a man in the house. I told her straight that Bruce Hudson and I have known each other for some time.

"Bruce Hudson? It is a nice name. How long have you known each other?"

"About six months. He is a pilot in the same company. He flies from San Francisco to Honolulu once or twice a week."

"I did not know you have a boyfriend. I am glad you have someone special. I hope he is a nice fellow."

"Yes. He is very nice and kind. We only see each other when he flies over here to stay overnight. We just did not get around to meet anyone. I am sorry."

"Well, should I fix breakfast? Or should I leave?"

"Mom, don't leave. I will introduce you to Bruce. Who knows he could be your future son- in-law!"

I did not mean to say that, but it was too late. When I said "your future son-in-law," her eyes started sparkling like stars. Her pretty face had the nicest smile, just like Mr. Okuma's. Now I could recall my mother had the same smile as Mr. Okuma's.

She said, "I'd better make more coffee."

Bruce Hudson came out of my bedroom in his robe.

"Bruce, this is my mother, Mrs. Keiko Richardson. Mom, this is Bruce Hudson from San Francisco."

When he saw my Japanese mother, he looked a little puzzled, but bowed slightly. Bruce was reluctant to discuss his life in San Francisco, and he had never asked me about my parents. Therefore, he was not told anything about my family or my being a hapa haole.

"It is nice to meet you, Bruce. I am Mary's mother."

Bruce smiled and embarrassedly said, "It is a pleasure to meet you, but I am sorry I met you like this. Let me take a shower and change my clothes. Excuse me."

Bruce hurried back to the bedroom; my mother commented on how handsome he looked. "He seems a very nice person. Are you both in love?"

"Yes, I think we are."

"Well, it is a blessing. I am glad you finally found someone. How well do you know him?"

"I guess well enough for six months."

"Do you know about his family?"

"Yes. His father once worked for the American embassy in Japan. He speaks some Japanese. He has two younger sisters. I think his parents live in Chicago. Both of his sisters live in San Francisco. Mom, he is not intimidated by me. He is not a male chauvinistic person. I really like the idea of having someone like him. I hope he will be my Prince Charming in the future, but I don't know yet. We will see."

"Do you know him well, such as what kind of relationships he had in the past, or if he still keeps a relationship with someone else in San Francisco or hiding a wife or a girlfriend like that?"

Once I asked Bruce if he had ever married in the past. He said he was married once for a year. Since he was reluctant to discuss more on his past marriage, I did not pursue further.

"I think he was married once a long time ago."

"Does he have any children from the previous marriage?"

"I don't think so."

The thought of children did not come to my mind when he said he had only been married for a year. I assumed he was divorced without a kid. Now I could recall that whenever I tried to ask him about his life in San Francisco, he always changed the subject.

My mother was busy preparing breakfast for three, instead of two. The aroma of coffee permeated into my bedroom. Bruce was getting dressed in his uniform. He was to fly back to San Francisco at noon. I had a couple of days off from flying. After taking a quick shower, I put on a casual dress for breakfast. My mother was busy preparing some French crepes.

While I was growing up, my mother's hobby or dream was to perfect French cuisine. During my early years, my father and I often became her guinea pigs or tasters for her new recipes.

Once my father tasted a new recipe of hers, and he did not like the taste of it. He swallowed a chunk of meat in a hurry, and it got stuck in his throat. He tried to cough it out several times, but he could not do it. His face was turning red.

My mother made my father stand up and held him from behind. Her thin arms clenched around his stomach, and she told me to thrust my body against his stomach with all my mighty strength. I did what my mother told me to do. My entire body went toward his stomach, and at the same time, my mother tightened her arms and jettisoned the air toward his mouth. Suddenly, the chunk leaped out of his mouth. His face was almost purple by then. He started coughing with a relief. Boy, we almost lost him. We were scared, so was my father. We huddled and cried a lot for a while. My father hugged us and thanked us several times. My mother and I were still crying.

After that incident, he has been very careful swallowing any food, unless he has chewed many times. When he did not like her recipe, he just left the food on his plate. My mother took it as his feedback.

With the help of her tasters' feedback, she perfected her French, Japanese, and other cooking. Her friends from the symphony or neighbors loved to be invited by her to her occasional dinners or luncheons. Whenever my father came home, he anticipated her good cooking. I have been the luckiest person to eat her good cooking for all my life.

The French crepes with various fruits were prepared as our breakfast. Bacon and eggs were also on the table. As usual, the breakfast was fabulous. At the table, my mother asked Bruce, "Do you know Captain John Richardson?"

"Captain John Richardson in our company? Yes, I flew with him for several months as his copilot, probably five years ago."

"He is Mary's father. He lives in Los Angeles."

He looked at me and said, "Mary, you did not tell me anything about your father."

"I thought I did. Well, I guess I did not tell you because you never asked me about my family. Sorry."

Bruce was right. I never mentioned my father as being Captain John Richardson who was thought to be a legend in our company. I never mentioned my mother being a concert pianist, either.

When I think about Bruce Hudson now, it seems obvious that he intentionally did not include anyone else in our relationship because of his secret life in San Francisco. He was afraid that somebody might recognize him. That was the reason he did not want to meet my family or friends. It was foolish or naive of me to wait for the next level of our relationship. There was no next level on his part.

If he asked about my life or my family in detail, he knew he had to reciprocate by telling his life in San Francisco. That was the reason he had never asked me about my parents. Neither did he care to know about my past relationships because he knew he had to reciprocate.

As a result, he was not informed of any details of my family, including my mother being Japanese, my parents' separation, my father being Captain John Richardson. Most importantly, he did not know I was a hapa haole. He probably thought I was a haole, or a kamaaina Portuguese, just as other people thought I was.

After he found out my father was Captain John Richardson, he became quiet and acted somewhat awkward. He seemed to be anxious to get back to the airport. He thanked my mother for the breakfast, kissed me on my cheek, and left in a taxi.

That was the last time I saw him. He never contacted me after that. I tried to call him on his cell many times but to no avail. His flight schedule was changed to New York. My heart was aching.

After about a month of heartache, I finally asked my father, "Dad, do you know Bruce Hudson?"

"No, who is he?"

"Someone said he used to fly with you as your copilot years back. I don't know how he looks like, but he is supposed to live in San Francisco." I lied about Bruce.

"Oh, that Bruce. Yes, he was my copilot, and we flew together years back. I forgot which route we flew, but he was a very conscientious pilot, a nice fellow, an excellent pilot. I think he flies from San Francisco now."

"How well do you know him?"

"How well do I know him personally? Let me think. Why do you ask?"

"I have a friend who wants to know about his personal background. I was told to find out from you since he was your copilot." I lied again.

"Well, if I am not mistaken, he was married to one of the ticket agents at the airport and had a child. Later, I was told he had another child. He used to show me the pictures of his wife and daughter. His wife was a beauty. Their girl looked like an angel."

"Are they still married?"

"I think so. I saw them in San Francisco a couple months ago."

I was sure my anger inside of me was showing on my face. My heartache was replaced with an unknown numbness inside. My head was spinning for no reason. My hands were cold. I was not thinking straight. I had to sit down to avoid a fainting spell. All the blood from my body followed the gravity down to my feet. In the process, my head and heart emptied. I could not think, could not feel anything.

My father did not pay any attention to my change. He was typing some e-mails on his laptop. I sat down on a couch beside his desk and gazed at the horizon of the city lights of Los Angeles for the longest time.

My father was still busy writing something on the computer. He probably thought I was enjoying the sight of the city lights from his high-rise condominium.

My empty skeletal frame remained on the couch; my eyes stared at the city lights obliviously like an android or zombie until I heard my father's rumbling voice.

"Mary, are you all right? You are awfully quiet. Do you want to watch a movie? I will fix popcorn."

I sat in the living room, stared at a movie with him, and ate popcorn, but I did not comprehend the movie plot because my brain left my body a long time ago. My father was falling asleep on the couch, so I turned off the movie and motioned him to go to bed by poking his shoulder.

I went to my bedroom, stood up at the window, and stared at the city lights again. When the scene of a man and a woman with two children at Fisherman's Warf flashed back, I felt rage again. The man that day was Bruce. He did not fly to Chicago; he was in town with his family.

I felt cheated and betrayed by the person I thought I was in love with and trusted. I thought he was my Prince Charming and my destiny. My anger did not allow me to cry. The feeling of being cheated hurt my ego more than my heart.

I could not forgive Bruce's dishonesty. I thought about telling his wife and letting her know he cheated on her, but I did not do it. I did not want to do it for the sake of his children. I decided to bow out from this fraudulent affair and move on. I convinced myself my life is much bigger and better than his deceitful life.

Days passed by. My desire to see Bruce gradually disappeared. The feeling of being betrayed remained deep inside of me for the longest time. My anger would surface occasionally when I thought about him, especially in bed. In any rate, time has been a good healer for the wound.

Chapter 10

A SECRET

As a young child, I used to go to shopping with my mother. I quite often noticed some men turned and looked at my mother. As it happened so many times, I told my father about it. He said, "Because your mother is beautiful."

Whenever I imagined my mother, I always pictured her face with fair, creamy complexion and a beautiful smile. She dressed elegantly just as a movie star in a magazine, and she always looked beautiful. Her movement was vivacious, robust, and yet gracious.

However, my mother had a dark secret. My father and I had hidden her secret from her friends and neighbors for years. She had suffered from a mental illness called anxiety neurosis, the old-fashioned name is hysteria.

The illness could be triggered by the patient's obsessive jealousy toward her husband or lover. If the patient suspects her husband's unfaithfulness, the illness might be triggered. However, the anxiety neurosis could be controlled by following the steps of anger management.

Everybody seemed to have the same kind of anxiety, and most people could control it, but my mother could not. She could become violent when it was triggered. My father knew how she acquired the illness, but he had never revealed the fact. It happened a long time ago, before I was born. Allegedly, my father caused it. That was the reason he had always felt responsible for my mother's illness. Whatever it was, my parents were tight-mouthed about it, even to each other.

Moreover, my father and I made sure to keep her illness a secret from our acquaintances and neighbors. Neither neighbors nor her friends had ever suspected she had suffered from the illness, even my mother's best friend, Mrs. Kitano.

I don't remember how old I was, probably in primary school, quite young, when I witnessed the disaster caused by my mother's illness for the first time. It happened before I came home after visiting Alice, who lived in the same neighborhood.

All my father's clothes, uniforms, and shoes were scattered down the stairs and onto the garage. Dishes were broken, pots and pans were all over the kitchen upstairs, and my father's car was gone.

My mother was shaking on the sofa like a leaf and crying. I was frightened. I thought someone broke into our house and injured my mother. I ran to her and embraced her. She embraced me back while sitting down on the sofa. Her whole body was tremulous.

"Mom, what happened? Are you hurt? Are you okay? Who did this?"

She looked ashamed and whispered, "I…did it. I am sorry." She sobbed quietly. Her hair was in disarray, and her pretty face was smeared with tears.

"Where is Dad?"

"I don't know."

"Was he here?"

"Yes, but he went away."

"Why did you make so much mess?"

"I don't know."

I kept embracing her until her trembling stopped. She was mumbling something about lipstick stains on my father's shirt.

I held her hand and led her to the bedroom as though she was the child. I turned up the bed and tucked her in. I used a warm wet towel to wipe her puffy eyes and face.

She thanked me and said, "Your father is having an affair. He had a lipstick stain on his shirt. Look."

Suddenly, she sat up straight against the headboard and showed me my father's uniform shirt with a red mark stain near its collar. I did not realize she brought his shirt to the bed. Her eyes were filled with tears again.

Even though I was young, I had seen some movies with my babysitter while my parents were away. So I understood what an affair meant.

My father took a girl alone to dinner, without my mother. They had a nice dinner with a glass of wine and chatted with beautiful smiles. One thing I could not figure out was why the girl had to soil my father's white shirt with lipstick.

"Dad should take you to dinner to have an affair instead of that girl so his shirt should not be stained by her lipstick. She is a messy girl."

I was angry with my father taking a girl to have an affair instead of my mother. As a result, he got his shirt stained by her lipstick.

I knew my mother did not like to see my white dress stained with chocolate ice cream. I thought I understood how she felt about the lipstick stains or any kind of stain on my father's white shirt or my white dress, so I cried with her.

After my mother went to sleep, my father came home. I helped him clean up the house. We both did not say much; especially I did not say anything to my father because I was angry with him for having an affair with a girl in the restaurant. Most importantly, his shirt was stained by her lipstick.

After I helped him clean most of the stuff around the house, I decided to get some rest. Without saying anything to my father, I quietly closed my bedroom door behind me. He was still cleaning up the mess.

I felt sorry for him, but I thought he deserved to be punished because his shirt was stained. If he did not take that girl to have an affair, his shirt should not be stained. My mother was angry because of her lipstick stain.

However, when I thought about the time I stained my white dress with chocolate ice cream, I remember that my mom looked startled by the size of the stain, but she did not seem to be angry.

She took me to the restroom, washed off most of the stain, and said, "When we get home, I will soak it in bleach water. I hope the stain will come off. Please be careful the next time you eat chocolate ice cream. I don't want to see any more stains, especially on your white dress."

She kissed me, held my hand, and walked to the car. She was not angry with me at all. She did not slap me or did not throw anything at me.

Why is she so angry about the lipstick stain? Is that lipstick stain hard to come off? Couldn't it be washed off in bleach water? Is it why Mom is so upset?

When I was reading a picture book at the windowsill, I heard a knock on the door. It was my father. His voice was very low, almost whispery.

"Mary, you are the only one who can help me. You know I love you and Mom very much, but Mom thinks I have been sleeping around with someone when I was away for two nights on a scheduled flight."

"I thought you are having an affair with a girl."

"Well, that is what Mom thinks…an affair."

"Do you have to sleep with a girl when you have an affair?"

My father's face turned red.

"No. I don't. Mary, listen, I need your help. Would you please explain to your Mom that the red mark on my uniform shirt was not a lipstick stain? See, we use this red crayon marker to inspect the aircraft by marking a check on the inspection sheet. Somehow this red marker got on my shirt."

He brought a crayon marker and stained it on a piece of cloth. It really looked like a lipstick stain on the cloth. He wanted me to show it to Mom and let her compare with the red mark on his shirt.

"Dad, I tell you why Mom is angry. She is angry because she does not want to see any stain on white clothes, especially a lipstick stain. The lipstick stain is very hard to come off. That is why she is angry. I have been very careful not to get chocolate stain on my white dress."

My father looked puzzled. "I know that, but that red mark on my uniform is not a lipstick stain. Mom thinks that came from lipstick, but it did not. Please help me."

"So you want me to show the stain on this cloth and let her compare with the stain on your shirt?"

"Yes, my dear Mary. Yes. You are very smart. When you talk to Mom, don't forget to use this marker to stain this piece of cloth in front of her eyes first and then let her compare with the stain on my shirt. Understood? If you could prove my innocence, I'll owe you a lot for the rest of my life. I love you very much."

He hugged me and disappeared in the guest room. I was perplexed and not quite convinced why the lipstick stain brought so much commotion between them. I decided, however, to represent my father because I wanted my parents to be friends again.

A few minutes later, I marched right into my parents' bedroom with a piece of cloth and the red crayon marker my father gave me. My mother was asleep, but I touched her gently to wake her up. I asked her to sit up straight because I wanted her to look at something.

After she sat up straight, I used the crayon marker and drew a bold line on the cloth in front of her eyes.

"Mom, take out Dad's stained shirt and compare with this. The stain on his shirt did not come from the girl's lipstick. That came from this crayon marker. That girl did not have a lipstick. She had this crayon marker to stain Dad's shirt. I am very sure he is not going to take her out to have an affair anymore. She is such a naughty girl!"

My mother's eyes were widened with bewilderment. Her mouth was wide open, but speechless.

While she was comparing the two stains, my father was watching us by standing up at the door. When my mother saw him, her pretty face lit up. She stood up and went to embrace Dad.

"I am sorry, John. I love you very much."

I heard Dad's moan when Mom's lips covered his lips. I should be embarrassed, but I felt relieved instead. This time I felt as though I accomplished something very big. I understood how those heroes felt when they saved the world.

I had seen TV news, hearing about some children who were abandoned by their divorced parents. I felt as though I saved my parents' marriage and saved myself from being abandoned by them. I felt very happy. My father winked at me when I left those lovebirds alone in their bedroom.

A few weeks later, my father told me my mother was taking a class called anger management, to help control her illness. He also explained all about anxiety neurosis. That anger management class must have helped her a lot because I did not see the outburst of her illness for a long time.

After many years' remission of her illness, my mother found a note in my father's uniform jacket one day. It read,

> Hi John,
>
> Thank you for a nice conversation and drinks. You were incredibly sexy and I thoroughly enjoyed you last night. Ummm…hope to get together soon. Probably on the next trip? Call me.
>
> Kate

My mother's illness flared up uncontrollably. That anger management class did not help. As she threw everything at my father, he did not have any choice but to leave the house in a hurry.

My mother locked herself in the bedroom. I was flabbergasted when I witnessed my mother's outburst. She acted like a crazy person, throwing everything at my father, ripping off his shirt and trousers.

The house looked as though a tornado went through the living room and kitchen. I had to tiptoe to get a broom. I carefully swept broken dishes first, then put away pots and pans. When my father came home, he helped me clean the house without saying anything. He looked tired and distraught.

I was already a teenager, so I knew all about what an affair meant, what adultery meant, and what a lipstick stain meant. Therefore, I decided to confront my father to hear his side of the story for the sake of my mother.

"Mary, I did not know the note was in my jacket. Yes, Kate is one of the flight attendants who are occasionally assigned to my flight, but I had never had drinks with her nor had conversation with her alone. I swear I had never ever spent time with her. Most importantly, I have never been called John by any of my flight attendants. They always address me as Captain Richardson."

He looked innocent, but I was not convinced. I acted as an interrogator in the courtroom. "Why do you think she put the note in your jacket like that? Is she single? Is she infatuated with you?"

"I don't know. I don't know anything about her background. Everybody knows that I am happily married and faithful to your mom."

"Is she young?"

"Yes, she is very young. She could be my daughter."

"Where was your uniform jacket?"

"I always hang it in the crew closet. Why?"

"Are any of your copilots named John?"

He thought for a minute and said, "Yes, John Monahan. He flew with me when the note was placed in my jacket."

I informed my mother that the note was placed in Dad's uniform jacket by mistake. That note was meant for a copilot named John Monahan. My mother was not convinced. She thought I was taking Dad's side.

"No, Mom. I know Dad well. He is telling the truth. No flight attendant would ever call Dad, John. Some people don't even know his first name. He had been always called Captain Richardson. So he is telling the truth."

"But if they were intimate, I am sure she would call him John."

"No, Mom. She is too young. He said she could be his daughter. Besides, Dad had seen John Monahan and Kate at the airport café often. They seemed to be in love."

My father did not say anything about their relationship, but I just added to convince my mother because I really believed what my father had to say when I interrogated him. I knew he had adored my mother, and he had been faithful to her for all his marriage life. He often said he was crazy about Mom, and she was the most intriguing person in his life.

"Mom, I want you to remember that Dad loves you very much. He said he has been faithful to you since he married you. So please believe him and trust him. Go tell him you are sorry. He has been worried. He looks very distraught and sad."

At the dinner table that night, my mother made my father his favorite handmade sushi. They both looked very happy. Again, I felt relieved.

That outburst was seemingly the last one I witnessed as far as I can remember. If she reminded herself Dad had been faithful to her, I did not think her illness should be triggered.

Even thought I had a miserable school life when I was young, I had the best home life with my parents. My parents were the best kind of parents. Despite of my mother's illness, she had been my wonderful, loving mother for all my life. My father had been my perfect and ideal father who had inspired me since I was a child.

When I was young, I often thought about my parents' loving relationship and dreamed about having my own family just as theirs and living in a house on a hill just like them so I could capture the perfect sunset from my own house and live happily ever after. That was my dream for a long time when I was a child.

When Eric Johnson was around, I really thought that he and I could have that future together and have a family just as my parents did. Eric could love me faithfully and unconditionally. Moreover, he could be crazy about me for the rest of my life, and we could live happily ever after with some children. That was my dream while Eric and I were together.

However, Eric and I went our separate ways. I went to college and Eric moved to Seattle to make a living to support his mother and two sisters. Eric was college material, but unfortunately, his mother could not afford to send him to college. When I thought about life in general, I felt sorry for Eric because his life was not as smooth as mine was. I concluded his destiny and my destiny were not meant to intertwine.

While I was growing up, my father often took me to fly his Cessna. He told me all about flying airplanes. He emphasized that if I ever decided to become a pilot, be the best and skillful one. In order to become a skillful one, I must practice, practice, practice, and obtain a lot of flying experience. Eventually, I might be able to acquire the instinct of flying any type of airplane.

My father also emphasized that I should go to an aviation college to learn all about airplanes, maintenance, mechanics, physics, aerial dynamics, and other aviation facts. I am glad I took his advice to finish aviation college.

While we flew together, my father also told me many other things. He talked about mostly his growing up with his parents, the Nakayas, and the people he met in college and in military. Those topics were repetitious, but I did not mind hearing them a million times because they were mostly happy ones and related to me as his daughter.

While flying, I also immensely enjoyed the view of the endless sky and beautiful blue ocean below. I marveled the invention of an airplane and imagined myself bowing in front of the Wright brothers.

The beautiful sights of the Pacific Ocean and the Hawaiian Islands were imbedded in my mind. If heaven ever existed, I thought, the sky above the Hawaiian Islands could be it. The sunset brings an awesome orange glow to the blue sky as though heaven were in a festive mood, welcoming some new arrivals from the earth.

Suddenly, I thought I saw my mother in an elegant attire traveling through the clouds to reach the beautiful blue sky above the Hawaiian Islands that might be called heaven.

My mother might have already arrived there without saying goodbye to us. My dreadful thought flashed back again. When I felt warm tears in my eyes, I turned my face toward the window.

Chapter 11

PARIS

When I had a summer break in high school, my father decided to take my mother and me to visit Paris. As it was my first visit to Paris, I was so excited that I secretly brushed up my French before the visit. My father had probably flown there before, but it seemed he had not explored much of Paris, known as the City of Lights.

My mother was born in Paris and educated in the French language during her childhood. In other words, Paris was her birthplace and her hometown. Her father was the Japanese ambassador to France. After she finished high school in Japan, she returned to Paris and studied in Sorbonne University as music major.

She spoke French like a native Parisian. When I was a toddler, she only spoke French to me. I thought French was my native language although my father did not understand a word I said. He spoke English and Japanese to me. My parents' language was Japanese. I was confused, but I was quick enough to switch from one language to another. My parents were amazed by their young child's ability.

They were always careful when they spoke their secrets in front of me because if they spoke in one of those three languages, I knew what kind of secrets they were talking about.

When I became older, my mother thought I had forgotten French since we had not conversed much at home. I did not tell her, but I understood every word she spoke in French. I had taken many language classes, especially French, in high school.

The day before the trip, at the dinner table, my mother was thanking my father for the trip.

"John, thank you for taking us to Paris. I am glad we all are going to Paris together. You and Mary will never regret visiting Paris. I think Paris is the most beautiful city in the world. I have a friend named Liliane there. We have not seen each other for almost twenty years. In fact, I have not seen Paris for twenty years. Paris is considered my hometown because I was born there and grew up there."

As she talked about Paris, her eyes were sparkling with excitement. Her beautiful face and cheeks were rouged like a young girl.

My father interrupted, "Keiko, the stove is smoking!"

My mother ran to the stove and came right back and kept talking.

"Oh, I forgot what I was going to say. Yes, Paris has many places we can visit. I will show you every corner of Paris. You will love Paris."

My father and I helped set the table for dinner; her talk of Paris was nonstop. She was so excited about the trip that she forgot to make her special dressing for the salad, so we used olive oil and vinegar instead.

"Keiko, you will oversee everything when we get there. You have the language. Is your French okay?"

"I guess so. I have not spoken much French lately, but I will be all right."

"By the way, did you get the medication for calming your anxiety of flying?"

"Yes, my doctor gave me some sleeping pills."

"I will remind you to take that before we board the airplane. Remember last time we went to Tahiti. You were shaking like a leaf."

My father obtained three free airline passes from his company. We were to spend one night in Atlanta, then fly to Paris the next day. Our stay in Paris would be for twelve days.

Family Secrets

At the departure gate in the Honolulu Airport, my father reminded my mother to take a sleeping pill too soon. While waiting for the boarding announcement, my mother's head was rested against my father's shoulder, and she was sleeping soundly. We tried to wake her up, but she did not respond, so my father held her waist, and I held her from the other side. We dragged her to the aircraft. Everybody thought she was drunk or sick.

We let her sit between us. I put a pillow against her head and covered her legs with a blanket. She soundly slept without eating or drinking almost nine hours until we arrived in Atlanta.

The next day, from Atlanta to Paris, she took some sleeping pills again and slept for almost eight hours. When she woke up, she stretched out her arms and innocently said she had a great rest.

When we arrived at the Charles de Gaulle (CDG) Airport, it seemed the airport was disorganized in its means of transferring passengers. The bus had to stop at all separate terminals for transit passengers before we reached the main terminal. It took almost forty-five minutes to get to where we were supposed to be. Additionally, it took one hour to get through the immigration and customs.

Since my father was a pilot, he seemed to know about the CDG's notoriously disorganized air terminal.

"Using the buses to transport passengers is too outdated. They should use trams or trains, like Atlanta Airport does."

My mother was disappointed as well. "I do not remember the airport was like this before. Everything looks old and dirty."

As we went through the immigration counter and customs, I noticed my mother was speaking French fluently, just as a Parisian would. She said she had not spoken French much lately, but she seemed to have no problem bringing her familiar language back into use. I was very proud of her; so was my father.

At the information desk, she got a map and directions to the hotel by asking many questions. Our personal tour guide was so efficient that my father and I predicted this trip would be a great one.

We rode a shuttle bus to Porte Maillot and took a taxi to the hotel. Because of my mother's language, we did not have any problems with our taxi driver. Some taxi drivers would drive the longest way possible to reach the destination in order to inflate the fare, but my mother knew exactly where we were going, so our taxi fare was not inflated.

The apartment of my mother's friend, Liliane, was in Pont de Neuilly. Our hotel was in the nearby business district called La Défense on the hill. At that time, they were building La Grande Arche Monument and the largest shopping mall in Paris. The streets were therefore congested.

My mother and Liliane had lived together for many years in the Latin Quarter district near Sorbonne University. They went to school together and played in the symphony together. Liliane had been a violinist for years. She had never been married.

When Liliane met us at our hotel, she embraced Mom and they cried a lot in front of us. We were officially introduced to Liliane, but she seemed to know all about us already. My mother probably sent our pictures or my pictures when I was much younger.

Liliane said to me in English, "Mary, you are no longer a child. You have grown up to be a beautiful teenage princess. You have handsome parents as well. Your mother and I are just like sisters for a long time."

She embraced me and shook my father's hand.

"Here are three tickets for this weekend's concert. I am very sorry I cannot take you around the city because of the summer concerts."

My mother said in French, "Liliane, do not worry about taking us around. Remember I used to live here, so I know every corner of Paris. Thank you for giving us tickets for the concert. We will be there. By the way, we would like to invite you to dinner one night before we go home."

Liliane nodded and smiled at us.

Our hotel room was on the highest floor of the building. From the balcony, we saw the city sights: the Eiffel Tower on the right, the Arch of Triumph in the center, and farther left, Sacré-Cœur at Montmartre.

Family Secrets

The room had two queen-size beds and a huge bathroom. I did not mind sharing the room with my parents. I really liked the choice of our hotel, especially, seeing the famous Eiffel Tower from our own balcony.

The Eiffel Tower was built in 1889 for the Universal Exposition. I did not see the sparkling lights when I went to Paris with my parents for the first time. However, in the past several years, whenever I visited Paris, I made a special effort to see the sparkling Eiffel Tower from Tracadero, especially at night.

The sight of the Eiffel Tower from Tracadero is awesomely panoramic, indescribably magical, and magnificent. The sparkling lights could be shown at night from 10:00 p.m. to 1:00 a.m. every hour on the hour for ten minutes during the summer evenings. The sparkling illumination was installed in 2000 but stopped in 2002. In June 2003, once again, sparkling lights started sparkling.

The next day, we took a tour of the Eiffel Tower. The sight from the top of the Eiffel Tower was unforgettable. Everything looked very small; cars, buildings, and streets down below looked just like a miniature city made of matchboxes.

One day, we took the Metro to visit the Montparnasse building, the tallest building in Paris, to see a 360-degree view. From the top of the 59th floor, we viewed the city of Paris in more realistic size; cars, houses, and buildings did not look like matchboxes. The 689 feet height of the Montparnasse building was much shorter than that of the Eiffel Tower, which stood the majestic 1,063 feet high over the City of Lights.

We also took the Metro to the Louvre. We were going to spend the entire day there, but the line was too long, so we decided to walk all the way to Champs-Élysées. I did not know how many miles from the Louvre to Champs-Élysées, but to me it seemed like a hundred miles. In any rate, we started walking through Tuileries Garden–Concorde and to Champs-Élysées. The summer sun was unbearable.

We made some stops for my father's photo opportunities. As I was already exhausted from walking a hundred miles, I sat on the lawn to rest at every stop. My parents were in good shape, my mother especially. She had walked every morning, seemingly, since I was born. As my father had been playing golf for years, walking did not bother him either.

Therefore, walking did not exhaust them at all. Me, the youngest one, was in bad shape. I felt aches and pains in my muscles as though I were their seventy-year-old grandmother. However, I did not tell them about my aches and pains.

At an outdoor café on Champs-Élysées, my muscle pain was finally eased by sitting on a chair. While eating lunch, I watched the people on the famous street. My parents were discussing something.

Thousands of people passed by where we were sitting: some following a tour guide, some looking for a restaurant, some waiting for someone to lunch, some taking pictures of the crowd, some walking in a hurry to reach their destinations, and some fashionably dressed Parisians carrying their shopping bags.

After lunch, we walked to the nearby Arch of Triumph. My father wanted to view the branched-out streets and the buildings from the top, so we paid to climb the steps, no elevators. My parents did not complain, but my seventy-year-old body felt aches and pains again.

The next day, we visited Cimetière du Père-Lachaise, the most famous and the oldest cemetery in Paris. Famous French artists, musicians, politicians, singers, movie stars, and notable people are buried there.

While inside this huge cemetery, we visited Chopin's tomb. There were many fresh flowers in front of the tomb. Those flowers were from his fans. The narrow pathway was almost filled with flowers. Even though he died in 1849, his music was still alive in the music lovers' hearts as well as my mother's heart as a pianist.

My mother said, "Liliane and I picnicked here often. One day, we brought violins and practiced in front of Chopin's tomb. Many tourists came by and listened to our practice. They thought we were a couple of starving musicians who wanted some inspiration from Chopin as well as gratuities from the listeners. Yes, we wanted some inspirations, but we did not expect any gratuities or donations. Nevertheless, the tourists left tons of francs, the French currency at that time, in my violin case. We could not believe how generous and sympathetic those people could be. On the way home, Liliane and I went to one of the most exclusive French restaurants and dined." My mother laughed and looked very happy reminiscing about her life in Paris.

I was amazed how well my mother knew about Paris and the Parisians, and how they think. She easily located the historical places, museums, castles, and even famous restaurants.

She told us how Parisian women think about other women. The married women think that all women around them, single or married, are threats to their own marriages. Therefore, married French women do not seem to have real friends.

Recently I read a book titled *Almost French*, written by an Australian author who moved to Paris and tried to assimilate herself into Parisian society because her beloved live-in boyfriend was French. In that book, she delivered a somewhat similar view of the married women or women in general in Paris.

One day, we decided to visit Sorbonne University, the school which my mother graduated from many years ago. It is located near the Pantheon. We walked from Notre Dame to Sorbonne University.

The summer sun was shining, but the tall buildings on the incline threw shade on the streets so that there was no direct summer heat. Instead, we felt a cool breeze coming through between the tall buildings.

My mother wanted to show us the campus, but the entrance to the main school buildings was gated and guarded by two police officers.

They wanted to see a student or faculty ID. My mother told them, in French, that she graduated from Sorbonne many years ago, and today, she brought her family from the United States of America to show them the school campus. One of the officers kindly escorted us inside to view the courtyard for five minutes. They allowed us to take some pictures.

I saw two statues in front of the main administration building. If my memory is correct, one was a famous French scientist and the other was a French philosopher. Both graduated from Sorbonne University over a century ago.

I could not recall exactly how many floors were in the buildings, but they looked tall—at least seven stories—and well maintained. I saw some students running up the wide stairs to the next floor, probably to their next class, and some students sitting and studying on the steps around the courtyard. All the classroom buildings were quiet. I figured all summer classes were in session.

Four sides of the buildings around the courtyard are connected. The campus is almost two blocks long and a block wide. The large courtyard is therefore a rectangular shape. All the surrounding buildings outside the main campus also belong to the university.

The outdoor café in front of the main gate was occupied by many students who looked busy discussing and comparing their notes. Those students seemed to be Sorbonne's future scholars. I imagined my mother and Liliane walking the street with their violin cases.

After visiting Sorbonne University, we went into a traditional French restaurant at the Latin Quarter district to have lunch. My father and I ordered one dozen escargots (French snails) each. Escargots were heavily cooked in garlic and olive oil and served in shells. The taste was exquisite, especially with French bread.

Even though my mother had cooked fabulous French dishes in the past, she never served escargots at home because she dislikes snails. That was therefore my first-time eating escargots.

My father ordered another dozen for his lunch. I was not that hungry, so my appetizer became my lunch. While my mother was finishing her French specialty soup and sandwiches, she kept pinching her nose and exclaimed, "John, please don't speak to me for several hours. Here, this stick of chewing gum might help."

She took out two sticks of chewing gum from her bag after we finished escargots. My father blew his breath to his cupped hand to smell garlic, and then he put a stick of chewing gum in his mouth. She gave me the other stick.

One day, we ate breakfast at one of the eateries on Rue Montorgueil. That long street housed traditional French shops and markets. Both sides of Rue Montorgueil included bread shops, fish stores, cheese stores, colorfully decorated vegetable and fruit stands, flower shops, meat markets with horsemeat, many eateries for the local Parisians, wine shops, clothing shops, jewelry stores, drug stores, cosmetic stores, gifts shops, and some family-oriented restaurants for the Parisians in the neighborhood.

It seemed the morning was the busiest time for Parisians to get fresh flowers, vegetables, fruits, and meats. The markets on Montorgueil had been there for centuries and catered to the indigenous Parisians.

The shoppers and the storekeepers seemed to know each other, and they were exchanging the neighborhood news and information. Well, from my eavesdropping, they were gossiping about their acquaintances and neighbors.

After breakfast, we bought some seasonally harvested cherries at the fruit stand and ate them on the way to the Metro. I remember they were plump and juicy.

Since we visited so many places, I forgot the names of those historic places. However, I still remember how I felt when I visited the Notre Dame Cathedral and Sacré-Cœur at Montmartre.

The visits to those churches made me think as a teenager that human history had revolved around the churches, temples, and religious worshipping places since human civilization had begun.

My mother and I used to go to a Catholic church when I was young, but I was not impressed by the church's rituals, praying or worshipping God whom I had never met. I asked my mother once, "Where does God live? Why doesn't he come visit us and shake hands with us as Father Montanez does? Mom, have you met God before?"

My mother could not answer. She was not a devout Catholic, but when she was in a private school in Paris, going to church was one of the daily rituals she had to follow.

In high school, studying world history, I remembered the people in Europe and in the Middle East shed so much blood in the name of God for many centuries. They wanted to prove their religion had the right God and killed each other in the name of their God.

The suicidal terrorists related to the Islamic belief acted upon the name of their God to kill other humans as well as themselves. Did their God allow them to do that?

I was overwhelmed and distressed by thinking about all the religions in this world: Jewish, Islam, Protestant, Catholic, Hinduism, Buddhism, Shintoism, and other small religious cults. Most of them do not respect other religions because they think their God is the right God, and they therefore think that their religion is the right religion or a better religion.

My father believed in *human decency* as his religion. He literally hated the religious people who tried to recruit him to their faith by saying that if he did not believe in their God, he would be burned in hell.

I am like my father. I believe in human decency and I want to be decent for the rest of my life. I want to be kind, thoughtful, generous, helpful, honest; yes, that is decent.

When we visited the Louvre, I was just overwhelmed by the Louvre's fourteenth or fifteenth-century paintings and statues that carried religious themes. Yes, I saw Leonardo da Vinci's *Mona Lisa* and some other paintings. Regretfully, however, I was astounded by the volume of the exhibits and lost interest in seeing more of the Louvre. I felt illiterate for not knowing the names of those ancient artists or sculptors.

Moreover, I found out the Louvre did not house the paintings of the indigenous French impressionists: Claude Monet, Pierre-Auguste Renoir, Paul Cezanne, and Paul Gauguin. I just sat at the main lobby and waited for my parents to finish the tour. At that time, I. M. Pei had not built the famous Pyramide du Louvre yet in the lobby.

On Saturday night, we dressed up and went to Liliane's concert. I was told the symphony she belonged to was one of the oldest and best in France, and even in all of Europe. The concert was superb. It was so crowded that we could not meet up with Liliane afterward.

The day before we were going home, we took Liliane out for dinner to the restaurant of her choice. Surprisingly, she chose a Japanese restaurant. She knew a lot about Japanese food. She said she used to crave for sushi after my mother left for Japan. Apparently, Liliane ate my mother's homemade sushi often at their apartment.

When we parted at the restaurant, Liliane started crying, so did my mother. Liliane profusely apologized that she did not have the time to visit with us, especially with my mother.

I heard what my mother said to Liliane in French. "Do not worry. We will write to each other often. By the way, Liliane, don't work too hard. Take some time off to visit me in Hawaii. We have a nice house on the hill, and you can look out to see the Hawaiian sunset. It is beautiful. You can stay with us as many days as you want."

Liliane nodded several times in tears. They both embraced each other again. When we left in a taxi, she was waving at us in tears until we turned into the corner. I watched her tall, thin silhouette as she waved.

That was the last time any of us saw Liliane. While I was in college, my mother called to tell me that Liliane died of breast cancer.

On the way home from Paris, again my mother slept peacefully. From the window, I saw the Atlantic Ocean down below. It looked ominous with the dark-blue color, almost black unlike the Pacific Ocean.

While staring at the Atlantic Ocean, my thinking became as dark as the Atlantic Ocean. I thought about my intimidating childhood by a psychotic child, religious prosecutions in history, people's hate crimes against different races or homosexuals, criminal acts of mentally ill patients, terrorists, obsessively jealous people, and psychotic liars.

While we were crossing the Pacific Ocean, my thoughts became as bright as the blue ocean below, which was so unlike the Atlantic Ocean. My mind filled with thoughts of Alice's smiles, Nina's laughter, Eric's kisses, my own sunset, and my dream of becoming a pilot. Somehow, I felt elated thinking about all my dear friends, especially my sweetheart, Eric.

When the ocean color changed to aqua blue, I knew we were closer to paradise. Home sweet home!

Chapter 12

ALICE AND NINA

After my affair with Bruce Hudson ended, I simply said to my mother that Bruce and I broke up. I was sure she wanted to know the reason of the breakup, but she only said, "I am sorry. Are you all right with it?"

I nodded several times. After that, my mother had never brought up the subject of Bruce Hudson. She probably thought if I wanted to tell her all about my breakup, I would come tell her as I always had done in the past. However, she probably interpreted this breakup as too personal since I did not come to tell her, so she decided to leave me alone.

I was ashamed of myself getting involved with a married man. The only solution to forget all about the fraudulent relationship was to travel. After the trip, I was able to bury Bruce Hudson deep in the ground and decided never to bring up his name as long as I lived.

Several months after I buried Bruce Hudson, Alice came to visit me from Maui. Nina dropped everything and joined us. Whenever we were together, we always planned to spend the night at my place. We stayed up late to make our night longer.

My dear friends, Alice and Nina, were married and have children. Rearing their children, looking after their husbands, and taking care of the daily household chores had been a lot more hectic than they said they had anticipated as their destiny.

Although they seemed happy being with their families, they said that they would not mind switching roles with me and enjoying the freedom of a single person.

Even though we had not seen each other that much, we made sure to call each other on the phone to stay in touch. Nina and I had lunched together occasionally, whenever I had the time to stop by her office near the airport. She had been helping her husband with his shipping company while her children were at school.

Alice lived in Maui too far away from Honolulu, but whenever Alice came to Oahu, Nina and I made sure to meet up with her and have a slumber party at my place.

Since Alice and I did not have any siblings, we naturally acted as though we were sisters for life. We would chat on the phone often. I would also send birthday presents and postcards to my godson Gregory, who thought of me as his inspiration.

Whenever we three were together, our friendships were rekindled. We bonded just as before and acted as though we were silly teenagers again.

After spreading a large picnic blanket to cover my bed and many pillows around, we put our favorite junk foods including Portuguese doughnuts called Leonard's Malasadas on a big wooden tray in the middle; we three were all situated for a slumber party. We could talk anything and everything in pajamas. We did not have any secrets among us.

Alice and Nina talked about their husbands and children in details. They told me all about their lovemaking with their husbands. They also wanted to know all about my exciting life as a pilot and my love life.

I did not want to bring up the subject of Bruce Hudson, but I decided to tell them all about my fraudulent relationship. They were as angry as I was, and at the same time, they were sympathetic about my situation.

Alice said in a sisterly voice, "Next time, when you get involved with a man, make sure to get his home address. If your date does not give it to you, just think he must be hiding something. Do not hesitate to ask your date many blunt questions such as 'Are you married?' 'Do you have a girlfriend at home?' and look right in his eyes to see if he has any hesitation. If he has some hesitations, he might be married or have a girlfriend at home. A long-distance relationship has some dangers, so don't be naive."

Alice continued, "I am not an expert, but from my common sense, if your date is not interested in meeting your family or friends, he might be hiding something as well. Be aware of the deceitful men who might try to take advantage of a long-distance relationship. Be a detective before you become a lover. You are such a beautiful girl. I guarantee that you will meet someone special soon. Remember, marriage is not everything. Live well and enjoy your single life as much as you can. We love you, kiddo."

Nina agreed with Alice by nodding.

"Yes, Moms. Thank you for your advice. I will be careful next time. Yes, I will be a detective before becoming a lover."

We laughed and ate some more junk food and sweets. Malasadas tasted great.

Now we changed the subject to a gossip.

Alice suddenly sat up and said, "Do you remember Sue?"

"Who forgets Susanna Mendosa? Occasionally, I still have nightmares seeing Sue as a wicked stepmother of Cinderella. By the way, do you remember Eric Johnson, my first love? My high school sweetheart? He wrote me a letter after many years. It was probably eight or nine years ago. I almost forgot who he was. Well, strangely he wanted to locate Susanna Mendosa. He did not ask me how I was doing. He just wanted to know if I happened to know Susanna Mendosa's whereabouts or if some of my friends knew her address. Since I really did not know where she lived, I simply wrote him I did not know her address."

"Hmmm... That Eric Johnson wanted to know Sue's address? Did you hear from him after that?" Alice asked.

"No."

"Hmmm... I am just curious. Did you say Eric wrote you from Seattle?"

"Yes. I guess he had lived there since he moved to Seattle."

"I was told Sue married a son of a wealthy family in Seattle and her husband died of a rare disease shortly after their marriage. She was pregnant, so she decided to come home to have her child in Maui."

"Wow, I did not know that. Do you think Eric had met Sue in Seattle?"

"I don't know. Well, in any rate, let me tell you all about her mother, Mrs. Matilda Mendosa."

Alice continued, "She is the founder of the Clubhouse, which is also the headquarters of the Kamaaina Portuguese Society. I am currently serving as the elected president of the organization. I had been the volunteer accountant for years, but this year, some of the board members and the previous president campaigned for me to be president against several candidates including Sue. Mrs. Mendosa campaigned for her daughter. The election was held at the New Year's party this year. You should have seen Sue's face when the result was announced. Mrs. Mendosa thought Sue should be elected because she is the daughter of the founder. The election was overwhelmingly for my favor."

"Is Sue of Portuguese descent?"

"Yes. She is a Kamaaina Portuguese, probably third generation just like me. Because of Mrs. Mendosa's donation to build the Clubhouse twenty years ago, the organization became prosperous under a nonprofit status. We have been able to generate the income from the facility rentals."

"Mrs. Mendosa must be a very generous donor."

"Oh, no. She did not donate the money out of love. Her donation was something to do with the IRS. I believe her ego was the biggest factor on that donation as well. According to the board members, she made sure her name was carved on the marble in front of the Clubhouse."

"Did she donate the entire cost?"

"Oh, no. She just donated the down payment. The organization still pays the monthly mortgage from the rental income every month. I don't know how much she donated, but it was just the down payment. She is such a bragger. She tells the guests from the state or other organizations that she saved the organization from a financial difficulty twenty years ago. She tells it as though she had paid the entire cost of the facility. She has tried many times to control the organization as her own company. Once I heard that she transferred a substantial amount of the organizational funds to her own bank account. When the accountant caught her transaction, the board was going to report it to the police as embezzlement. However, since she returned the money, the board dropped the case."

Alice put a piece of malasadas in her mouth and continued. "I was told she really thought the money was hers like the dividends on her down payment. The rumor was that her fortune was depleting for some reasons and she needed the money at that time. That was just a rumor, but they said it was quite a scandal for a while. The board almost suspended her from the organization."

"How did she transfer the fund to her own bank account?"

"It was easy. She was one of the signature authorities of the bank account. If the accountant acted in her favor, none of the board members would have ever noticed her embezzlement. I don't know how she had done it without getting the accountant's approval, but she did it. Therefore, they took her name out from the signature authorities after that."

She put a piece of malasadas into her mouth again and continued. "The income of the organization comes from the membership fees, individual cash donations, and facility rentals. However, the income and accounting book must be open to every member and the IRS as a public domain."

"Who is the accountant now?

"Sue is."

"Did the board approve of her?"

"Yes. Mrs. Mendosa showed Sue's résumé to the board, bragged about Sue's accounting skills, talked about Sue's marriage to a wealthy husband who left his fortune to Sue, and said her daughter might donate some of her fortune to the organization just as her mother did twenty years ago. She also added Sue would be the better accountant than the previous one. She insinuated that I had done a lousy job. I was an accountant for almost five years and the organization became prosperous. Can you imagine that? I can't stand that woman. What a family!"

Nina said, "I am not a psychiatrist, but Sue and her mother must be suffering from a mental illness, like adult ADHD, bipolar disorder, or schizophrenia. Remember she was always hyper when she was in the classroom?"

"What is ADHD?" I asked.

"Attention Deficit Hyperactivity Disorder."

"Is that a mental illness?"

"Sort of. I don't know. Anyway, I read about ADHD or bipolar disorder that usually runs in the family, but it could be controlled by medication."

Nina wiped her mouth with a napkin and gestured to Alice to continue.

"In any rate, when I handed over the accounting book to Sue, I named my husband, Daniel Thomas, as the auditor of the book, just in case. Sue did not like that. She wanted her mother, Mrs. Mendosa, to be the auditor because Daniel is not of Portuguese descent. Daniel is a spousal member. Nevertheless, the board members know his contribution to the organization as a lawyer and a certified accountant, so they unanimously chose Daniel to be an auditor. After Mrs. Mendosa's embezzlement incident, the board took her title as the registered agent of the IRS and gave the title to Daniel Thomas years back. Now she has no title, except the engraved name as founder. The board members do not like the Mendosa family because they treat the board members like their servants."

Alice started eating potato chips instead of malasadas. Nina and I took some bites on malasadas and I asked, "How did Sue become the accountant?"

"The organization relies heavily on volunteers. The board did not have any choice but to choose the person who volunteered. Sue volunteered to be an accountant, so she became an accountant. I am the elected president. Daniel was the chosen auditor by the board. Of course, none of us get paid. It is volunteer work."

According to Alice, over the years, the Clubhouse spent some money to renovate and expand the facility so that it could accommodate at least three hundred people. The rent is reasonable. Therefore, the rental schedule is always full. People would rent the facility for wedding receptions, anniversaries, birthdays, board meetings, class reunions, family reunions, and other special occasions. Many volunteer officers would be glad to oversee the rental setup and schedules. The organizational assets had increased steadily while Alice had served as a volunteer accountant for many years.

"By the way, does Sue remember who you are?"

"I don't know. Since Mrs. Mendosa seemed to be hiding her husband's imprisonment in Honolulu from everybody, Sue might be avoiding me because I know her family secrets. By the way, Sue's daughter, Natalie and Sue are listed as Mendosa, Sue's maiden name, and yet she wears an expensive wedding ring with a big diamond. I often wonder why she did not use her husband's last name for Natalie. Anyhow, her marriage probably took place a few years after high school because her daughter is already a teenager."

"Is she still outspoken and acts psychotic?" I asked.

"No. Strangely, she is very quiet as though her personality has changed. Her quietness worries me a lot. She acts very secretive, enigmatic, and ominous just like a criminal would act."

"What happened to her father after he was indicted?"

"I heard he was imprisoned because of some illegal stock trading or embezzlement. Mrs. Mendosa divorced him immediately after the scandal. She transferred her husband's fortune, the assets of their mansion, and fled to Maui with Sue. After his imprisonment, nobody seems to know his whereabouts. Remember Sue used to brag about how rich they were, having ten thousand books in the mansion. Mrs. Mendosa tells everybody her fortune came from her side of the family. It seems I am the only one who knows about their past or their family secrets, but I have not said anything about their past, even to Daniel."

"Did you say those three women live in the same house?"

"Yes. You should see their house on the beach. Mrs. Mendosa must have gotten a powerful lawyer to get everything her husband had before he was jailed."

I stopped eating the junk food. I could not eat anything anymore. I was full. "I hope Sue would not bother you as she did to me in the past. She was such a wicked person when she was young. Please be careful. I would not trust her."

"I would not either. I told Daniel to be careful too."

My childhood friend Alice was a promising and ambitious corporate lawyer in a law firm in Honolulu after graduating from a law school in mainland USA. Alice's parents were lawyers who had lived in the same neighborhood where I grew up.

When she fell in love with her colleague, Daniel Thomas, they both decided to marry. She was almost thirty. Her husband, Daniel, was offered a senior position in a law firm in Maui. So Alice sacrificed her career and followed her husband to Maui. During her pregnancy, she had worked as a part-time legal assistant to help some nonprofit organizations including the Kamaaina Portuguese Society.

Alice's grandmother, who used to bake cookies as big as my palm, passed away when Alice was in college. Her parents were killed by a car accident while they were traveling, shortly before Alice's baby was due, so Alice did not have anybody but me. She asked me to take a week off from my job to help her out with her baby.

Daniel was elated to see his baby boy in good health. He profusely thanked me when I was helping Alice. Gregory looked plump and healthy. He resembled a mixture of Alice and Daniel with red hair like Daniel. Naturally, I became Gregory's godmother.

When my godson Gregory was a toddler, he called me Annie May because he could not pronounce "Auntie Mary." I used to fly there for his birthdays. The years I could not attend his birthdays, I sent him numerous birthday gifts. Alice thought I was spoiling Gregory.

Whenever I visited foreign countries, I sent him postcards. Gregory wrote me many thank-you cards in his childish penmanship. He often wrote me and told me his dream was to be a pilot just like me. In any rate, we had built a good rapport between us.

Alice still practiced law on a part-time basis, but her main concern was to take care of her beloved husband and her son's schooling. Now Alice had an additional responsibility as the president of a nonprofit organization.

Nina, my other dear friend, is a native Hawaiian of Polynesian descent. Her parents used to operate a large convenience store in the neighborhood where we grew up. They sold it when Nina finished high school and moved to Pearl City where their other children lived. Nina was the youngest child.

Nina graduated from college in California and came back to be hired by one of the internationally known companies in Honolulu. She met and married Tom Clayton from Pearl City, who worked for the same company.

She worked until her first baby was born. In the meantime, Tom's father died, and he had to take over the family business in Pearl City. Nina's oldest child is in junior high now and two are still in elementary school. Currently, she helps her husband at his shipping company while the children are in school.

"Mary, when can I switch the role with you? I am so tired of being a wife, a mother, a homemaker, an office manager, and a lover. I'd really like to be you and fly a jumbo jet to anywhere I want to go. I need a vacation."

"Nina, I should envy you because you have your beautiful children and handsome husband. I have none, except my parents. You can enjoy them as much as you can. Your freedom comes later. You and Tom can vacation all over the world after your children grow up."

"It will be a long way off, but I guess this must be my destiny. I had better be thankful for what I have. Mary, I want you remember something. Every marriage comes with tons of responsibilities, obligations, headaches, and heartaches that you cannot anticipate now as someone who's single. So enjoy your single life without any obligations and responsibilities. Nevertheless, whenever you find your Prince Charming and get married fast, Alice and I could come to your bedroom and supervise your lovemaking as your dear friends, just because we love you."

We laughed aloud together.

Alice added, "Remember, be a detective before jumping in bed with your date. We love you, kiddo."

I nodded.

"Thanks, Moms."

We stopped talking as the night fell deeper.

Chapter 13

Eric Johnson

Alice called me several months after we got together; she asked me if I still had Eric Johnson's address. It had been so long ago, I did not know where to look for it, but I finally found his address from my computer. I called Alice back and gave his address.

"This address may be old but try it. Why do you need his address?"

"Our twentieth high school reunion is coming up soon. We are locating those who did not attend or never listed their addresses in the tenth alumni book. Eric Johnson was one of them. I will be serving as one of the committee members again. Nina will be the chairperson for the twentieth reunion. You are a committee member as well according to the list I received from Nina. Did you get one?"

"No, not yet, but I will be glad to help. Do we have more committee members?"

"Yes, six more. You and Nina are supposed to reserve the reception facility in Waikiki Beach area and negotiate the hotel deals for out-of-state alumni. By the way, do you happen to have Eric's phone number as well?"

"No."

"Well, I must write him to see if it is all right to publish his home address in our alumni address book and remind him we will be having the twentieth high school reunion soon. I'll also tell him Sue lives in Maui, if he still wants to locate her."

"Do you think he still wants to locate Sue? By the way, since Sue did not finish high school with us, she would not be involved in this reunion, right?"

"Right."

"I am glad. I just don't want to see her face as long as I live."

"I know what you mean. Well, I will write to Eric Johnson. I hope he remembers me. I will tell him that you have been working as a pilot for one of the major airlines. I bet he does not know that. When he writes me back, I will let you read his letter. I will talk to you soon."

I did not want to start the subject of Eric Johnson. He was my forgotten and ancient past. He had been nobody for me for many years.

Several weeks later, Alice called me. She told me to sit on a chair first. I did not know the reason, but I took a chair at the kitchen table.

"Eric wrote me a ten-page letter to let me know how he has been doing in Seattle. Are you sitting down? I am talking about Eric, your first love. Are you there?"

"Yes. What about Eric?"

"Well, let me read his letter so you would understand. It will be a very long letter, but be patient."

I was not interested in Eric's letter. Besides, I had a scheduled flight to fly. I was leaving for the airport. "Alice, I have to meet my flight. Please send me a copy of his letter."

"Sorry. Okay. I will get some copies and mail them to you. Right now, I am just flabbergasted and speechless. Anyhow, read the letter first and call me."

"Okay, I will be back tomorrow."

The letter arrived a few days later. I was hesitant to read his letter. I felt as though I was getting involved with my forgotten past and was about to dig up something undesirable from the old tomb. The letter was left unopened on the kitchen table for several days. Alice called me to see if I read Eric's letter or not, so I did not have any choice but to read it.

Dear Alice,

Yes. I remember you. I always thought that you three, with Mary and Nina, were the smartest and nicest girls in my class. Thank you for writing me. It has been so long since I heard from any of my classmates.

This letter would be a long one, but hear me out. I would like to explain how Susanna Mendosa came into my life after I left Honolulu. I wanted to let Mary know the same thing before, but I knew how Mary felt about Sue, so I decided not to bother Mary.

When we moved to Seattle, we lived with my mother's relatives for a while. My mother worked for a Chinese restaurant, and I worked in a factory at the seaport. My sisters went to school.

After Mary left for college, I had missed Mary for the longest time, but I knew Mary's life was on the right track, so I decided to bow out from her life.

When my family got situated in an apartment in Seattle, Susanna Mendosa phoned me. Somehow, she tracked me down all the way to Seattle. She said someone told her my whereabouts, so she located me. Since she was attending school in Seattle for a while, she wanted to get together with me as a friend.

Besides, she wanted me to look at some old papers. She gave me her phone number and told me to call her anytime. As I did not call her back, she left several messages on the phone.

Since I remembered her dishonest and psychotic personality when we were in school, I did not feel like calling her to meet her, so I did not return the call.

However, one day she showed up at my work right before I was going home for the day. She probably got my company's phone number from my sister and located my workplace. It was the first time I saw her after so many years later.

Sue dressed very elegantly and looked very pretty. I thought I was seeing a different person. She did not show any image of Cinderella's stepmother. Her personality seemed to have changed too. She drove a brand-new sports car.

She politely asked me if she could give me a ride home. Since I was taking a bus home, I agreed to ride with her. On the way home, she wanted to show me some important papers, so we stopped at a restaurant.

At the restaurant, she took out her bank statements. It had a list of monthly draft transactions. She explained that the draft was made to pay Eric Johnson's school tuition for three years. I was stunned.

When my parents were divorced, my father signed on the divorce decree and agreed to pay my high school tuition until my graduation or at the age of eighteen. As the school had never contacted us for the tuition, my mother and I thought that my father had been paying for all that time even though we did not know his whereabouts. I had no idea that the tuition debt was drafted automatically from Susanna Mendosa's savings account for three years.

She explained how it happened. Her father, the chairman of the school board, was informed that Eric Johnson in his daughter's class was about to be put out due to his unpaid tuition.

When she heard about it, she cried hysterically and told him that Eric was like her childhood boyfriend, her most important person in her life since elementary school. Eric could be her Prince Charming, could be her father's business partner in the future.

She cried, cried, and begged her father to retain Eric in school with his power. She told him to use her inheritance money to pay Eric's tuition every month so he could go to high school with her.

Sue was his only beloved child, and he had always done whatever his daughter asked him to do. He agreed to set up the monthly draft from her savings account. Mr. Mendosa was going to talk to Eric's mother later so she could repay the tuition to Susanna Mendosa in the future.

In the meantime, Mr. Mendosa was indicted. Sue and her mother fled to Maui. Nevertheless, the tuition draft remained effective as planned.

Sue said she just discovered the draft transaction recently when she transferred some of her money from the savings account to the checking account. Her father put more than enough money into her savings account before the draft started. As she became eighteen, her trust fund was transferred to her savings account as well.

I thanked Sue and told her that I would like to pay for the debt in an installment payment plan. She said she was not interested in collecting the money. She just wanted me to know the fact of my high school tuition. She also said that tuition was not that much since her father arranged to put some scholarship fund into Eric's tuition. If she needed the money, she would ask me in the future.

However, she requested one favor from me. She wanted to get together with me as a friend while attending school in Seattle. Then she asked me if I were still involved with Mary. At that time, I was still missing Mary and thinking about her often, so I did not say anything. I think she interpreted we were still together. She looked as though she was determined to win me back from her rival, Mary.

She started picking me up almost every day after work. My friends at work were kidding me about my rich girlfriend with a sports car. Some met Sue. We often stopped at one of the exclusive restaurants for dinner. Since I could not afford the price, she paid. She did not mind paying, rather insisted paying.

I thought to myself that Sue must be splurging her inheritance money for our dinner. I felt somewhat uncomfortable. If she were an old woman, the waiters at the restaurant might have thought I was her gigolo.

She said she was going to school, but she did not look like she was attending any school. Moreover, she never told me which school she was attending. She said she was studying to be an accountant for her mother's company.

One day, she invited me to have dinner at her apartment. She lived in an expensively furnished apartment more like a hotel room with a kitchen.

I thought to myself, if she kept living like that, her savings account should be depleted fast. The takeout dinner was on the table with a candle. The room was lit with several candles... very romantic. We finished an expensive bottle of red wine together on that night.

She dressed seductively and treated me like a king throughout the night...I was flattered. We made passionate love after dinner. While we were in bed, she asked me if Mary's lovemaking was as passionate as hers was.

At then, I told her that Mary and I were no longer together...we decided to go on separate ways, and I have not seen or heard from Mary for some time.

Strangely, she threw her arms up and started sulking. I thought she should be glad because I was not involved with Mary or anybody else, but she did not look happy. She rather looked remorseful.

Shortly after that, she vacated the apartment and moved away without saying goodbye to me. The apartment owner did not have her forward address since the room was rented weekly or monthly bases.

She only lived in that apartment for two months. It seemed she did not come here for schooling. She came here to track me down. I tried to locate her, but nobody seemed to know where she went. About four or five months later, one of my friends who met Sue at work told me that he saw Sue in the fish market at the pier. He also said she looked pregnant.

I knew then she was still living in Seattle. However, I was overwhelmed by the news of her pregnancy. I figured she was carrying my child and felt responsible. So I went to the fish market looking for her every day, but she did not show up. She was gone. Years later, I wrote to Mary if she happened to know Sue's address or whereabouts.

Alice, I assume Sue lives in your neighborhood. Do you see her often? Is she married? Does she have a child about the age of sixteen or seventeen? If you don't mind, please let me know anything and everything about Sue and her child without Sue knowing it.

The address you used was my mother's address. Currently, I live with my girlfriend and her son. Yes, you can publish this new address. Yes, I will try to attend the reunion with my girlfriend. Please send me an invitation.

I am very proud of Mary and genuinely happy for her because her dream really came true. Stay in touch.

Thank you,
Eric Johnson

I was flabbergasted and speechless just as Alice was. Now I could put all the pieces together to fill Sue's lies. She was supposed to be a wealthy young widow, her husband was supposed to be a son of the wealthy family in Seattle who supposedly died of a rare disease before her daughter was born, and her wedding ring with large diamond was supposed to be given by her wealthy husband.

Whoa, what a liar she had been. Sue had been the same person as before, lived in the grandeur delusion, and lied like a pirate. She must have been suffering from a mental illness called Grandeur Delusion or Grandeur Hallucination, if such mental illness ever existed in medical books.

She had her old grudge as well as her obsessive jealousy against Mary because she had lost every race against Mary when she was in school...race in beauty...race in intelligence...race in love relationship...race in popularity. She always lost. Whenever she thought about Mary, she could not stand it. When she received the bank statements on Eric's tuition, she decided to track Eric down, assuming he was still Mary's precious love. She wanted to destroy Mary in love race by winning Eric this time.

However, in order to attract Eric, she remembered she must dress elegantly like Mary and looked pretty like Mary because Eric was always mesmerized by how Mary looked in school. Therefore, she spent lots of money to change her attire and looks. That was how she looked pretty and attractive to Eric when he saw her after so many years later.

Furthermore, she bought an expensive car to mesmerize Eric and let him know she was financially secured unlike Mary. Sue wanted to use Eric to challenge Mary, but she did not know Eric and Mary were no longer together. Eric was no longer Mary's sweetheart. Her victorious smirks were useless...the trophy called Eric was useless. A one-woman race without the rival was meaningless.

In reality, her winning trophy was merely a factory worker with no future. Her mother would be furious and might risk losing her family fortune or inheritance. She panicked. She threw the trophy away and vacated the apartment in a hurry.

Nevertheless, she did not know she was already pregnant. Her revenge came with a problem...pregnancy. When she found out her pregnancy, she thought about telling Eric, but she knew Eric would marry her for the sake of the child.

She knew he was merely a factory worker with a meager wage. She pictured her mother's disapproving look. Therefore, she decided to make up a story. She stayed in Seattle until her story plot was completed.

She probably wrote her mother saying she met a son of a wealthy family while attending school and married in Las Vegas, that her husband gave her a wedding ring with large diamond—she probably used a chunk of her inheritance money to purchase the largest diamond ring she was able to find in Seattle.

She probably described how beautiful their apartment was, how rich his family was, how humongous the mansion his parents owned. They were elated to hear the news on their first grandchild. Her husband was so ecstatic that they wanted to buy a huge house soon for the baby. Unfortunately, her husband had suffered from a rare disease and suddenly died.

She probably described how sorrowful the situation she had been in for months. She did not want to have a child in Seattle. She wanted to be with her mother who was knowledgeable of everything, especially about babies. It would be wonderful to have a child in Maui. Therefore, she wanted to come home. As a result, Mrs. Mendosa made a baby room in her mansion and welcomed Sue.

Alice called me. We talked about Sue for a long time comparing our theories but came to the same story line. We did not know how to handle the situation. However, we decided to keep Eric's letter secret from everybody including Nina and Daniel.

"Mary, Sue might be suffering from a mental illness. She is a psychotic liar. If anyone tries to reveal her lies, she might harm the person. As Sue had lived and believed in her lies as a wealthy widow for so many years, if Eric tries to confront Sue, she would deny it and she might hurt him just to silence him. She probably thinks nobody knew about her pregnancy, not even Eric. She does not have any clue that Eric has been looking for her for years."

"I bet no one would believe Eric's story except us."

"I will write Eric that he cannot show up in Maui to claim his daughter or ask her daughter's DNA test. It could be very dangerous. Sue might think Eric wants to destroy her reputation. The scandalous talk would hurt her ego as well as her grandeur delusion and her reputation. If she found out that I was the one who gave Eric her address, I would be in danger as well."

"Please write to Eric about the danger of confronting Sue. I hope he understands how Sue's mind works."

"I will. I heard Mrs. Mendosa knows some rough underground people in Honolulu. We must keep Eric's story secret. I am not going to tell Daniel anything about Eric's letter, but I worry about Sue's mental status toward Daniel's audit as well. I feel like she and her mother are conspiring something against the organization or against us personally. This is just my hunch."

"Alice, please just be careful. They are not as normal as we are. They are sick. You know most murders are caused by mentally ill people. Please hide Eric's letter somewhere safe so no one could find it. When you write to Eric, make sure to do it discreetly. Tell Eric not to contact Sue. If he writes her, she would probably find out who gave her address and she might turn on you. Please be careful."

"I will."

I heard Alice's almost whispery voice on the other end of the line. That voice almost sounded as though she was sensing some premonition or trouble on the horizon.

Chapter 14

GRANDMOTHER

The time was still passing slowly. I ordered a cup of coffee just for myself. My father's eyes were still closed. The first-class cabin was quiet. Most of them were still watching movies.

When my father heard a clicking sound from my coffee cup, he opened his eyes. I asked him if he wanted a cup of coffee. He nodded, so I got the flight attendant's attention.

"Dad, have you been to Okinawa before?"

"Yes, many years ago. Just at the Kadena Air Base, for some fuel stops on the way to Vietnam, but never explored the island. I remember the island was surrounded by a beautiful ocean and clear sky, just like Hawaii."

"Did you know Mr. Okuma lives in Okinawa, now?"

"Yes, your mom told me. They write to each other. He moved to Okinawa when he retired. Have you heard from him? Oh, I forgot. Your mom told me you went to Okinawa for something and you wound up staying with Mr. Okuma, right?"

"Yes, I stayed with Mr. Okuma last month after attending a conference."

Attending a conference was a lie. I was on a secret mission; in other words, I was researching my mother's past, to find out why she was disowned by her parents. Even though the word *disown* was stuck in my mind for many years, I had not done anything about it. I wanted my mother to reconcile with her parents before it was too late.

As far as my mother was concerned, her parents had died, and they were buried an ancient time ago. She refused to bring up the subject of her parents. Therefore, the story pages of my Japanese grandparents had been left blank. I had not had any information to fill those pages.

On the contrary, the story pages of my grandparents on my father's side had been filled beautifully with many episodes of their kind, humane, decent, and loving deeds to their neighbors, students, and to their own son. Because of that, I knew my half came from the decent ancestors, but my other half was left blank.

I only knew a little about my Japanese grandmother; she was a good cook and baker who could bake cookies as big as my palm, but I still did not know what kind of person she was. Moreover, I did not know anything about my grandfather. I often imagined my own Japanese grandfather like Mr. Okuma.

Through my secret mission, I wanted to find out the fact of mother's disownment, and at the same time, I wanted to find the way for them to reconcile. The only person I knew who might know about my mother's past was Mr. Okuma, so I decided to start my secret mission or my first research with Mr. Okuma. I really hoped Mr. Okuma would offer any information that might fill the puzzle.

However, this one-person mission had to be a secret, especially from my mother. After I arranged my annual vacation time for my secret mission to see Mr. Okuma, I asked my mother.

"Mom, do you hear from Mr. Okuma? You told me he moved to Okinawa when he retired from the symphony. Does he still live there?"

"Yes. He lives in Okinawa. It has been almost ten years since he moved."

"Wow, time flies fast. I have not talked to him for a long time. I should've at least talked to him on the phone once in a while. He probably forgot all about me by now."

"Oh, no, he always talks about you saying how proud he is of you. He still calls you My Little Cute Mary. He has been working on music compositions as his retirement projects. I think he had published several compositions since he retired. One was played in the symphony in Okinawa last year. I was very happy for him."

"I really want to see him since I am going to Okinawa for a conference. I would like to spend some time with him after the conference. Do you have his address and phone number?"

I lied to my mother about a conference because I did not want her to know I would be going to Okinawa just to see Mr. Okuma.

She took out her personal address book and copied Mr. Okuma's address and phone number by squinting. "I need a pair of reading glasses soon. By the way, if you go, take some Kona coffee. He loves that coffee. Once in a while, I send him some bags of Kona coffee."

I called Mr. Okuma on the phone the next day. He was surprised to hear my voice. It had been too long. His robust voice revealed his good health. I spoke in Japanese. "Hello. Mr. Okuma, this is Mary from Hawaii. How are you?"

"Who?"

"Mary Richardson from Hawaii." I pronounced my name in the Japanese way.

"Mary, My Little Cute Mary?"

"Yes. I am not little anymore, but yes, this is Your Cute Mary. How are you? You sound wonderful!"

"I am fine. What a surprise! Is your mother okay? Father? Where are you?" He probably thought I was calling him for some kind of emergency matter on my parents.

"They are fine. I am fine too. I am at home in Honolulu. I am coming to Okinawa next week. I just wondered if you would be in town. If you do, I would like to visit you."

"Yes. I will be in town. How long can you stay?"

"For one week."

"It is not long enough. Can you arrange to stay longer, ten days or two weeks? Mary, I'd really like to spend time with you just as we did before in Hawaii. It has been too long. I would like to see you. Remember, I am supposed to show you my sunset. I have a perfect place for that. Just wait and see. Extend your stay. I will pick you up at the airport. Just let me know the arrival time. Rearrange your schedule and call me back."

I could tell Mr. Okuma was ecstatic. I felt relieved to hear his robust voice, and at the same time, I felt as though I was going to see my closest relative…my own grandfather whom I had never met. After I arranged two weeks off from my work, I called him back and gave him my arrival time in Naha.

"So you went to Okinawa. How was Mr. Okuma?"

"He looked great, very happy, and robust. He did not look his age."

"He could be over eighty by now."

"I think so. Anyhow, he has a beachfront condominium. He lives on the top floor, the fifth floor. He has a large balcony in front of the living room. His living room has a huge glass window facing the East China Sea. You can sit and watch the ocean without any obstruction. We saw the perfect sunset almost every day from his balcony."

"I am glad he has the place he wanted. He always talked about owning a place just like ours on a hill so he could look out the sunset."

"I am glad too. He has two bedrooms, kitchen with a dining area. In his living room, his grand piano and study desk are placed against the window so he could look out the ocean to be inspired. He said he found the one thing he missed most when he lived in Tokyo was the sunset on the ocean. He said he took it for granted. Now he appreciates the sunset on the ocean each day."

"I am glad he went back to Okinawa. I understand how he felt about his birthplace or hometown."

"Dad, you should see his living room. Almost one wall from the top to the bottom is filled with tons of books just like a library. He showed me some books written in English. They were all about Okinawa, its history, culture, people, politics, geography, international relations, even statistics. He said he collected that English version just for me. He said I might be interested in learning about my own heritage. I did not know what he was talking about first, but I figured later he was talking about my grandmother."

"Yes, Mr. Okuma and your grandmother are from Okinawa."

"Dad, I did not tell you, but I met my grandmother in Okinawa."

My father looked inquisitive.

"At the airport, a woman who came with Mr. Okuma embraced me tightly and made a scene by weeping with oceans of tears in front of the airport crowd. She embraced me so hard that I could not breathe. Finally, Mr. Okuma told me she was my grandmother. Then I started embracing her tightly and made a scene, sobbing with tons of tears with her. We wetted each other's shoulders and faces. She was so happy to see me, kept saying I have grown beautifully in a quivery voice and kept crying. She said it in English. I did not know she could speak English."

"Yes, she spoke English when I met her in Tokyo. She also spoke French. I guess she learned the languages when she lived in Paris. Wow, you must be surprised seeing your grandmother for the first time after so many years."

"My grandmother looked young and pretty, just like Mom. We had joyous cries at the airport. The people who saw us had tears in their eyes too. Dad, they smiled at us with their teary eyes. I guess our tears were contagious. On the way to the parking lot, Grandmother held my hand as though I was a little grandchild. In the car, she took out my picture that was probably taken when I was in fourth grade, a long time ago. My cowlicks were showing on that picture, but I looked cute and innocent. She probably kept that picture for years. It looked wrinkled and faded a little."

"Do you have cowlicks?"

"Yes, Dad! I still do. When I was going to school, Mom had to press down every morning with hair spray."

"I have never seen your cowlicks. Let me see."

He tried to see my cowlicks on my head, but I said, "Dad, you don't see my cowlicks now because I pressed them down with hair spray this morning. You would probably see them after I wash my hair."

He was looking at top of my shoulder-length hair curiously for a while and tried to remember something.

"Does Mr. Okuma have cowlicks?"

"Yes, but he does not seem to know how to control them. I told him to use hair spray. But I thought his cowlicks are cute on his head."

"Yes, I thought so too when he was conducting the symphony."

"Dad, you may not know it, but I had longed to see Grandmother for a long time. When I was a child, I wanted her to bake cookies as big as my palm, just as Alice's grandmother used to bake. Mom told me she was the best cook and baker in her neighborhood when they lived in Paris. Anyhow, I did not expect to meet Grandmother in Okinawa. I thought she lived in Tokyo."

"I thought so too."

"Grandmother told me Ambassador Itoh passed away ten years ago. After his passing, she sold the house, moved back to Okinawa, and opened a restaurant. Do you think Mom knows about Ambassador Itoh's passing?"

"I don't think so unless Mr. Okuma told her, but you know your mom. She does not want to know anything about her parents. She does not want to talk about them either. So I don't know if she knows about her father's passing."

I almost said something very important about Ambassador Itoh, but I decided to wait. "Did you know Grandmother and Mr. Okuma were childhood friends? They went to the same school from elementary school to high school in Okinawa, and then they both received scholarships and went to the same music college in Tokyo and graduated."

"Mr. Okuma told me something like that a long time ago. He said they practically grew up together. They have been very good friends for years. How was she?"

"She looked great. I don't think Mom knows Grandmother lives in Okinawa, does she?"

"I don't know. I will ask her, when we get home."

Suddenly, my father got quiet. He probably thought—asking my mother could be impossible, if something fatal had happened to her.

"I saw Grandma every day. She brought some grocery to Mr. Okuma's house and cooked hot meal lunches for us often. One day,

I asked her to bake cookies as big as my palm. Yes, she baked them just for me. My dream came true. They were big and delicious. Mr. Okuma and I feasted on those cookies for several days."

I glanced at my father. He was still quiet. He was probably thinking about my mother's unknown condition in Hawaii. He looked frustrated, but he probably wanted to carry a conversation just to escape from his dreadful thoughts. "Your mom told me she learned the basics of cooking from her when she was young."

"Grandmother wanted us to eat dinner at her restaurant every night. After sunset, we drove to her restaurant in the city every night. As soon as she met us at the restaurant, she held my hand and led me to a special table. She treated me like a princess. She did not eat with us, but she sat with us between helping her customers. She often brought her regular customers to our table and introduced me as her only grandchild on earth with her tearful eyes. Then she proudly introduced me as a female pilot in the United States."

My father's eyelids looked heavy, so I stopped talking to him. He fluffed up his pillow behind his neck.

"Dad, are you sleepy?"

"Not yet. By the way, I met your grandmother many times at Mr. Okuma's concert parties, but I had never had the opportunity to meet Ambassador Itoh, your grandfather."

Again, I wanted to say something about Ambassador Itoh, but I decided to wait. "Dad, did you know Grandmother was a violinist before she married Ambassador Itoh?"

"I think I heard about that when I was in Tokyo. I think Mr. Okuma and Grandmother played in the college symphony together during music school. Mr. Okuma won numerous awards as a pianist. So was your grandmother as a violinist."

"I bet you did not know my grandmother is a direct descendant of the Shō Dynasty."

"The Shō Dynasty of the Ryukyu Kingdom?"

"Yes. Okinawa was a small kingdom for many centuries. It was called the Ryukyu Kingdom before the country of Japan invaded and conquered it by force at the beginning of the seventeenth century. That was the end of the Ryukyu Kingdom." I was going to say something else, but I could not remember what it was. Was it about Okinawa or Mr. Okuma? Besides, my father looked tired, so I motioned to him to take a nap. He nodded and adjusted his pillow and closed his eyes. Even though his eyes were closed, he might be thinking about my mother's whereabouts, probably imagining her in the hospital.

I pushed the window shade up a little and stared at the clouds that were floating with no concern of our time. My thought went back to Okinawa.

One day, Mr. Okuma and I rode a sightseeing bus all day to see the island. The tour guide on the bus looked happy to learn I understood Japanese.

She asked me if Mr. Okuma were my grandfather. I nodded several times in a hurry just as I did to the waitress at the hotel restaurant in Hawaii when I was young. When Mr. Okuma came back from his photo opportunity, the tour guide smiled at him without saying anything. He looked puzzled.

We lunched at a restaurant overlooking the ocean. The ocean was blue, and the sky was clear just as Hawaii. The sun was hot, but the sea breeze helped cool down the surroundings.

The outing with Mr. Okuma reminded me of the time we went to Disney World in Florida after my college graduation. I saw Mr. Okuma's same satisfying expression on his handsome face with his beautiful smile just because I was with him.

After the trip, we stopped at Grandmother's restaurant. Sachiko, my grandmother's niece, and her husband welcomed us. Grandmother was out for a meeting. Sachiko and her husband had managed and cooked for the restaurant since the restaurant opened ten years ago. They brought our usual dinner. Mr. Okuma tried to pay for our dinner, but they did not accept his money, just as Grandmother would not. Therefore, while I was in Okinawa, I ate free dinner every night.

Family Secrets

Every evening after dinner, Mr. Okuma and I did our rituals: he worked on his composition at the desk next to his piano, and I did my reading in my bedroom.

I really enjoyed my quiet time in my bedroom reading. However, I realized I did not come here to read books or learn about my heritage. I came here to accomplish my secret mission.

I asked Mr. Okuma if he did not mind walking with me on the beach every morning. My intention was to make some time alone with him and research on my mother's past by asking some simple questions to motivate him to give me more information.

Mr. Okuma was delighted to walk with me. He remembered he walked a long way home from shopping with me in Hawaii. Besides, he said he would love to stroll on the beach early in the morning when it was still cooler.

Every morning, we walked slowly on the paved pathway along the beach. My investigation had begun. During our slow walk, I calculated to entice Mr. Okuma's answers by asking some simple questions without arousing his suspicions. First, I wanted him to talk about himself and hoped that would come to the intertwining point with my mother as a result. Those questions could be, What was your childhood like? How did you know my grandmother? Did you go to the same school with her?

He gladly answered all my questions and gave me more information in the process. He was a good storyteller. I was taking many notes in my head. He wanted to tell me all about my grandmother because he thought I would learn more about my own heritage from his reminiscence as well as from the information he provided.

Chapter 15

MASAO OKUMA AND YOSHIKO SHŌ

I could not remember what I was going to say to my father before, but now I remembered what it was. I wanted to tell him all about Mr. Okuma and my grandmother, including their secret that was unveiled to me for the first time while I was walking with him in the morning.

Masao Okuma was a son of the crop share farmer who lived in the Shō Dynasty complex. Masao's father worked on the dynasty's vast farmland to harvest rice, sweet potatoes, vegetables, sugarcanes, and other crops. The crop share farmers would work for the allocation of the harvested crops as their wages. There were pigs, chickens, and goats for the farmers to tend as well. There were four more families lived in the complex.

Masao's mother worked as a domestic helper inside the complex for the Shō family. At the harvest time, the wives of the farmers worked with their husbands on the farm after leaving their children with Masao's mother in the complex.

Therefore, Mrs. Shō gave Masao's mother a big playroom for the children to play. Mrs. Shō's three girls played with the farmers' children in the same room as well. Masao Okuma, Yoshiko Shō, and other children practically grew up together in the complex.

Senator Shō often traveled to Tokyo to attend the congressional sessions. Mrs. Sho oversaw the household chores and her children's care with the help of Masao's mother. Mrs. Sho was a kindhearted person. She gave more than enough food and clothes to the farmers and shared the harvested crops generously when Mr. Shō was away.

Although the Ryukyu Kingdom was dismantled two or three generations ago, the direct descendant of the Shō family kept their vast land properties, wealth, and the royal names for decades.

My grandmother Yoshiko Shō was the oldest child of their three girls. She was therefore considered the direct descendant of the Shō Dynasty since her parents did not have a son.

When Okinawa officially became a prefecture of the Japanese government, it did not matter whether they were poor or rich; the children in the village went to the same pubic school in the district. Therefore, Masao Okuma and Yoshiko Shō went to the same school.

The school was on the hill. Several villages were along the beach, and some were at the foot of the hill. The beautiful scene of the blue ocean with a straight line of the horizon was seen from the classroom windows as though it were a painted picture on the wall.

All the schoolchildren from all the villages had to walk four or five miles to school. Masao walked with Yoshiko and other children from their village.

As Yoshiko was a scrawny little girl who had a hard time carrying her heavy book bag back and forth to school, Masao helped her carry it. The Shō family witnessed Masao's kindness as a warning sign. They did not want the son of a crop share farmer to be interested in their princess.

Nevertheless, Masao and Yoshiko already bonded as good friends or siblings. Masao carried her book bag all the way to the corner of the complex and then he let her carry it home. He waited at the corner until the princess entered the complex and then he entered.

They repeated the same routine for years until the princess got taller and stronger to carry her own book bag. The princess liked Masao's kind nature.

When they became teenagers, the princess started practicing violin in the music club. Masao decided to join the music club just to be with the princess. The music teacher told the club members to bring their own musical instrument if they want to be in his music club. Since Masao did not bring any instrument, the teacher let him use his piano until he was able to purchase an instrument such as a violin, guitar, clarinet, flute, or a drum set.

He knew his parents could not afford to buy any musical instrument, so he had worked very hard to master the piano. In fact, he wanted to use the teacher's piano as his instrument since he could not bring one.

He drew the keyboard on a long sheet of paper and practiced the finger movements at home by looking at a music sheet. He studied to read music and memorized the keyboard position and the sound of each key. He practiced maneuvering his fingers on the paper keyboard silently for many hours at home.

His younger brothers curiously watched his brother's finger movements on the keyboard sheet. They did not have any clue what he was doing. Sometimes in the dark, before sleeping, Masao drew the keyboard in his head and practiced. At school, he reproduced his learning from the paper keyboard.

The music teacher was surprised how fast Masao mastered the piano. His finger movement was meticulous, and the music came perfectly. He thought Masao was gifted in piano.

Masao Okuma still does not believe he is gifted in piano, even to this date, but my grandmother disagrees. He believes his talent was born out of desperation or out of necessity.

He was able to stay in the music club without purchasing any instrument. He felt as though his hard work paid off or his wish came true. He wanted to practice music with the princess and walk home just as they did before. There were no other children after practice, so they talked loudly and freely just as two siblings. Sometimes, they argued, laughed, sang, and recited some poems. Masao always carried the princess's violin case for her.

They never failed to sit on a big rock at the beach, watched the sunset, and then raced back home, but Masao had to wait at the corner until the princess disappeared into the complex.

In the music club, the teacher let Masao use the piano as though that were Masao's own instrument. His rapid learning of the assigned music made the music teacher very happy, but he had no clue that Masao practiced his finger movements on the paper keyboard for hours at home. Soon, he was able to hum each note by looking at the music sheet.

One day, Masao was given a thick book of music sheets. He played each page in front of the teacher and completed the entire book in one week. The music teacher was amazed how fast Masao could master the piano and how well he was able to play.

The teacher had never thought of the paper keyboard Masao used for hours at home. He knew Masao did not have a piano at home, so he concluded Masao's fast learning came from his giftedness.

One day, the music teacher let him listen to the famous prelude of Beethoven No. 5 on the record player. Masao was captivated by the music and felt as though he were destined to be a musician for the first time. He imagined himself playing piano in front of the audience. After a week, Masao asked the teacher if he could play Beethoven No. 5 in front of the club members.

When the teacher heard Masao's powerful Beethoven No. 5, he thought that Masao's giftedness should not be buried in this small school. His giftedness should be introduced to the music world as a music prodigy just as Chopin or Mozart.

While listening to Masao's performance, the princess looked as though her heart was struck by a Cupid's arrow for the first time. After the performance, he bowed curtly. All the club members including the teacher stood up and gave him a standing ovation. The princess was utterly mesmerized by looking at Masao's handsome face that was beaming with a smile.

The music teacher was determined to introduce Masao as a gifted pianist or prodigy to the music world. He taught him many technical finger movements and things Masao needed to master. The princess stayed and practiced her violin until Masao was released from the lesson. The teacher recognized the princess's talent as well, so he personally helped the princess too.

The teacher entered both their names in a music contest. Masao played a piece from Chopin, and the princess played a piece from Vivaldi. They both won. The teacher entered them to many talent contests. They kept winning throughout high school. Because of their talent and the teacher's recommendation, they both received scholarships to enter the same music college in Tokyo.

Before Masao's departure to Tokyo to attend college, Mr. Shō gave the direct order to his parents by saying, "Your son, Masao, cannot see or cannot associate with Yoshiko Shō while he is in college. Otherwise, your whole family should be evicted from the complex."

His parents begged Masao to stay away from the princess. He felt sad, but he obeyed his parents.

In Tokyo, he lived in a small apartment. Masao's scholarship was for tuitions, books, and some spending money. Some spending money could not cover the apartment rent, so he took a part-time job as a piano player at an exclusive hotel restaurant five nights a week.

Later, he cut down from three meals to one meal a day in order to make ends meet. His tall figure became thinner.

Even though Masao saw Yoshiko in class, on campus, or at the symphony practice, he had avoided her. Yoshiko did not know the reason. It made her very sad. She also noticed he was getting thinner.

One day, she appeared at his apartment door. She wanted to come in. She was holding two bags full of grocery. Masao was hesitant, but he let her come in.

The princess cooked delicious supper and they ate together. She asked him why he had been avoiding her at school. He told her about her father's message.

She looked furious. "It is absurd. My father cannot do such a thing in these modern days. I am not a royal princess. The Shō Dynasty is gone a hundred years ago. We might be wealthy, but he has no right to tell you what to do or how to lead your life. It is just absurd."

The princess begged him to give her his apartment key so she could help clean or cook for him. She was determined to help him one way or the other since he lived in poverty. She might just be rebellious against her father, but her friendship to help him was genuine. Masao gave her his spare key, but he told her to come to the apartment discreetly.

Masao saw the princess almost every night in the apartment. She cooked supper for him and ate late together after his work. It seemed she studied and practiced violin while waiting for Masao to come home from the restaurant.

Masao walked her to her place late in the evening after supper. While walking, they talked a lot about their future as musicians. Sometimes, they played like little kids on the street. Whenever Masao saw a puddle of water on the street, he carried her on his back. When they came closer to her apartment, Masao waited at the corner to see her off and then ran home.

They were fond of each other, but they were not lovers. Their relationship was more like a brother and a sister. For four years in college, the princess helped Masao with nutritious supper almost every day. That was a great contribution to Masao's budget and health.

Their music skills were sharpened by participating in the symphony practice on campus. Well, Masao's music skill was sharpened at work too. Occasionally, the princess came to the restaurant to do a duet with Masao. The customers really liked the duet they performed with piano and violin. They praised them for how skillful musicians they were.

However, Masao's dream was to become a symphony conductor in the future. He took many classes preparing to be a symphony conductor. That was his ultimate goal or ambition.

Shortly before their graduation, the princess came to his apartment in tears and pleaded Masao to marry her or take her away from Tokyo. She did not give him the reason of her urgent pleading, but she kept saying her dream was to live with him as his wife and share the joy of music for the rest of her life because Masao had been the only love for her.

He held her in his arms, wiped her tears, and told her she was the only love and forever love for him as well, but he told her to wait for a while. He needed to get a good job so Mr. Shō would approve of him as his daughter's future husband. She shook her head fiercely and cried again. He held her tightly and whispered to her—as soon as he obtained a teaching job or symphony job, they would see Mr. Shō together. It would be very soon. She stopped crying, but she looked desperate.

When he walked her home, he held her hand as though he was assuring he would marry her as soon as possible. He waited at the corner to see her off as usual. That was the last time he stood to see her off.

Masao did not know the princess was in the middle of a political marriage plan between the Shō family and the Itoh family. The Foreign Minister Itoh wanted the Shō family's wealth for his son. The Shō family wanted the title for her daughter's future husband.

Before graduation, the marriage plan progressed rapidly without the princess's input. The Foreign Minister Itoh had already secured his son's ambassadorship. Mr. Shō was satisfied for the sake of his daughter's future and transferred a substantial amount of money to the newlywed.

Masao read a newspaper article with some pictures: The newly appointed ambassador Ritsuo Itoh, son of Foreign Minister Itoh, and Yoshiko Shō, a daughter of Senator Shō, were married in front of three hundred guests including the honorable prime minister, congressional staff, senators, foreign dignitaries, business executives, local government officials from Okinawa, friends, and families. Ambassador Itoh and Mrs. Itoh would be moving to Paris for his new assignment as ambassador to France shortly after their honeymoon.

When he read it, he knew then the meaning of Yoshiko's urgent pleading. He cried loudly by pounding on the wall. It was too late. His dearest lifelong love was gone forever. He wished it were just a nightmare. He felt as though his dream…being a symphony conductor…did not mean anything anymore without the princess.

Instead of looking for a teaching job or a symphony job after the graduation, he just stayed on his part-time job at the restaurant and played all Chopin's music to ease his broken heart. He valued

Chopin's piano music greatly and hoped that he would write some music compositions like Chopin in the future.

One day, probably a month later after the newspaper article, the princess showed up in Masao's apartment. At that time, Masao thought she had already left for Paris with her husband. Therefore, he thought he was seeing a ghost in the dark. He backed off and waited.

The princess smiled in the dark and said, "I will be leaving for Paris tomorrow. I just came to say goodbye and brought your key back. I also want to thank you for your friendship with me for all my life. I will miss you very much. I want you to remember that my dream was to be your music partner and your wife. I have loved you all my life." Suddenly, she broke down.

Masao embraced her in his arms and said in a quivery voice, "Oh, my dearest princess, I have loved you and adored you all my life. You are my forever love. I have been in love with you since I carried your book bag. I am sorry I did not take you away when you asked me to. I am sorry. Please forgive me. I know it is too late, but remember you are my forever love and I love you for the rest of my life."

"You are my forever love as well. I love you. I will be thinking about you."

They embraced and cried together. Masao cupped the princess's face and kissed her for the first time. On that night, they made love for the first time.

Mr. Okuma was hesitant to talk more of their relationship, but he continued. After several years later, he received a letter from the princess.

Dear Masao-san,

After you read this letter, please destroy it. This secret is just between us. I want you to know the daughter I bore is ours. I don't need to prove it to anyone. I know she is ours. I am very happy.

I will nurture her and give her a good care, so do not worry. Please destroy this letter.

Your forever love,
Yoshiko Itoh

I was flabbergasted, but now I realized I was walking with my real grandfather. My eyes were moist. I stopped and turned to Mr. Okuma and gave him my big smile. He knew what my big smile meant.

"Does my mother know about this secret?"

"No. No one knows. You are the first one to hear this secret. When the time is right, I will tell your mother, or you can tell her instead of me when the time is right."

"I will tell her when I get home. I am sure she will be glad to know you're her biological father."

"Visiting you and your family in Hawaii was mostly your grandmother's idea. Since she could not do anything to prevent the disownment, she pleaded me to visit you in Hawaii to see if you and your mother lived well without being hungry. Your grandmother thought your mom married a poor American solider. She also gave me some money to buy things you needed or wanted. So I did the honor every time I visited you. It was a secret between your grandmother and me."

Mr. Okuma showed his beautiful smile just as my mother's.

"Did my mother suspect that your visit was something to do with my grandmother?"

"No! I don't think so. I was very careful on that matter."

"I am glad you are my grandfather. In fact, you were always my make-believe grandfather for all these years. It must have been very hard to keep that secret from me for so many years."

"Yes. It was, but I decided to wait for you to grow up first so you would understand my relationship with your grandmother better."

"Now, I understand why you had never married. My grandmother was your forever love."

"Yes. She was my dearest friend and my forever love. I did not want to marry anyone else. Another reason I did not marry was you and your mother. I have loved you both, even though I could not say aloud. Whenever I thought about you and your mother, I was always happy and proud. Besides, I always considered your grandmother my forever wife, so I did not need another wife."

He laughed aloud and said, "When I saw your cowlicks for the first time, I told myself, 'My Little Cute Mary is definitely mine, my granddaughter.'"

"Have you seen my mother's big smile? Her big smile is just like yours. Do you think my grandmother saw many resemblances in both of you? That was why she declared my mother as yours?"

"I guess so. Your grandmother thought your mom got my musical talent as a pianist as well. She said she could not believe how fast your mother mastered the piano when she was a child. Yes, she also said your mom's smile and other expressions reminded her of me when she was growing up."

"Did Ambassador Itoh suspect my mom was not his?"

"According to your grandmother, Ambassador Itoh wanted a son instead of a daughter. He had been upset with your grandmother because she did not seem to bear any more children with him. So he made an excuse to keep a mistress somewhere in the countryside for many years, and he finally had a son with his mistress, but he died of influenza when he was a child. Your grandmother wanted to leave Ambassador Itoh so many times, but the society would not allow such a thing, especially in the political society."

Someone stopped Mr. Okuma, he chatted for a while and finally introduced me as his granddaughter to his acquaintance. I was very happy. I nodded affirmatively several times.

I concluded he was ready to reveal his secret to everybody even to my mother, my father, and his friends. Now Mr. Okuma is no long Mr. Okuma to me; I would call him Grandpa Okuma, or simply Grandfather. Moreover, I felt very proud to be his grandchild.

Although I did not find out about my mother's disownment from Mr. Okuma, it did not matter too much to me now. The disownment of my mother was ended at the time of Ambassador

Itoh's passing. She had to deal with the current reality with her mother. Mr. Okuma wanted me to unveil the fact of my mother's birth when I returned home. Later he would write to my mother.

However, as far as my mother was concerned, her resentment toward her parents was still there. Unveiling the secret of her birth could be very difficult. She might be confused, and it might upset her more. She may not forgive them. Now it seemed my mother could never know the secret of her birth. It might be too late. My heart was sinking.

Chapter 16

OKINAWA

It had been three weeks since I left my grandparents at the airport. Their eyes were moist and looked sad as though they came to say their last goodbyes to their only grandchild.

They probably thought I would not be coming back to see them again because of the distance. I assured them I would be back to visit them soon. I also told them that I would call them on the phone often. They saw my sincerity in my eyes and looked hopeful.

"I must come back to visit you because you are the only grandparents I have in this world." I winked at them.

They nodded with their teary eyes. Somewhat my grandmother was startled when I called them grandparents. She probably did not know the family secret was out. I embraced them tightly.

At the departure gate, the airport crowd knew we were weeping for goodbyes, unlike the joyous cries at the arrival gate. They glanced at us sympathetically with their somewhat moist eyes. This time they did not wear any smiles. They looked sad and sympathetic in general when they saw us.

My secret mission was more than a success. Meeting my grandmother for the first time and finding out Mr. Okuma as my real grandfather, that was enough to fill the blank pages of my storybook.

Again, my grandparents on my mother's side were as equally decent as my father's side. I was happy to complete the blank pages that were left unfilled for so many years.

With all my grandparents' greatness and decency, I avowed to be decent for the rest of my life just as they were. I felt very proud to have my musically talented grandparents, although I had not inherited their talent.

On the other hand, I felt obligated to inform my mother that she is the product of those two people's forever loves. Most importantly, her musical gift was given by them as well.

When I thought about being their only grandchild, I felt ashamed of myself because I had not produced any of their descendants. I might still have some possibility, but I could not foresee my future. I thought about Bruce Hudson for a second, but I shook my head. I waved to my grandparents at the departure gate.

When the airplane was ascending from the island of Okinawa, I was thinking about how I could tell my mother about Mr. Okuma, and how I could persuade my mother to reconcile with her mother. I really hoped she would not resent me for finding out her family secrets.

After reaching a high altitude, I dozed off and had a dream. I was in a beautiful Okinawan kimono and strolling with my grandmother and one more person on the other side. We were in the courtyard of the Shuri Castle where the Shō Dynasty had resided for several centuries. I was a princess. My grandmother held my hand talking to the person next to her, but I could not see that person. The voice sounded like my mother. Their conversation sounded very gentle and loving.

I woke up. The dream was somewhat odd, but the kimonos my grandmother and I wore were so colorful that remained vividly on my mind for a while. I saw those kimonos in the market when I went shopping with my grandmother in Naha.

Family Secrets

The vivid color made me think about my own heritage being partially an Okinawan descendant. I learned enough history, culture, and other things while I was with Mr. Okuma. I stared at the clouds below and recalled the things I learned about my heritage.

Around the twelfth century, there were three small kingdoms on the island of Okinawa. Those three were called Hokuzan (northern) principality, Chuzan (central) principality, and Nanzan (southern) principality. They fought each other for many years. However, at the beginning of the 1400s, the Ryukyu Kingdom was unified by the southern principality leader named Hashi Shō, the direct descendant of the Shō Dynasty. After the unification of three principalities, the kingdom had thrived and became prosperous by trading with China.

After the death of Hashi Shō in 1469, the direct descendants of the Shō Dynasty had continued to govern the islands. The Ryukyu Kingdom under the Shō Dynasty had ruled the island of Okinawa and seventy surrounding islands including the Amami Island, the Miyako Island, and the Yaeyama Island until 1879.

The kingdom had traded with the country of China, exporting various sea-harvested products including dried or marinated fish, minerals such as salt and sulfur, woodworks, fabric materials, fabric dyes, boating materials, some botanic plants for medicine, etc. The Ryukyu Kingdom imported in return various agricultural products, sweet potatoes, vegetable seeds, tools for farming, potteries, porcelains, and music instruments.

They also sent the scholars to learn China's language, culture, technologies, political and education systems, usage of musical instruments, and medical treatments by herb medicines as well as by traditional Chinese medicines.

The Ryukyu Kingdom enjoyed Chinese influence on performing arts, but over the centuries, the Okinawans created their own unique performing arts, which are much different from Japanese or Chinese performing arts.

Okinawa is known as the Island of Song and Dance. The three-stringed *sanshin* (guitar) was introduced by China, but since the Okinawans used it so frequently and widely for centuries, it seems that the sanshin is synonymous with Okinawa.

Karate (martial arts) originated in China, but now karate is synonymous with Okinawa as well. Many foreigners come to Okinawa to learn traditional karate from karate masters.

Geographically, the archipelago island of Okinawa runs from northeast to southwest; the east side is surrounded by the Pacific Ocean and the west side is surrounded by the East China Sea. The length of Okinawa is about sixty-six miles, and its widest width is about nineteen miles.

Since the island is located on the convenient sea route to China, the Westerner's great ships started appearing on the horizon of the East China Sea around sixteenth century. The Ryukyu Kingdom became an easy prey of any country's invasion at that time. Especially, the country of Japan was keeping an eye on the Ryukyu Kingdom for some time. They wanted the Ryukyu Kingdom's seaport rights as well as the prosperous business relationship with China.

In 1609, the country of Japan (Satsuma clan) invaded and conquered the Ryukyu Kingdom by force. The island became a Japan's territory, but they still let the Shō Dynasty rule the kingdom. They just wanted the kingdom's seaport rights to trade with China as well as with Southeast Asia. Foreign trade was the foundation of the Ryukyu Kingdom's economy, but the country of Japan seized the seaport rights from the Ryukyu Kingdom and used it for their own advantage.

In 1879, the Meiji government in Japan transformed the Ryukyu Kingdom into a prefecture. The Ryukyu Kingdom was annexed to Japan, and the Shō Dynasty was no longer the ruler of the Ryukyu Islands.

Even though Okinawa became a prefecture, the Japanese government did not allocate enough funds or budget to support the people of Okinawa in any means. There was no plan for the island's modernization or jobs. The island was simply neglected for many years by the government of Japan.

Most of the islanders were farmers and fishermen who were meagerly self-sufficient. They lived on fishes, seaweeds, shellfishes, other harvests from the sea, as well as agricultural products such as sweet potatoes, sugar canes, rice, pineapples, tropical fruits, and vegetables. The people who had money were probably the merchants in the city at the time.

On the farmland, farmers shared pigs, goats, and chickens with the families and relatives. Mostly, they lived on the island's staples such as rice and sweet potatoes.

They used the land and sea resources maximally to survive. The children helped their parents to farm or fish instead of going to school.

The Japanese education system was implemented, but the poor families rather wanted their children to work on the farms or to babysit their younger siblings instead of going to school. Because of it, most of the older generations were illiterate. The island's poverty situation made the people illiterate. It was a vicious cycle. As a result, most Okinawans remained poor and uneducated for a long time.

In the beginning of the twentieth century, the young Okinawan males started immigrating to South America, Hawaiian Islands, the mainland USA, Canada, and other countries to seek the betterment of their lives.

Due to their uneducated and poverty background, the foreign countries took advantage of the Okinawans. Their labor was cheap, but they were known as hard workers; therefore they were hired massively. The young Okinawan males' exodus began. Their exodus was somewhat desperate to escape from their poverty situation. Mostly they were hired to work at pineapple fields, sugar cane fields, berry farms, citrus farms, and any agricultural fields.

The workers were to come home after they earned enough money, but most of the Okinawan workers rather wanted to make the foreign country as their new homes because there was no promising future or jobs in their hometown in Okinawa.

They wanted to fight the loneliness in the foreign country rather than to live in poverty at home. The massive picture brides from Okinawa started joining those male immigrants and established their own families in the foreign countries.

The current population of Okinawan immigrants worldwide was estimated to 350,000. Currently, they are bearing fifth, sixth generations worldwide since the emigration started a century ago.

At the end of WWII (1941–1945), the island of Okinawa became the last battlefield between Japan and the USA and tragically lost the lives of 130,000 mostly Okinawan civilians.

Japan surrendered to the USA in 1945. The peace treaty was established between two countries. Japan gave the island of Okinawa including the entire Ryukyu Islands to the United States under the treaty of military strategic watch for the Pacific Ocean Rim. From 1945 to 1972, Okinawa remained under US military occupation.

During the US military occupation, the island was governed by two governments: the Ryukyu government and the US military administration. The dollar currency was used. Long awaited modernizations were introduced. Electricity became available to all islanders' households. Public transportation became more available.

Many employment opportunities became available in the military bases. English language was widely spoken. Automobiles were brought in or imported mostly by Americans; therefore the traffic system became the same as the USA. Twenty percent of the island's population were American soldiers and their families.

Compulsory education was strictly enforced. The children were taught in Japanese language, and all the textbooks came from the Japanese government. Therefore, the Okinawan educators followed the Japanese curriculum just as before.

The islanders kept the Japanese language as their official language as well as their nationality as Japanese. Yet they were to have an Okinawan passport to visit relatives in Japan. When the Okinawans were to visit foreign countries, they had to have two passports—one from the Okinawan government and another one from the Japanese government to prove their Japanese nationality. The identity of Okinawans during the US occupation era was confusing to the Okinawans as well as to other Japanese citizens in the mainland of Japan for a long time.

Many mainland Japanese did not know the Okinawans were Japanese citizens. They thought the Okinawans were from a foreign country. Some Japanese refused to recognize the Okinawans as Japanese citizens. Sometime that attitude revealed their discrimination or their superiority toward the Okinawans just as the same attitude they had toward Koreans and Taiwanese when the Japanese Empire was in the full swing before WWII.

In 1972, Okinawa reverted to Japan and officially became a prefecture of Japan once again. The traffic system was reverted to the Japanese way, and many accidents occurred during the transition. The governor is elected every four years; senators and congresspersons are elected to represent the prefecture of Okinawa. The central government of Japan allocates the same governmental budgets without any prejudice. Moreover, the island's long-awaited modernization rapidly progressed with its prosperity.

Many beautiful beaches with exclusive resort hotels were built; highways and roads were widened and improved. Vacationers from mainland Japan and neighboring countries such as Taiwan, China, Philippines, and Southeast Asia have steadily increased every year. Because of the beautiful beaches, Okinawa has become the paradise of Japan for vacationers, just as Hawaii is for the United States.

Karate (empty hands) was introduced to the world over the years as Okinawa's indigenous martial arts, although its formation was heavily influenced by Chinese kung fu many centuries ago.

The performing arts known as Ryukyu Buyou (Ryukyu Islands Dance) and Taiko/Parankuu (Drum) Dance are unique. Many dance stories were derived from the enjoyment of their surroundings: tropical flowers, white sand beaches, the blue ocean, the blue sky, ocean waves, boats, the full moon, the beautiful sunset, etc.

Among Mr. Okuma's book collection, the anthropological theory of the Okinawans caught my eyes. It described the two-wave theory about Japanese ancestral species as well as the Okinawans. In the theory, the two waves were explained.

The first wave of human dwellers came from the continent of Asia to the archipelago islands of Japan to hunt and fish. They dwelled along the coastlines from the north of Hokkaido to the south of the Ryukyu Islands (Okinawa). However, those dwellers in the center part of archipelago, currently known as the mainland Japan, were eradicated by a disease. Nevertheless, the northern dwellers and southern dwellers survived. The descendants of surviving dwellers in the north were thought to be Ainus, in the south were thought to be Okinawans. The distinctive features of the first wave species are recognized by the plentiful hair on men's chests, bigger eyes, and darker complexion.

The second wave of human dwellers arrived from the continent of Asia as well. They had survived this time. Those dwellers were more refined, fair skin, smaller eyes with no hair on men's chests. The second wave species are thought to be the current Japanese. The species from the first wave and the second wave were mixed over many centuries, but the first wave species had dominated in genes. Therefore, the Ainu and the Okinawans still share distinctive features. This is just a theory, but when it comes to some resemblance of Ainus and Okinawans, I somewhat agreed with the theory. I thought about my grandpa Okuma's big eyes and plentiful hair on his chest.

Characteristically, the people on the island are happy and leisurely with not much concern of punctuality. The Okinawans believe in peace and friendliness, the spirit of Ichariba Chodei shows the people's friendliness. The spirit is translated as "Once the islanders meet other islanders, they become sisters and brothers." In other words, they feel a kinship among Okinawans once they meet. That spirit is a principle of the islanders' friendliness. The outsiders, other than the islanders, would receive the same friendliness and generosity once they get to know them well.

The book titled *The Okinawa Program* was written by three authors: one Japanese medical doctor and two American brothers, one MD and one PhD in anthropology. That book was a result of their twenty-five-year-old research on the islanders' longevity that was ranked as the longest in the world. Many one-hundred-year-olds remain active on the island of Okinawa. The book introduced their diet and lifestyle to the world. When the book was published, those authors were interviewed by Oprah Winfrey. She praised their work in her interview.

The book credited the Okinawans' longevity to their diet and their lifestyle that include their frequent socialization with friends, relatives, and families as well as ancestral worships. The book emphasizes that the Okinawan's certain diet and their no-stress lifestyle have proven the Okinawans' longevity. Many Okinawan cooking recipes were included in the book.

It has been three weeks since I came home from Okinawa. I was determined to have a heart-to-heart conversation with my mother and unveil her birth secret, but I could not do it—I became a coward.

I was afraid that unveiling her birth secret might cause her to resent Mr. Okuma and me. She might think I went to Okinawa just to dig up her past. I desperately needed my father's help to unveil her birth secret. Now it might be impossible for my mother to know the fact of her birth. She might have left us without saying goodbye.

Chapter 17

GENERAL PALMER

I glanced at my father. His eyes were closed, probably dozed off this time. Our time on the airplane was passing too slowly. It seemed that someone was purposely stalling our time. I peeked out by pushing up the window shade a little; all fluffy white clouds below were floating motionlessly as though the universe came to a standstill on purpose.

The noise of the aircraft was the only one alive to indicate we were still on the move. Everything else seemed to be lifeless including the first-class passengers who were watching movies silently. If something happened to my mother, every minute could be critical, but the time did not seem to be cooperating.

My father woke up and sat up straight. He looked ashamed because he dozed off on his wife's critical situation. Nevertheless, he seemed to be very anxious to tell me something very important.

"I was dreaming about General Palmer. I don't know why, but he was in my dream. By the way, did you know Mr. Okuma was a very good friend of General Palmer?"

"Wasn't he your boss in the military when you were stationed in Japan?"

"Yes. Mr. Okuma and General Palmer met at the Tachikawa Air Force Base when they had a music festival there. General Palmer loved classical music and jazz. He used to play the saxophone in a marching band when he was young. Sometimes he entertained his troop by playing saxophone. In any rate, they became very good friends as musicians, even though they did not speak each other's languages. Mr. Okuma sent two concert tickets to General Palmer every time his symphony played in Tokyo. I often accompanied General Palmer to attend the concert as his interpreter. We rode a train to Tokyo and shared a room to stay overnight because of the train schedule. We were like a father and a son. He was a soft-spoken, kind person, easy to smile at any time, and friendly. Everybody liked him. I always thought my friend, Richard was very lucky to have a father like him. He reminded me of my dad."

My father had a faraway look in his eyes as though he was remembering General Palmer and Richard, and his own father who died many years ago.

"Richard was my best friend throughout MIT. I spent three Christmases at his grandparents' house in Maine. After Richard's mother died overseas when he was young, he was sent back to the state of Maine to live with his grandparents, but every summer, he visited his father, wherever he was stationed. Richard practically flew all over the world to visit his father. They were very close, and General Palmer had great hopes for his son's future."

I nodded because I heard all about them before. His eyes were again moist. I knew why.

After they graduated from college, they spent a year in a flying school. Richard wanted to join the US Air Force to be a fighter jet pilot, just as his father. On the other hand, John's dream was to become a commercial airline pilot for one of the major airlines. Since John and Richard were drafted, they both decided to join the US Air Force as fighter jet pilots.

While they both were in the Air Force flight training camp, Richard wrote to his father in Tachikawa USAF, Japan, asking if his friend John Richardson and he could be stationed in Tachikawa under his father's command. However, for some reasons, Richard was sent to the Philippines, but John got an order to station in Tachikawa Air Base. They both were fighter jet pilots, but in different places. It was during the Vietnam War.

Richard wanted to make a professional career in the military just as his father, so being in the Philippines did not bother him at all. He rather liked it. Seemingly, he was determined to follow his father's footsteps by frequenting to the war zones in Vietnam. It was somewhat Richard's dream came true. He wanted to establish himself as a fighter jet pilot in the military.

On the contrary, the military career did not entice John much. His dream was to fly a jumbo jet after his military duty. He had never forgotten the jumbo airplane model his father helped him assemble before he died. Besides, John did not like the idea of flying a fighter jet to kill people in war. He believed that his deceased parents, especially his father, would want him to be a commercial pilot instead.

My father looked determined to tell me more about General Ronald Palmer.

"I did not meet General Palmer when I first stationed in Tachikawa. Richard told me to see him, but I did not make any effort to meet him in his office. He was the highest commander in the air base. I was just a fighter jet pilot. However, General Palmer personally came to see me in my room three months later. I was flabbergasted when I first met him in my room. He resembled Richard a lot. He said he heard all about me from Richard. He told me the reason he came to see me was to find out if I could speak Japanese. I was sure Richard wrote him about my Japanese. As I said yes, he immediately asked me if I could accompany him to a symphony concert on that Saturday as his interpreter. I told him I would be honored. That was how we knew each other and often attended Mr. Okuma's concert."

Two cups of coffee arrived. My father sipped some coffee. His voice suddenly became whispery because someone in the cabin looked at him as though he was hinting our conversation was too loud.

"After that, I accompanied him to everywhere, whenever he asked me. At the very first concert, I saw your mother onstage. Yes, your mother stole my heart at that time."

I nodded. I knew what he was going to say next.

"I have never forgotten seeing your mother for the first time. General Palmer and I sat in the best seats in the house. When I saw her as a solo piano performer onstage, my heart leaped out of my body as though my heart was struck by Cupid's arrow that was transported to your mother's heart. I was mesmerized and overwhelmed with her beauty, music, and performance. At then, I told myself, I had to marry her no matter what."

I heard his Cupid's arrow story a million times in the past, but I did not mind hearing it over and over, so I nodded with a smile. His eyes were oblivious…faraway.

"We were invited to a party after the concert. We had a hotel room near the concert hall for that night, so we accepted Mr. Okuma's invitation to the party. Your mom was there. She was with her mother and a man who looked very stern and older. I wanted to talk to her, but the man did not give me any chance. Therefore, I admired her from a distance. I thought your mom noticed my stare and reacted favorably."

He sipped more coffee and looked around to see his voice was whispery enough. My father had never told me about his courtship with my mother in details before. He probably had waited for me to grow up to understand the grown-up's courtships or relationships.

On the other hand, he had probably been anxious to reveal his love story in detail for some time, but he just did not have the time to be with me. Sitting together on the airplane for almost six hours was the longest time we had ever spent together. Therefore, he probably thought now was the time to reveal whatever he had in mind. I was careful not to discourage him, so I showed my enthusiasm by leaning over to hear him talk. He was leaning over toward me in order to talk softly as well. He was whispering into my ear.

I had some hunches that his talk might lead to complete my secret mission—what caused my mother's disownment by her parents and how her mental illness was triggered…or developed. I was really hoping all our family secrets would be revealed through his talk today.

"Mr. Okuma finally introduced your mom as Keiko Itoh. Additionally, the man was introduced as her fiancé. Your grandmother, Mrs. Itoh, was introduced as Mr. Okuma's childhood friend. I learned your mom's name for the first time, Keiko Itoh. She did not speak much English, so I spoke Japanese to introduce myself. She was surprised and looked very impressed by my Japanese."

He sipped coffee and continued. "I still remember her sparkling eyes with the nicest smile. After the introduction, she looked as though she wanted to chat with me more, but her fiancé sternly took her away and started mingling with other musicians. While I was with General Palmer, my eyes were searching for Keiko Itoh at the party. Nevertheless, I was already heartbroken by learning that Keiko Itoh was engaged to that stern-looking man."

My father coughed several times by covering his mouth and sipped some more coffee.

"For several weeks, I was heartbroken, but I remembered Keiko Itoh's favorable smiles, so I kept praying to see her again. General Palmer and I attended another party. I saw Keiko Itoh and her fiancé. She was looking at me as though she wanted to talk to me again, but her fiancé was beside her. Your grandmother came to where General Palmer and I were standing. She came and informed us in English that her daughter's wedding would take place within two months. She wanted to invite us as Mr. Okuma's friends. General Palmer positively nodded for us, but I was contemplating on something else like how to stop her wedding. In any rate, I felt desperate to do something."

My father was about to sneeze, but he stopped.

"On that night in the hotel room, I told General Palmer how I was smitten by Keiko Itoh and really wanted to know her or marry her. I told him Keiko Itoh was my love at first sight. General Palmer wanted to help me see how Keiko Itoh felt about me first. So he told me to call Mr. Okuma on the phone to invite Mr. Okuma, Mrs. Itoh, and Keiko Itoh to eat lunch with us the next day before we went back to Tachikawa. It was late in the evening, but I called Mr. Okuma in Japanese. He was delighted. I was wondering why General Palmer asked Mrs. Itoh to come with them, but later I knew exactly why he did it. He wanted her to interpret for him and Mr. Okuma. Mrs. Itoh spoke English quite well."

My father stared at his coffee cup obliviously and continued. "The next day, Mr. Okuma in a nice jacket, Mrs. Itoh in a kimono, and Keiko Itoh in an elegant dress met us at a restaurant in Ginza.

General Palmer purposely made Keiko Itoh and I sit together around the large round table. General Palmer sat next to me. Keiko's mother sat between Mr. Okuma and General Palmer. The table was for eight people, so three empty chairs between Keiko Itoh and Mr. Okuma. General Palmer made Mrs. Itoh interpret their conversation, so she was busy doing it. Keiko Itoh and I chatted in whisper so that they could not hear us, but we put on some poker faces. Both of our hearts were pounding during lunch. Our feelings were mutual. I saw Keiko Itoh's rouged cheeks. She looked so beautiful."

My father coughed again. I turn off the air vent for him. He nodded to thank me.

"While we were eating, Mr. Okuma and your grandmother had watchful eyes on us, but General Palmer had them involved in his conversation, so they did not have the time to eavesdrop on us or observe our activities. I whispered to Keiko Itoh and told her I really wanted to see her soon alone and squeezed her hand gently under the table. She blushed but nodded. She gave me her business card with a private phone number under the table. I kept holding Keiko Itoh's hand as long as I was able to hold under the table without arousing anybody's suspicion. We both were very happy, but we still put on our poker faces."

He gulped his remaining coffee and continued in his whispery voice. "I took a train from Tachikawa to Tokyo one afternoon and met Keiko Itoh in a coffee shop in Ginza. She looked so happy to see me. Again, both of our hearts were pounding equally. We were chatting and playing like two teenagers in the coffee shop. I told her I was the luckiest and happiest man in the world, dating the most beautiful and most talented lady in Tokyo. She laughed aloud because she thought I was just exaggerating. Then I confessed truthfully that I was lovestruck when I saw her at the concert for the first time. She blushed and wore the most beautiful smile on her face. Her eyes were sparkling."

A flight attendant brought two bottles of water and took our empty coffee cups with her. He thanked her and opened the bottle top, but put it on the table instead of drinking. I kept my bottle on my table without opening it.

He continuously whispered, "I went to Tokyo on my own at least once a week. General Palmer was very happy to learn that Keiko Itoh was smitten with me equally. He kept saying, 'Follow your heart.' Most of the time, Keiko Itoh and I met in a coffee shop and walked a park to the train station for my return. We talked a lot…about everything including her engagement to the man whom her father, Ambassador Itoh, arranged. The man's father was a senior senator and a wealthy one, seemingly he promised to get a majority support for Ambassador Itoh to become the foreign minister after the marriage of his son and Keiko Itoh. In return, Ambassador Itoh promised him his son's ambassadorship to Spain. Keiko Itoh's mother did not seem to like the political marriage arrangement for her daughter, but she could not say much to Ambassador Itoh. Keiko Itoh said she did not like her fiancé or did not love him. She wanted to escape from the situation before too late."

My father finally took a sip from the water bottle and continued. "One particular afternoon, while we were walking in the park, she broke down and said, 'Please take me to Tachikawa with you today. I don't feel like going home. My fiancé will be taking me to dinner tonight for some final arrangement for the wedding.' She kept sobbing by covering her face with both of her hands. I did not know what to do. Instead I felt the urge to kiss her. So I cupped her teary face and kissed your mom for the first time. She was still crying, so we sat on the bench for a while. I was contemplating how to solve this urgent situation."

My father's voice was low so no one could hear him but me. We were at the last row against the wall, so no one possibly could hear us.

"Finally, I decided to take her with me to Tachikawa. We rode a train together. We held hands and sat quietly on the train. I remember it was a chilly night. Keiko Itoh did not have a warm jacket, so I put my jacket over her shoulders. Her pretty face was smeared with tears, so I wiped her face with my handkerchief. She smiled, but more tears came down. We both were quiet. I was thinking and thinking what to do next. I knew I was the only one who could take her away and save her from marrying her fiancé. I was determined to take her away because I was madly in love with her. I knew she was madly in love with me too, but we did not look happy. We both looked like fugitives who were running from the law."

My father seemed to be recalling how they looked on the train. I remembered my grandmother came to Mr. Okuma and begged him to take her away before she married Ambassador Itoh.

"When we arrived in Tachikawa, I put her in a small motel outside the military base for the night. I went straight to General Palmer and told him everything about her situation. She did not love the man. She wanted me to take her away from the political marriage her father arranged. Now she stayed in the motel for the night. I asked him what I should do next. General Palmer told me to call Mr. Okuma to relay a message to Mrs. Itoh first saying that Keiko Itoh would be staying in Tachikawa for a while, so Mrs. Itoh should not be looking for her daughter. So I phoned Mr. Okuma. Then General Palmer and I went to see Keiko Itoh in the motel. General Palmer told us, we both should get married as soon as possible. The next day, General Palmer again asked me to call Mr. Okuma that Keiko Itoh needed her passport and birth certificate. General Palmer was going to use his power to arrange our marriage. He needed Keiko Itoh's legal documents as well as mine."

My father seemed to be thirsty. His water bottle was almost empty. So I gave mine.

"Several days later, Mr. Okuma brought Keiko Itoh's passport and birth certificate, but he wanted to see Keiko Itoh in person to find out what was going on. I was flying on that day, so I did not get to see Mr. Okuma. According to General Palmer, they spent a lot of time talking. Apparently, Keiko Itoh told him that she decided to follow her heart instead of marrying the man whom she did not love. Mr. Okuma seemed to understand how she felt, so he promised he would help her as much as he could."

My father had a sip from my water bottle.

"General Palmer worked hard to get all the paperwork processed so we could marry soon. In the meantime, your mother and I decided to rent an apartment outside of the base. I did not know what kind of turmoil happened between the Itoh family and the man's family, but the Japanese magazine scandalized it, saying Keiko Itoh, the famous and hopeful pianist for the symphony, left her fiancé for an American soldier. Her upcoming wedding ceremony was abruptly canceled. A son of the wealthy senior senator was hospitalized due to his emotional anguish. My name was published, John Richardson, a poor American soldier who seemed to be a gold digger or fame seeker. They had my pictures from a concert party. Since I could not read Japanese, your mother read it for me. We were just flabbergasted. Nevertheless, the Japanese neighbors at our apartment were very sympathetic and kind to us, especially to Keiko Itoh."

Chapter 18

CONFESSION

Somehow, my father looked hesitant whether he should continue the rest of his story or not, but he apparently decided to continue.

"Mary, before I fell in love with your mom, I had a personal problem. It is a long story."

He paused for a minute. "Shortly after I came to Tachikawa, a young Japanese woman who was assigned to clean my room came with her Japanese supervisor. It must have been a routine for them to visit a new tenant in the barracks so that the tenant would know his room would be cleaned while he was gone to work. When the supervisor introduced her to me in English, I spoke Japanese to introduce myself. She looked stunned and mesmerized by my Japanese. Her eyes were sparkling. She had an attractive face, but her body was somewhat obese. Whenever she cleaned my room, she placed one stem of fresh flower in a small vase. She did not do it for anybody else but did it for me. I was flattered by her good gesture."

My father's eyes were somewhat downward as though he was ashamed of his feeling.

"One day she left a message written in Japanese on a rice paper sheet. It was folded nicely and placed under the flower vase. She apparently did not know I was illiterate in Japanese. You know I had never studied to read or write in Japanese, but I spoke the language.

She assumed I could read her Japanese message. As I could not read the message, I put it in the desk drawer and went to bed. That night, she sneaked in my bed and seduced me to make love to her. I resisted her for a while, but she caressed my naked body in bed. I was aroused. Foolish of me, I made love to her. She said she would like to come every night to give me some pleasure. Immediately, I regretted what I had done, but it was too late. Nevertheless, I wanted to prevent the further relationship with her by installing a lock from the inside. Mary, I want you to know this incident happened several months before I met your mom. Anyway, she attempted to come in my room many times by using her master key. She never knocked on the door because she was probably afraid that she might wake my neighbors up."

Indeed, my father was courageous. He really had to have the courage to confess his dark secret to his only child. I should be honored to be trusted, but I rather liked to hear his Cupid story. I really liked it as a child because that was a happy story. At bedtime, I used to beg my father to tell me all about the baby whom the Cupid wanted my mother to keep in her stomach until the baby was ready to greet her father. The baby's name was Mary, and she was the best-looking baby in the entire hospital, just like a baby Cinderella. When my father tucked me in bed after the story, I really had a dream of my being Cinderella in a beautiful castle and lived happily ever after.

As my father's voice was too whispery, I had to cup my ear with my hand.

"Nevertheless, she continued putting fresh flowers with many short messages while I was at work. As I could not read the Japanese messages, I saved them in my desk drawer. One day, her Japanese supervisor came to see me in my room and told me that the young housekeeper was going to file charges against me. It was going to be a rape charge. She claimed that I raped her in my bed. Her Japanese supervisor wanted to hear my side of the story before he was to take to the highest rank, General Palmer. I was flabbergasted. I took all her messages from the drawer and gave them to him to read. While he was reading, his face turned red with anger. He apologized to me and told me to forget all about the charge; he would take care of the matter. I still did not know what those messages were. However, those messages save me from her rape charges. After that, I did not see any more flowers on my desk."

I thought his confession was over, but he was determined to continue.

"However, one day, I was ashamed to say, my past haunted Keiko Itoh. The woman showed up at our apartment. She probably learned from gossip magazines that John Richardson, who she slept with, was getting married to the famous pianist Keiko Itoh in Tachikawa. Since she lived in Tachikawa, it was easy for her to locate our whereabouts. She came to visit Keiko Itoh while I was at work. The woman told Keiko Itoh that John Richardson was already married to her and she was carrying his child. She showed a fraudulent marriage certificate and made Keiko Itoh overwhelmingly startled."

My father's voice got lower than before. "She told Keiko Itoh to vacate the apartment immediately because the apartment was supposed to be hers since her husband, John Richardson, rented it. As Keiko Itoh was petrified to learn the unfaithful, deceitful, despicable behavior of her husband-to-be, she was just speechless and could not move. The woman took Keiko Itoh's physical paralysis as her defiance. So she took out a kitchen knife she brought and attacked her. Keiko Itoh screamed her lungs out. Luckily the neighbors rushed in, restrained the woman, and called the police. Keiko Itoh's arm was almost slashed, but her long-sleeved sweater prevented the injury. When I came home, Keiko Itoh threw everything at me like a mad person. All the dishes were broken, and pots and pans were thrown at me. Since we did not have much of anything in the apartment, she stopped throwing, but she was shaking as a leaf. I went to hold her, but violently rejected me by saying, 'Don't touch me!' She was violent, but I was able to hold her tightly. I held her from her back until her trembling stopped. I whispered to her and asked her why she was so violent. She did not know why, but finally she told me about the woman. Later, one of the neighbors came to tell me that the woman almost killed Keiko Itoh, and luckily the police came and took her away for questioning."

He paused for a while. "I was ashamed. I understood her reaction toward me after being traumatized by that woman. I explained my mistake and begged her for her forgiveness profusely. I also told her it happened several months before I met her. She seemed to be confused and cried a lot that night."

He did not say anything about my mother's illness, anxiety neurosis, how she acquired it, but now I understood how her illness had started…by a traumatic situation.

"Did she forgive you?"

"Yes or no. Your mom wanted me to find out if the woman was indeed carrying my child. I went to see the Japanese supervisor and told him about the attack the woman made to Keiko Itoh. He apologized to me again as though it was his fault hiring her as a housekeeper. He gave me her parents' address, and he thought she might still be living with her parents. I took Keiko Itoh with me to confront her whether she was pregnant or not. If she were, we were going to ask her what she wanted us to do about the baby. Keiko Itoh was determined to tell her that John Richardson would be her husband whether she liked it or not because she loved him very much."

My ear was still cupped with my hand so I could hear my father's whisper better.

"When we arrived at her parents' house, she was reluctant to come out to meet us. When she came out, her stomach was rather slimmed down, but we asked her to make sure. She said she had a miscarriage due to her emotional stress being fired from her job. Keiko Itoh questioned when the miscarriage took place before the attack or after. She said before, so Keiko Itoh concluded she had lied because when she attacked her, the woman clearly said she was carrying John Richardson's child. Keiko Itoh confronted her further on that matter. Finally, she confessed she was not even pregnant. After we went back to the apartment, Keiko Itoh made me avow to be faithful for the rest of my life; otherwise, she would not marry me. So I did it by kneeling in front of her and then asked her to marry me officially."

Family Secrets

My father looked peaceful. His dark secrets were now out of his system. However, I was very sure he still felt guilty because his mistake caused my mother's mental illness and made her suffer from anxiety neurosis for years.

"Where did you get married?"

"Our marriage took place in the military court in front of a judge. Mr. Okuma and General Palmer came to witness it. I bought a large diamond ring for Keiko Itoh. She thought I was heavily in debt, but I told her not to worry."

He glanced at his wedding ring and continued. "After our wedding, I wanted to take Keiko Itoh somewhere for our honeymoon, but we saw a gossip magazine saying Keiko Itoh, a promising young pianist, daughter of Ambassador Ito, married John Richardson, an American soldier. Because of the abrupt cancellation of the wedding, the son of the senior senator, the groom-to-be, was hospitalized and the senior senator himself was hospitalized. The son suffered from his emotional anguish or trauma. The father suffered from a mild stroke. Now the senior senator is planning to file a lawsuit against the Itoh family. They tried to get monetary compensation for their sufferings. The amount was not disclosed yet, but it was thought to be at least ten million yen. We were stunned by the magazine scoop, so we stayed home instead of taking a honeymoon trip."

He looked regretful for not taking my mother on a honeymoon trip.

"Several days after the gossip magazine, Mr. Okuma visited us with some wedding gifts. He said those were from him, but I thought they came from Mrs. Itoh as well. Mr. Okuma brought a legal document that stated Keiko Itoh's official disownment. The Japanese document included the signature seal of Ambassador Itoh and Mrs. Itoh. It stated, 'In quest of the monetary compensation for the party's sufferings shall be denied by the Itoh family due to the fact of Keiko Itoh's official disownment by the family. Thus, regarding Keiko Itoh's whereabouts shall be of no concern to the family. Any future contact by Keiko Itoh to the family shall be prohibited permanently. Keiko Itoh's disownment shall be officially confirmed, hereby.' Mr. Okuma said the document should save the

Itoh family from the lawsuit, but he looked very sad. That was how your mother was disowned by her parents."

"Did that document prevent the lawsuit?"

"I guess so because they dropped the case."

"How did Mom feel about her disownment?"

"She understood it but cried a lot. She mainly blamed her father, Ambassador Itoh, for arranging the political marriage without her consent. She felt she was betrayed by her mother as well because she went along with her husband to arrange the marriage."

"What happened to both of you after you were married?"

"General Palmer got a military housing inside the base for us, and we lived there until my transfer. Mr. Okuma often visited us in the military base with General Palmer's special permission. He kept bringing some cookies. Even though Mr. Okuma kept saying he bought the cookies from the bakery near his house, your mom knew those cookies were from her mother. She cried, seemed to be missing her mother a lot, especially when she found out she was pregnant with you. I was sure she wanted to talk to her mother or ask her many questions about pregnancy. She did not say anything much, but she cried a lot."

He finished drinking his water. My father went back to the subject of General Palmer. He told me all about what General Palmer did for them and what happened to Richard and General Palmer.

Since Vietnam War was heightened and thousands of causalities being reported every day, General Palmer was worried about the safety of my father, John, and his son, Richard. John flew to Vietnam occasionally, but Richard's visit to Vietnam from the Philippines were frequent. General Palmer hoped the war would be over soon for the sake of his son.

After General Palmer learned of Keiko Itoh's pregnancy, John received a transfer order. The Hickam Air Force Base in Honolulu was John's destination. He did not know the significance of his transfer at that time, but later he learned General Palmer arranged the transfer because he wanted John and his family to be safe by staying far away from Vietnam. As commanding officer, General Palmer was determined to protect John from being one of the statistics.

Family Secrets

A month after John's transfer to Honolulu, General Palmer faced the worst possible news from the Philippines. His son, Richard Palmer, was killed in action. He was so devastated losing his only child that he could no longer tolerate to remain in the military. He hastily retired and moved back to his home state, Maine.

According to Richard's grandparents, in Maine, General Palmer took his son's death so hard that he secluded himself in a room—lost a lot of weight, no desire of doing anything around his parent's house, no plan for his retirement. His siblings tried to help him, but he was too heartbroken. One day, he was found dead on the bed. His broken heart ceased his will of living. It was a natural cause. When my parents heard about the death of General Palmer, they, especially my father, grieved for him and Richard for the longest time. Mr. Okuma was grief-stricken as well.

"Where did you live when you came to Honolulu?"

"Well, we lived in the temporary housing in the military base for several months. My military duty was almost over. So we decided to look for a house. We really needed a house for the baby. Your mother wanted a house on the hill so that she could see the famous Hawaiian sunset, but she did not think her dream would come true. When we drove around the Diamond Head area, we saw a house on the hill for sale. The owner wanted to sell the house fast because the husband was already transferred to Arizona. The wife and the children would be moving as soon as they sold the house. The price was reduced drastically, but they wanted the substantial amount of their equity so that the buyer could take over the mortgage. It was a very good deal, but your mom shook her head. She thought we could not afford to come up with the amount they were asking for. Nevertheless, the owner gave us a tour around the house. When we came to the terrace, your mom looked as though she was hypnotized by the scene of the ocean and the sunset. I think she fell in love with the house instantly. So did I."

I could picture my father with his pregnant wife looking at the sunset from the terrace.

"She asked me if we could borrow money from the bank to pay their equity or if we could afford to buy the house. I nodded without saying much in details. The next day I paid for their equity and signed the mortgage transfer. Your mom really thought I robbed a bank overnight. I explained to her the savings I had from my parents' inheritance. She looked stunned because she did not know I was rich. She thought I was a poor soldier. So did the gossip magazine."

My father finally had a smile on his face.

"Even though her stomach was getting bigger, she was decorating your room and the entire house tirelessly. I helped her put some baby furniture, nailing, putting some curtains. I told her to take it easy, but she kept working until your arrival. You were born healthy, pretty, the best-looking baby in the hospital. I bought your mom a grand piano as a gift because she gave me such a beautiful baby. When she saw the grand piano, she cried with the biggest teardrops I had ever seen in my life."

My father winked at me. He sat up straight. His eyes were so clear as though all the dark secrets were out of his system. Now he could start telling me the happy part of his life. I could tell he wanted to talk to me about his secrets for some time, but he just did not have the time. Flying together for many hours made it possible for him to confess, although he had to whisper most of the time.

Now it seems all our family secrets are unveiled. My secret mission is almost completed. However, I must unveil my mother's birth secret to her soon. Hopefully, it is not too late. I must provide her a chance to reconcile with her mother so that we could live happily ever after without any family secrets.

Suddenly, I realized that I have withheld my mother's birth secret from my father. I remembered that I was supposed to tell him about it at a restaurant tonight, but it did not work out due to this urgency. So I must to do it now.

"Dad, do you think Mom and Mr. Okuma resemble a lot, their smiles, their shiny black hair, and their big eyes?"

"All Japanese have shiny black hair." He laughed softly. We were no longer leaning toward each other, but still whispered.

"Oh, Dad! Do what I ask you to do. Just imagine Mom's smile and Mr. Okuma's smile and their eyes. Don't you think they look alike? Oh, another thing, Mr. Okuma and I have cowlicks."

"What are you trying to tell me? Mr. Okuma is your grandfather?" He laughed again jokingly.

"Exactly. Yes, Mr. Okuma is my biological grandfather. This means Mr. Okuma is Mom's biological father."

My father looked puzzled, but he became curious. He wanted me to continue my explanation. I told him what Mr. Okuma told me. I told him everything what I learned from my visit with Mr. Okuma including his growing up with my grandmother. My father was stunned because he did not suspect anything like that. He thought Mr. Okuma and my grandmother were just childhood friends. However, he seemed to be very happy to know about the relationship between Mr. Okuma and my grandmother…their forever loves.

My father agreed to help me unveil my mother's birth secret together and convince her to reconcile with her mother. Nevertheless, my father and I got quiet thinking about my mother's unknown condition in Honolulu. His dreadful thoughts seemed to be the same as mine; she may not be with us any longer or may not be capable of recognizing us.

We were approaching the Honolulu International Airport. The announcement of landing made all the passengers put away the earphones and gather up their belongings. All the window shades were up. It was still bright outside.

Chapter 19

LOVE AT FIRST SIGHT

When we arrived at the airport, I turned on my cell and found Mrs. Kitano's voice message. She said she would be waiting at the arrival lounge. She and Mr. Yamagata would take us to the hospital.

They spotted us in our uniforms. I shook hands with Mr. Yamagata and thanked them both for picking us up and taking us to the hospital.

A tall man with a handsome face spotted my father. He looked rather haole, but I could not tell if he was a hapa haole or haole, but how handsome he looked. He could be a lookalike of George Clooney. My father was shaking hands with him.

"Mark. What a surprise! Why are you here?"

"My father called me to meet you and give you a ride to the hospital. We found out Mrs. Richardson was in Queen's Hospital. Well, I was spending my time here on Waikiki Beach. You must be Mary."

I nodded. "Yes. You are…Mr. Nakaya's son, Mark?"

"Yes. Nice to meet you. I heard a lot about you."

"Nice to meet you. I heard a lot about you too."

We shook hands. Mark looked stunned and somewhat mesmerized by me; so was I…by him. I finally met him—my rival. What a rival! Wow! He looked like George Clooney with black hair.

He took Kim's Caucasian genes, not much of Mr. Nakaya's. Just like me, I took my father's Caucasian genes. How handsome he looked with his nice suntan. I did not expect him to be such a handsome man. He also looked sexy in his jeans.

My father had never told me how Mark looked. He only bragged about his flying skills. If I knew he were such a handsome and sexy man, I would not mind a bit volunteering to fly them to Las Vegas or Palm Springs. Additionally, I would not mind learning how to play golf just to be with him. I was gasping, or I was swept up by "love at first sight?" I had never believed in such a thing…love at first sight, but it was happening to me.

I utterly forgot to ask Mrs. Kitano or Mr. Yamagata about my mother's condition because I was bitten by a love bug and my mind was paralyzed. Ironically, the love bug was my rival.

Since Mark did not know the direction to the hospital, I rode with him. While riding, I felt as though the love bug was sitting beside me with his beautiful fangs that had already injected the invisible venom into my heart. I heard the effect of the venom in my heart loudly, but I calmly directed Mark to take the highway to Queen's Hospital. By controlling my restless heart, I asked, "Mark, did you know what happened to my mother?"

"Yes. When my father asked me to locate which hospital Mrs. Richardson was taken to, I called the police department to find out your mother's whereabouts, the Queen's Hospital. She was hit by a dump truck from the driver's side. She has been unconscious since."

"Thank you."

I was quiet, but I could not control my rumbling heart inside of me. Mark's handsome face was concentrating on driving. Wow! I thought George Clooney has a lot of charms, but Mark has more sophisticated charms and sex appeal than the movie star has. He spoke with a sexy voice as well.

I was daydreaming…under the full moon on Waikiki Beach, the movie camera was rolling to take a love scene of George Clooney. He was holding an actress named Mary by her waist, and his other hand was caressing Mary's thigh. George Clooney's sexy lips were approaching Mary's lips. The camera was rolling. I shook my head. George Clooney was obediently following my direction to the hospital.

Mark was recalling something and said, "When my mother was suffering from cancer, she told me all about you. How pretty Mary looked, how smart and kind person Mary was. She kept saying if I would ever meet Mary, I would change my heart. She really wanted me to meet you. I did not know you are such a beauty. My mother was right. You are beautiful and seem to be just as she described. In any rate, I am very happy to meet you."

Now I recalled what his mother, Kim, said to me years ago. "I have someone I want you to meet. I guarantee you both would like each other. I will introduce you to this charming person soon."

I often wondered who someone could be after her passing. Now I know the charming someone was her own son, Mark. I did not tell him what his mother said to me. Kim was correct; Mark was handsomely charming. I finally met someone Kim really wanted me to meet. Miraculously, he became my love at first sight. Could it be Kim's supernatural gift from heaven to me?

As I had made a mistake in my love relationship in the past, I wanted to honor what my dear friends, Alice and Nina, said, "Be a detective before being a lover."

I must control my reckless heart that seemed to be acting feverishly since Mark appeared. As a detective, I must ask him many blunt questions, but I did not want to scare him. Of course, I would not jump in bed until I would find out he had no fraudulent background or lies as Bruce had.

We arrived at the hospital. My father was already there. They were sitting in the ICU lounge and waiting for us. My father and I were called to the surgeon's room to sign some papers before going to the ICU window.

My mother's swollen face and neck were bandaged, and numerous tubes were inserted into her mouth, nose, even in her wrists. Her closed eyelids were bruised. I could not tell whether her arms and legs were broken or not.

My father and I just stared at her once pretty face from the glass window. Somehow, I did not have any tears in my eyes. I was not crying. I could not cry. I was just stunned to see her motionless body. My father looked stunned, but no tears.

Due to my mother's low immune system and her unconsciousness, no one could visit her inside the ICU except the nurses and doctors. The hospital staff was monitoring the elaborate computer screen in the nurses' station.

Again, my father and I were called to the surgeon's office. The doctor had to explain what happened to my mother and her prognosis.

My mother was struck by a dump truck on the hill in our neighborhood. Since the dump truck was coming uphill slowly, the injury was not as bad as expected, yet the impact made her unconscious. Her facial bones and skull were slightly fractured, but the surgeon had already reconstructed them.

He thanked me for my verbal consent for the surgery that was left on Mrs. Kitano's phone. Her arms, legs, and other parts of body were not injured at all. He did not know how long she would be unconscious, but he thought the excellent condition of her vital organs could help her recover soon without any complications. The doctor was optimistic.

"What can we do for her now?"

"Nothing, the nurses will take care of her until she wakes up. If something changes on her vital organs, we will contact you. As far as we are concerned, Mrs. Richardson is in good hands. She seems to be a tough cookie. I could tell she is fighting back as hard as she could. You just pray for her fast recovery. Whenever you visit her, please check with us. We will give you the prognosis. Right now, you only can visit her from the window. Please bear with us. When her immune system improves, you would be able to hold her hands. We have your contact numbers, including your neighbor, Mrs. Kitano's. So do not worry too much."

He glanced at our uniforms and said, "Carry on your daily routine. We will take good care of Mrs. Richardson." He shook our hands.

We thanked the surgeon and joined Mark, Mrs. Kitano, and Mr. Yamagata in the ICU lounge.

Mr. Yamagata explained what happened to my mother in Japanese; when he heard a clashing noise down the hill while he was working at the driveway, he knew that was Mrs. Richardson's car because she just drove off saying she would pick up a jug of milk and come right back. So he ran down the hill. It was indeed Mrs. Richardson's car. The dump truck's front bumper crushed the driver's side. Mrs. Richardson's head was smashed with blood. He thought she was dead instantly.

The explanation continued; the dump-truck driver called an ambulance. They responded very quickly. The door was pried opened, and they took Mrs. Richardson on a stretcher. Mr. Yamagata rode in the ambulance with her to the hospital. At the hospital, he was told to contact her family as soon as possible. However, he did not know our phone numbers, so he got the airline's toll-free number from the reception desk. He talked to someone on the phone and said repeatedly, "Captain Mary Richardson must fly back to Honolulu urgently," in his broken English. They somehow relayed the message to the control tower and then to the cockpit. Everybody including Mark understood what Mr. Yamagata explained in Japanese.

After we chatted in the ICU lounge, we decided to go to my mother's house on the hill. Mrs. Kitano said she would be glad to prepare some supper for all of us. So Mark decided to drive me to the house. Besides, my father insisted Mark would come. Mrs. Kitano drove Mr. Yamagata and my father in her car.

I still could not believe I did not have any tears when I saw my mother in such a tragic condition in the hospital. When I had a dreadful thought about her when I was on the airplane, I cried; at least I had tears in my eyes. However, in the hospital, I did not have any tears when I was staring at my mother.

Somebody later explained to me about my psychological status. I was stunned and my mind was subconsciously refusing to include my mother's tragic actuality in my reality. I was in refusal stage; therefore, my tear ducts did not react. I could not cry, or I did not cry.

Mark was still injecting some invisible venom to paralyze me or hypnotize me while he was driving. Besides, I saw some electric sparks between his sexy lips when he spoke, probably to electrify me. I was not imagining—I really saw the sparks.

"Mary, are you dating anybody?"

"Umm…regretfully, no."

I thought Mark was a little rude to ask me some personal questions, so I changed the subject. "Mark, do you come here often?"

"Here in Honolulu? No. We went to Maui a couple of times before because we thought Waikiki was too busy."

I interpreted "we" meant he and his longtime live-in girlfriend I heard of. Yikes! Well, at least he was honest unlike Bruce.

"Yes, but Honolulu is a fun place to visit."

"Yes, even though this is my first visit, I am thoroughly enjoying being here. I can visit many good restaurants and shops. Swimming on the beach is relaxing with the perfect weather every day. No wonder everybody calls Waikiki Beach is the center of paradise. I am here because my company is offering me a home base position to Asia. So I came to investigate."

"Do you still live in San Diego with your girlfriend?"

"Who?"

"Your longtime girlfriend I heard of."

"No. We parted almost four years ago before my mother died. We had some problems, so we dissolved our relationship. I still live in San Diego but live alone now."

Whoa, my father did not tell me anything about his breakup with his girlfriend. "Are you dating anyone currently?" I became personal just as he was. Being a detective, I must ask some blunt questions. Alice told me to look in the eye when I asked blunt questions, but I could not look him in his eyes because he was driving.

"Umm…regretfully, no."

I had to ask one more blunt question to see a clear picture of his current relationship. "Are you and your girlfriend still seeing each other?"

"My ex-girlfriend? No. In fact, I don't even know where she lives now."

I stopped asking him anymore blunt questions. I thought I was getting too nosy. Even though I was not looking into his eyes, his voice was sincere and believable. I did not think he was hiding anybody or anything at home, unlike Bruce Hudson.

He seemed to be clean. I was sure he heard about me from my father, being single, living in a nice condominium. I believed he knew I was clean as well.

If I wanted to find out more on his relationships or background, I could ask my father or his father, Mr. Nakaya. In Bruce Hudson's case, I did not know anybody who could offer any information on him. Moreover, he lied about his relationship by telling me that he was once married for a year but divorced. I believed his lies.

Now I decided to tell Mark what I thought about him. "I heard a lot about you from my father. He always bragged about you, how excellent a pilot you are. In fact, I have been very jealous of you because he treats you better than he treats me."

My George rebutted, "What? No. I should be jealous of you because your father always bragged about you whenever I flew his Cessna. He said Mary is a much better pilot than anybody else because he trained you. You? Jealous of me?"

"Well, he had never asked me to fly his Cessna since he moved to Los Angeles because you were there. To him, you are his son whom he never had. Even though I did not know how to play golf, I do not mind flying you guys to Las Vegas, or Palm Springs, but I was never invited because I am a girl. Yes. You have been my rival and a threat to my relationship with my father for a long time."

Mark glanced at me. He thought I was crying.

"Mark, next time my father asks you to fly his Cessna, tell him Mary should be included in the circle because she is a pilot. If my father says okay, then you will be forgiven."

He glanced at me again and laughed with a sexy voice. "Okay, Captain Mary. I will. By the way, would you like to have lunch or dinner with me the next day or so? I will be here for three more days."

Whoa, my George Clooney is asking me to eat lunch or dinner with him? "Well, tomorrow, after my father and I visit my mother in the hospital, I am going to the airport to adjust my flying schedule to take two weeks off for my mother. Yes, probably for lunch tomorrow?"

"Perfect. Let's exchange our cell phone numbers when we get to your house."

When we arrived at my mother's house, I saw Mr. Yamagata shaking my father's hand. He had to go home to his wife. It had been a very long day for him. I thanked him again before he left.

Mark was very impressed by my mother's house. He was looking out the scene from the terrace. My father changed his uniform to his casual clothes. I went into my room and changed to a casual dress as well. Some of my clothes were left in my closet even though I moved out of the house.

Mark and my father were talking at the terrace while viewing the ocean. Mrs. Kitano and I were making supper together by using available food in the refrigerator. After supper, Mrs. Kitano was going home. It had been a long day for her as well.

She told me when she heard my message on the phone, she called Mr. Yamagata's wife and found my mother's whereabouts. She also called the surgeon and gave my verbal consent.

I thanked her for looking after my mother. She said my mother is just like her sister and she loves her.

Mark was to drive me home to my condominium. I embraced my father and told him I would come to pick him up the next day to see Mom. Mark was telling my father which hotel he was staying as he was leaving. Mark and I saw some debris at the corner where my mother's car was struck.

"Mark, which hotel did you say you are staying?"

"Sheraton"

"Which Sheraton?"

"Moana Surfrider Sheraton."

"We are neighbors."

"Would you like to stop for a drink after I park my car? I will walk you home."

"Okay."

The gigantic banyan tree was in the middle of the outdoor café. The live piano music was heard. Mark ordered two glasses of red wine for us. The full moon happened to be in the sky, as though it showed up to make us romantic or to command me to follow my heart, which was struck by "love at first sight."

Mark seemed to be very excited about having me for the evening. It was not a date. We just agreed to have a drink together before he was to walk me home.

The piano music reminded me of my mother's piano playing, and I thought about her for a minute, but when I remembered she was in good hands with the hospital staff, I felt relieved. I convinced myself by thinking that my mother would not mind for me to have a romantic night with George Clooney.

Mark wanted to walk on the beach before he was to walk me home. The full moon was still in the sky. There were not many people on the beach unlike in the afternoon. We both took our shoes off and walked along the waves on the sand. We were chased by the waves. I was screaming.

It reminded me of my childhood. The PE teacher used to bring just the girls in class to the beach for swimming lessons. We used to play with the ocean waves on the beach before the lesson. Each time the waves chased us, we screamed.

The teacher wanted us to stand at the edge of the waves to exercise before going into the water, but our feet were sinking in the sand with the waves. Again we screamed. Nevertheless, once we got into the water, we learned how to swim.

Mark and I were playing like kids with the waves. Suddenly, Mark held my hand for the first time, and he brought my whole body against him. I saw his handsome face under the spotlight called the moonlight. I also saw his sexy lips coming closer to my lips.

Suddenly, my whole body was melting. I was supposed to play a kissing scene with George Clooney in front of the camera. I thought they would shout, "Cut!" because I was falling on the sand dune by mistake, but I did not hear the movie director.

"Mary, are you okay?"

"Yes. Geor…Mark. I am okay."

I was flat on my back. Mark looked worried. He tried to lift me up, but instead he fell on top of me. Again, George Clooney's lips were approaching mine.

I did not care what the movie director would say about my kissing scene with George Clooney. I devoured his kisses like a crazy fan. The movie director could not separate us. He had to leave us alone. We were stuck together.

When I realized, we both were in my bed naked. Our bodies were glued together and the actress's lips and the actor's sexy lips were sealed together, and now nobody could separate them. Perhaps a bucket of cold water could separate George Clooney from Mary, or Mary from George Clooney, but Mary did not mind being stuck together with George Clooney forever.

I had no regrets because I did my detective job before I jumped in bed with my love at first sight. As far as Alice and Nina were concerned, yes, I had completed the assignment they told me to do.

"Mary, have you heard of love at first sight?" My George Clooney was whispering in my ear in bed.

"I had never believed in love at first sight, but I experienced it with you at the airport."

The movie star was reading a script.

"I was swept up in the passion of sex before, but this is different. My heart is pounding with such a delightful feeling that I had never experienced before. It is incredible and indescribable. It is genuine. I am confessing to you because I cannot contain this wonderful feeling just to myself. I hope you understand how I feel about you."

I nodded several times. I was very happy to hear his feeling as same as mine, love at first sight. I was going to say the same thing, but I decided not to say anything. Instead, I devoured his mouth again like a sex maniac. My love scene with George Clooney continued without any interruption from the movie director.

Mark's lovemaking was unadulterated and truthful unlike Bruce's. Mark's passion was wild, so was mine, but sincere and genuine unlike Bruce's. We both were mutually struck by love at first sight. This magnetic attraction was real unlike Bruce's. I did not know why I was comparing this relationship to Bruce's. Perhaps, I became wiser, not naive anymore.

Chapter 20

MARK NAKAYA

While Mark Nakaya was growing up, his father, Minoru, used to take him to the airport and let him learn many things about airlines and airplanes. Whenever Mark saw John Richardson at the airport, who was in a pilot uniform, Mark wanted to be a pilot. Mark was very much inspired by John Richardson in a pilot uniform, and he was determined to be a pilot just like John Richardson someday.

His father, Minoru Nakaya, treated John Richardson as his younger brother. As a child, Mark was always thankful if they involved him in their Japanese conversations. Mark spoke Japanese with his parents at home. He read and wrote Japanese. Kim and Minoru made sure Mark learned Japanese correctly by sending him to a Japanese language school on Saturdays.

Mark's mother, Kim, was born out of wedlock. Kim's mother was a Japanese Nisei who worked for a wealthy family as a maid. She and the son of the family fell in love. She got pregnant, but the family refused to hear about her pregnancy with their son. They quickly sent their son abroad and dismissed Kim's mother from her job before the baby was born.

Shortly after Kim was born, her mother passed away. Kim lived with her maternal grandparents and grew up in Gardena. She went to the same school John and Minoru went. Because her looks were more like Caucasian, her classmates called her with some derogatory names—*ainoko* for a mixed breed and *shiseiji* for an out-of-wedlock baby.

John and Minoru were very sympathetic about Kim's situation and tried to protect her from those hurtful name-callings at school. They became very good friends. Kim was a little chubby but had a beautiful Caucasian face and tall. Her personality was always compassionate.

After high school, Kim was hired to work for Minoru's aging parents at Beverly Hills. She was a hard worker, and the Nakayas liked her and trusted her. The Nakayas were also very happy about Minoru's marriage to Kim.

Shortly after Mark started school, his grandmother, Mrs. Nakaya, passed away, and a year later his grandfather, Mr. Nakaya, died. Their laundry business was already handed down to their daughter-in-law, Kim, instead of Minoru. Because of Kim's excellent management, the family business was thriving. Therefore, Minoru did not feel guilty about working at the airport.

To Kim, John Richardson was always her husband's, Minoru's, younger brother. He was invited to eat dinner with them whenever he overnighted in Los Angeles. Most of the time, Minoru met him at the airport and brought him home to eat dinner, then usually John overnighted at Minoru's house…and the next day, they both drove to the airport.

When John came to the dinner, Mark learned how to play Go from him and discussed many interesting things in Japanese. Mark really felt a kinship with John, so he called him Uncle John from time to time when he was young.

Whenever Mark brought up the subject of being a pilot, John said to Mark, if he wanted to be a pilot, be the best one by practicing a lot and getting the best training. With plenty of flying practices, eventually he would acquire the instinct of flying any airplanes.

Mark went to the local college just as his father did, but he was determined to become a pilot. He worked for his mother after school and on the weekends to pay for the flying lessons. Throughout his college years, he was busy shuffling three things every day: going to college, going to flying school, and working at his mother's laundry. He hardly had his own social life other than music practice with his high school friends on Sundays.

Mark met Lisa Webster when he was working for his mother. He delivered some clothes to her apartment in Beverly Hills. He knocked on her door, but no one answered. He did not know what to do, so he knocked on the door louder again.

The woman who had a towel on her head opened the door slightly, told him to hang up the clothes back on the door, and leave, then quickly disappeared in the bathroom. She was probably naked. Mark did what he was told. As he hanged the clothes on the hook behind the door, he heard the woman's voice.

"Please do not forget to lock the door when you leave."

Mark shouted, "I need your signature on the credit card slip!"

"Oh, you are welcome." The woman answered as though she thought she heard Mark was thanking her.

However, Mark had to wait to get the credit card slip signed. The credit card number was already recorded at the time of pickup, but at the completion of each delivery, the customer must sign the slip to complete the transaction. Mark sat on a chair near the door and waited.

The woman finally came out of the bathroom, but she was naked. When she saw Mark near the door, she screamed. Mark shouted at her to sign the credit card slip. So she stopped screaming and came to the door to sign the slip as Lisa Webster.

Seeing a woman's naked body up close for the first time, Mark's face turned red. For some reasons, his eyes were widened with curiosity. After she signed the credit card slip, she glanced at his handsomely shaped face and his well-built body from head to toe as though she were examining her merchandise.

He thanked her for her signature and apologized to her for her inconvenience. When he opened the door to leave, the woman tugged him on his arm and led him to her bedroom. She made him sit on the bed.

Without saying anything, she started unbuttoning his shirt slowly and caressing his torso and chest with her silky warm hands. She made him hold her oversized breast with both of his hands. Mark was petrified, but he was aroused quickly just as a young stud might be aroused. The woman looked much older than Mark, but she had a young-looking face and firm slender body. She seemed to know how to arouse a man.

When she unzipped his pants, she gently searched for Mark's erection and let it pop out. She slid her naked body down to the floor, knelt in front of his erection, placed her tongue over it, and started undressing him at the same time.

When her mouth was aggressively placed over Mark's erection, he was crazily aroused. After she undressed him completely, she made him lie down on the bed. Her naked body was climbing over him. Suddenly, she sat on top of his erection. Mark was inside of her. He thought he was going to explode. Mark's face was flushed with an indescribable joy. The woman made Mark change position without disconnecting their bodies. He did as he was instructed.

To his surprise, when he was on top of her, he began to thrust himself with his most satisfying manner without being instructed. Although it was his first sexual intercourse, he thought to himself, the thrusting movement he performed had to be the male animal's instinct. She moaned; so did Mark about the same time of his eruption.

He was lured to her bedroom every day as though he was hypnotized to reach her. Whenever she told him to come, he went, even in the middle of the night. His sexual satisfaction was just out of this world.

At school, he could not help but think about sex with Lisa. During flying lessons, he thought about her breasts and sex with her. While helping his mother, he could not stop thinking about Lisa's naked body and his climax.

He thought about sex every minute. He had commuted to Lisa's apartment for a year. He was the happiest young stud in this world during that time.

He graduated with a bachelor's degree as mathematics major. He could be a math teacher in high school, but he wanted to use his pilot license to work for a small charter flight company. Later he wanted to land a pilot job with one of the major airlines just as John Richardson did.

He wanted to marry Lisa so he could live happily ever after with their fantastic sex life, but Lisa did not want to marry him. Instead, she suggested living together with him by sharing the living expenses. Mark agreed.

Mark told his parents about moving out of the house to live with Lisa Webster. They were flabbergasted. They did not know he had a girlfriend named Lisa. Nobody including his high school friends knew he had a girlfriend.

Mark and Lisa had never gone out. The only place they were together was in Lisa's bedroom; they had never taken the time to go out. They simply stayed in bed to enjoy sex, nothing else.

Lisa knew Mark was a recent college graduate and began working for a charter flight company. Mark knew Lisa worked for a magazine company as a model. She showed him some pictures of her provocative lingerie line of work. She seemed to be doing well living in such a nice apartment for all this time. Mark believed that they should be very happy living together and having fantastic sex whenever they wanted without any concern of the time.

Before Mark moved out of his parents' house, Minoru and Kim insisted to meet Lisa in a restaurant for the first time. Mark's mother saw her as a slut or a hooker. She looked ten years older than her son. Mr. Nakaya was very disappointed in Mark's choice of women. They could see that Mark was swept up in the passion of sex; he was blinded. He could not see anything else but Lisa's naked body.

Mark did not neglect his career. He started commuting a long distance to his work, left early in morning, and came home around seven. Lisa supposedly went to the office for photo shoots at least three times a week. The rest of the week, she did her nails and face.

Every Saturday night, Lisa made sure Mark accompanied her to an exclusive restaurant in Beverly Hills for dinner. Lisa made Mark wear a tuxedo, and she dressed in an expensive provocative silk dress. They both looked awesomely handsome. Mark did not know the importance of this event every Saturday night for Lisa, but he followed her order. At the restaurant, some customers, especially the men, recognized her, but they seemed to be avoiding her.

Family Secrets

Mark had never met any of Lisa's friends. Mark had many friends from high school, but Lisa did not want to invite them to her apartment. Additionally, at his work, he was making some friends. He really wanted to invite his friends from work so that they could feast on Mark's cooking, which his mother, Kim, always bragged about, but Lisa did not want that at all.

Lisa also resented Mark for seeing his parents every Sunday, but Mark did not care. He told her that he would not mind using his Saturday nights for Lisa, going to the restaurant, but Sundays should be his days for spending his time with his parents and friends.

Mark went to see his parents without Lisa every Sunday. At his parents' house, he practiced music with his music group and entertained them with BBQ, mowed the lawn for his father, helped his mother with the accounting book, and sometimes, he accompanied his father to play golf.

As Mark looked happy, Minoru and Kim decided to stay away from the topic of his live-in girlfriend, so Lisa's name never came into their conversations.

Mark had landed a job with one of the major airlines as a first officer after working for the charter flight company for several years. Lisa did not show any interest in Mark's career. She had been secretive about her background. She had never mentioned her family, where they lived, what they did for their livings, how many siblings she had, and so forth. Occasionally, Kim had invited Lisa to have dinner with them, but Lisa always made some excuses. She had no desire of seeing Mark's parents, nor his friends.

After ten years of living together with Lisa in Los Angeles, Mark was transferred to San Diego as his home base station. He became a full captain. He was to fly between San Diego and Mexico City. Even though Lisa was reluctant to leave Los Angeles, she moved with him.

After they settled in San Diego for several months, Mark realized that he was already over thirty, no marriage, and no children. He asked Lisa to marry him, but she refused again. She said Mark was not rich enough to support her for the rest of her life. Besides, she did not want the hassle with kids. She rather wanted to marry someone who could guarantee her life as a wealthy woman. It did not matter whether she became a mistress. She just wanted to be wealthy enough to live in Beverly Hills or somewhere in Hollywood. Lisa said Mark had been a great lover, but he was not rich enough for her.

Finally, without any hesitation, she said she was going to leave Mark because she had a marriage proposal from a wealthy man in Beverly Hills who just lost his wife. She had already accepted his marriage proposal, so she should be moving back to Los Angeles.

Mark was flabbergasted. He could not believe what she was saying to him. He had lived with her for ten years and now she was going to leave him because someone wealthy old man proposed to her? How did it happen? Who is the man?

Several days later, Lisa took almost everything including cooking utensils, towels, a king-size bed, and all good furniture. She vacated herself while Mark was at work. She left a small kitchen table with two chairs and a small bed in the guest room. The apartment was emptied. Mark was outraged.

That night, he was reminiscing about his life with Lisa. There were so many unanswered questions. Why did Lisa want Mark to accompany her in a tuxedo to the exclusive restaurant in Beverly Hills every Saturday night? How did she meet the wealthy guy who just proposed to her? What kind of modeling job did she do to live in such an expensive apartment in Beverly Hills?

Mark's anger toward Lisa rather made him robust instead of being depressed. He kept himself busy every minute so he should not think about Lisa. Flying as a captain from San Diego to Mexico City became more important than his relationship with Lisa. When he saw the blue sky from the cockpit, Lisa became nothing. In other words, he realized his job was the most important thing in his life. Nothing could replace his job. He felt fortunate that he had the job he liked most.

Soon after Lisa left Mark, his mother, Kim, became very ill. The doctor found aggressive cancer cells in her pancreas. It was too late to apply any therapy to reverse the cancer. He predicted she could only live for a month. Mark's time allocation as a captain gave him enough time to stay with his mother. Minoru too took some time off from work to stay with Kim.

Before she got sick, Kim had already put out her business for sale and wrote a will for Mark and Minoru. They were to divide the profit in half. However, she emphasized not to give even a penny to Lisa. Mark did not tell his mother or father that Lisa had already left him for a wealthy man.

Kim must have sensed that Lisa was no long in Mark's life because she kept telling Mark to meet Mary. She kept praising how beautiful Mary looks, how kind and smart she is. Most importantly, she is a pilot just like Mark. She emphasized that Mark and Mary should have the same destiny. At that time, Mark did not want to think about any date or any woman. He really hated to start any relationship with any woman, so he just nodded with a smile and dismissed the topic of Mary.

Kim knew about Lisa all along as a prostitute. She had hired a private investigator to investigate Lisa Webster's background. After reading the investigation, she felt so sorry for her son for wasting so many years of his life on a hooker. She cried. Minoru cried too. At the end, they decided to hide the report. Nevertheless, before Kim's passing, she gave the envelope to Minoru and told him to give it to Mark at the right time.

Kim passed away quietly one afternoon in front of Mark and Minoru. She died within two weeks of hospitalization. She went too fast. Minoru and Mark were devastated and mourned for her death for a long time.

After his mother's funeral, Mark hated going home to an empty apartment, so he took a week off and stayed in his favorite city, San Francisco, and wanted to recuperate from his sad loss of his beloved mother. He walked to cross the Golden Gate Bridge, gazed at the sunset on the San Francisco Bay from a pier, and walked the hill from Fisherman's Wharf to the top.

After the trip, Mark finally decided to tell his father about Lisa's departure on the phone. Minoru did not say much, except, "Son, I am very sorry. I hope you will be all right."

Several days later, Mark received a large brown envelope from his father. Inside of the envelope, he found Lisa Webster's background investigation by a private investigator who was hired by his mother. The envelope was five years old.

The document contained Lisa Webster's numerous arrests on illegal sex solicitations since she was a teenager, as well as her service records with escort services in Hollywood. She had no relatives or siblings. Some wealthy clients bailed her out several times in the past.

When Mark read the investigation, he was outraged. He felt he was betrayed by the woman he thought he loved. All the pieces came together including her Saturday night events. She was sleeping with all those wealthy guys who came to the restaurant.

Now he understood the reason why Lisa insisted for Mark to wear a tuxedo. She wanted to make those men who slept with her jealous. She knew those men would come to the exclusive restaurant with their wives on Saturday nights.

When those wealthy ones saw her with a young stud who looked like George Clooney, they felt jealous, and at the same time their sexual fantasy or adrenaline was stimulated by recalling her dynamic, mesmerizing, and hypnotizing sex services. They wanted her.

Then the following week, those wealthy ones could phone her to fill her schedule to receive her intoxicating services. Her clients' most desirable time or unsuspected time was daytime…around lunchtime on the weekdays. Their wives would assume their husbands would be at work.

Mark had never suspected her daytime activities because she said she was working for a magazine company for modeling. He believed her.

He remembered once he became suspicious of her job. One afternoon around noon, Mark came home because he became ill at work. Lisa, dressed in a sexy dress, came down in the elevator. When she saw him, she said she had an important appointment in the office. She had to run, so she left in a hurry.

After she left, he tried to contact her in her office because he wanted her to pick up some medicine on the way home; the secretary said that Lisa did not have any appointment on that day. Later he asked her about her appointment. She said the shooting contract went well, the secretary in the office was typing up the contract. Mark knew she lied. That was the only time he became suspicious.

Now he realized her appointment was to meet one of the wealthy men in the hotel on that day. He imagined most of her clients were all wealthy ones who could afford her exclusive price. Those sexually captivated clients must have promised to marry her after their wives' future deaths. They were under Lisa's spell just as Mark had been for many years. She had been their sex goddess as well as Mark's.

When he started working for one of the major airlines, he only had to fly three days a week. So he was home with Lisa some weekdays, but Mark had never witnessed her suspicious activities. Apparently, she was very meticulous about booking her clients. That was why Mark did not have any knowledge of Lisa's fraudulent activities.

Mark realized how naive and stupid he had been for ten years. He was living with a high-class prostitute. He wasted a large portion of his life for nothing. He was angry with himself, but now he was wide-awake. He put the investigation report back in the envelope and pushed it into his overnight crew bag.

He searched for Lisa's belongings throughout the empty apartment. He found her Q-tip holder, shower cap, some lipsticks, fragrant soaps, handkerchiefs, and fancy panties. He shoved them in a plastic bag and disposed them through the garbage shoot in the building as though he were discarding filthy and smelly foods from the refrigerator. He took several showers to feel clean on that day.

Several weeks after Kim's passing, Lisa Webster moved back to Mark's apartment. She moved in with the key she had, cooked dinner, and waited on him. She planned to accept his marriage proposal.

However, Mark was with his father in Los Angeles, finalizing the sale of Kim's business. The property was in the prime location in Beverly Hills. The value was significantly appreciated. The laundry business was started by Mark's grandparents who handed down the business to their daughter-in-law, Kim.

The price of the property including the business transfer was a lot more than Mark and Minoru expected. The bank wrote two checks according to Kim's instruction in her will. Each received 2.5 million after the tax. They became instant millionaires.

When Mark arrived in his apartment, he was surprised to see Lisa Webster, who had moved back in as though everything were the same as before. Seeing Lisa angered him and made him ill. She dressed provocatively and came to kiss Mark, but he told her to stop it.

She said, "Mark, I changed my mind. I accept your marriage proposal. Please marry me. I will give you a beautiful son or daughter. Please forgive me for whatever I said to you before. We will have a beautiful marriage with fantastic sex for the rest of our lives. I love you very much."

"What made you come back to this poor man's life? I am not rich enough to support you for the rest of your life."

"Oh, yes. You will be rich. I read it in the newspaper. When your mother's business in Beverly Hills is sold, you will be rich. You will be able to afford me with some beautiful children. We could live happily ever after. So I accept your marriage proposal. I hope you have not changed your mind. I know you are crazy about me. I will make love to you whenever you want. You will be the happiest man in the world. Nobody can give you better sex than I can. Please marry me."

She started unbuttoning his uniform jacket, but he violently stopped her.

"I know your wealthy guy who wanted to marry you passed away last week. I read it on the obituary. I am not taking you back. Just leave the key before you leave. I will be staying in a hotel tonight. You must vacate this apartment by tomorrow. If you do not vacate by noon tomorrow, I will be calling the police or the landlord. Do not forget to leave the key. Here is something you can read."

He took out the large brown envelope from his overnight crew bag and slammed it on the kitchen table in front of her. Then he grabbed his crew bag and left.

Chapter 21

A Mysterious Fire

I found myself sleeping like a puppy snuggling against George Clooney's muscular chest when the phone rang. My father called to see if I knew where Mark was. I pretended and said he might be eating breakfast on the beach.

"Dad, I'll pick you up to see Mom, and then I need to go to the airport to get my flight schedule adjusted. I will take at least two weeks off to stay in town."

"Do you have your car in your place or at the airport?"

"I took a taxi to the airport last time. Yes, my car is parked here. I will pick you up soon."

"I think I will use my annual vacation time before I retire, but I need to ask Minoru something. I will plan to be here until Mom gets well. I don't have Minoru's cell phone number with me. That is why I was looking for Mark. He is not in the room."

"I am supposed to meet Mark for lunch. Do you want to eat with us so you can get Mr. Nakaya's cell phone number?"

"Okay. Call me before you pick me up. How long does it take for you to get ready?"

"About an hour."

"Okay."

George Clooney took the phone from me and placed it on the crater while smiling mischievously at me. He started caressing my naked body to arouse me crazily again. Our short love scene was repeated for the final take. We took a shower together. George Clooney and I looked very happy and handsome in the mirror.

I got my car out of the parking garage and dropped Mark off at the hotel while exchanging our cell phone numbers.

"I will meet you around noon for lunch. I will call you before we come. Get some rest."

I did not want George Clooney to be out on the beach alone because his fans might seduce him and make love to him while I was away.

My father looked rested. His eyes were clear and hopeful. In the hospital, the nurse smiled at us and reported, "Mrs. Richardson's vital signs are still very strong. She is getting some color on her face. It is a good sign. We are checking the monitor constantly. If there are any changes, I would personally call you. You can stay around here if you want, but you still cannot go inside yet."

We stared at my mother's face from the window for a while. I never recalled my parents to be hospitalized. This is the first time my mother being in the hospital.

When I was a child, I was hospitalized once. My pediatrician misdiagnosed me when I was sick and declared I had an infectious meningitis.

I was quarantined for several days. On the first night, I was crying aloud because I was scared to be in the enclosed tent that was steamed up with oxygen. I felt as though I was choking to death with the steam. I cried and screamed to be with my mother, but she was just looking at me helplessly from outside of the clear plastic tent with tearful eyes.

Finally, she could not stand to see me scream. She called a nurse to turn down some steaming oxygen. After she turned down the oxygen, the steam went away. Then she asked the nurse if it would be all right to touch her daughter. The nurse gave her a pair of plastic gloves and a plastic cover just like a space suit. I could not move because my arms were stretched out to both directions with some plastic tubes inserted.

My mother wore a plastic space suit with gloves and was ready to touch me. The covered square window was small, but she managed to use both of her hands to hold my hand. I stopped crying.

She could not hug me or kiss me, but I felt better. She held one of my hands until I fell asleep. My mother stayed with me around the clock and slept on a small couch next to my bed. My father came and held my hand just as my mother did with his space suit and gloves. His eyes were moist.

Several days later, my parents were told their daughter did not have meningitis. My parents were very angry with my pediatrician. After that, my mother found a new pediatrician.

The new doctor thoroughly checked me out and gave my parents an excellent report on my health. They looked very happy. I felt as though I became a normal and healthy child again.

After my father and I left the hospital, we stopped at our company operation center at the airport. Most of the people in the office knew what was going on with my mother and asked us about her. We told them what the doctor said.

Some office clerks were happy to see Captain John Richardson since they had not seen him after he moved to Los Angeles. They made some adjustments on my flight schedule and gave me two weeks to stay in town.

I called Mark. We met him at his hotel restaurant. The giant banyan tree shaded the café restaurant nicely; some sea breeze blew under the tree. We took a table in the middle, next to the tree trunk. I remembered Mark and I sat at the same table last night.

My George Clooney looked so sexy in his jeans. I knew my face was somewhat blushed by thinking about his naked body and muscular chest. My father did not seem to suspect anything.

He got Minoru's cell phone number from Mark and told us that he wanted to sell his condo and his airplane before his retirement. He wanted Minoru's help.

In the middle of our lunch, my cell phone rang hysterically. The phone call was from Alice. Her voice was frantic and quivery. I told her to wait for a second. I motioned to be excused from my father and Mark and went to the corner of the restaurant so I could hear her better.

"Mary, Daniel died in a fire at the Clubhouse."

I heard her sobbing on the other end.

"What? What happened?"

"While Daniel was in the office, a gas leak led to an explosion in the kitchen in the Clubhouse and blew up the office at the same time. The fire spread very fast because of the gusty wind."

"Are you sure Daniel was in the office?"

"Yes. Every Saturday morning, Daniel and I spend at least one hour to do some paperwork or account book for the organization, but this morning, Gregory and I stayed behind because of the phone call I got from Nina. I told Daniel to go ahead to leave in a separate car and we would meet him in the office a little later. So Daniel left alone. Gregory wanted to go with him, but I told Gregory to wait until I finished the phone call."

Alice explained in a quivery voice, "Nina wanted to know how many people already reserved hotel rooms and how many people are attending including their spouses and dates. I did not have the exact number, so I had to look at my notebook to tally. Anyhow, I was on the phone for a while with Nina. Gregory was finishing up his new kite. Daniel and Gregory were planning to fly their new kite on the beach today, and then we were going to eat lunch somewhere."

Alice stopped for a second and continued. "After I finished talking to Nina, we put the kite in the car and headed toward the Clubhouse. A fire truck passed by us with the loud siren. We saw the dark smoke in a distance, but we did not realize it was coming from the Clubhouse. When we came closer to the Clubhouse, we saw the police and the firefighters were blocking the road, so we parked the car on the side of the road and ran closer to the Clubhouse. Yes, the fire was at the Clubhouse. We looked for Daniel in the crowd, but we did not see him. I tried to call him on his cell. There's no answer."

Alice could not stop sobbing. Her voice was almost whispery.

"According to some witnesses, they heard the loud bang of the explosion twice from the Clubhouse, and then the fire gulped the entire complex fast before the fire truck arrived. I told one of the police officers that Daniel Thomas, my husband, was supposed to be in the Clubhouse. I saw Daniel's car was smoking. The wind was blustery. Gregory and I could not stop crying. We waited for a while, but the police officer promised to call us as soon as the fire was under control and wrote down our phone number. We went home and waited for a while. Finally, the police officer called and said the body of Daniel Thomas was sent to the hospital morgue. His body was burned and mutilated, but they wanted me to come and identify his body as soon as possible."

Even though Alice was sobbing, she continued explaining. "According to the fire department, the office and kitchen were totally blown up and destroyed. The documents in the file cabinet were irretrievably charred. The equipment in the office and kitchen were scorched. Daniel's body was mutilated by the explosion. Mary, please come help me. I just don't know what to do. I am frightened. I need you."

I heard her uncontrollable sobbing again. I felt tears in my eyes, so I turned around and wiped my tears with my fingers.

My voice got quivery. "Alice, yes, I will see you this afternoon. I will call you in thirty minutes and let you know my arrival time."

I explained to Mark and my father what happened to my dear friend's husband. I was sure Mark wanted to kiss me and wanted to say something, but he just nodded in front of my father. His beautiful eyes were longing for something, but I did not have any choice but to leave him with my father.

Alice and Gregory were waiting for me at the airport. Alice's eyelids were puffy, and Gregory's eyes were red. I embraced both without saying anything. Alice kept thanking me for coming.

She drove us to show the fire site that was located on the way to her house. The Clubhouse was away from the residential area, the large parking lot around it. Daniel's scorched car was the only car left on the parking lot. The building structure was big, and the architectural design of the charred wooden building looked modern. A part of the building wall in the back was still standing but scorched.

Alice did not stop; she just drove slowly so that Gregory and I could see the tragic remains. Some yellow tapes barred the fire site. The charred black debris was mounted, and the burned roof had caved in. The area of the kitchen and office were blown and looked bare. The marble monument with the engraved name of the Clubhouse and the founder's name fell to the side broken.

Alice wanted to stop at the medical examiner's office in the hospital morgue to identify Daniel's body. She went in alone. Gregory and I stayed in the car. Her eyes were red when she came back to the car. She quietly turned her car to the street and drove away from the morgue.

She also wanted to stop at the police department to file the investigation on Daniel Thomas's death. The police officer took the report and said he would send it to the investigation team to see if any foul play was involved.

When we arrived at her house, she called Daniel's parents in Chicago. She was sobbing on the phone. Her society friends and neighbors brought some food, a basket of fruit, ready to eat food, sandwiches, ham, cakes, and sweets. Some stayed with Alice and talked. Some helped fix coffee in the kitchen. Everybody seemed to be respecting Alice as the president of the organization.

I met Mrs. Lisboa, the chairperson of the board. When Alice introduced me, she nodded as though she were thanking me for coming all the way from Honolulu to help Alice. She had tears in her eyes when she embraced Alice in silence. They both went into Daniel's study and stayed there for a long time.

Gregory was in his room playing a computer game quietly. I went into his room and sat with him for a while.

"Gregory, are you okay?"

He nodded without saying anything. He was not into playing the game, just maneuvering his fingers. His red hair reminded me of Daniel's. I was sure that he was still too young to grasp his father's sudden death. I tried to cheer him up.

"Gregory, when you were born in the hospital, your father was the happiest person in the world. He was very happy because you were born healthy and redheaded. I was there. I know you will be missing him a lot. I think he will be missing you and your mom a lot in heaven too. Remember people say they are always watching out for the children from above. You won't see him, but your father will be watching out for you."

He wiped his tears with the back of his hand quietly.

"From now on, Auntie Mary and you will protect your mom. Let me show you my muscles and let me see your muscles. Do you think we can do the job to protect your mom with those muscles?"

I tightened up my muscle on my arm. I made Gregory tighten up his. We touched each other's plump muscles and smiled at each other.

"From time to time, if you want to cry, just cry. There is nothing wrong with crying. Cry your heart out. You might feel better."

"Auntie Mary, if Mom and I went to the office with my dad this morning, do you think we should be dead too?"

I could not answer him, so I knelt on the floor and embraced his small body and cried together. "Gregory, remember Auntie Mary will be with you for a while. So whenever you feel like crying, I will hold you and let you cry as much as you want. I will cry with you too." I held Gregory for a while.

He nodded and said in his quivery voice, "Auntie Mary, my dad and I were supposed to fly a kite on the beach today. We made a bigger kite this time. He really liked the picture I painted on the kite. I think I am still too small to fly the kite myself. I miss my dad."

I let him cry on my shoulder for a while and took him to the bathroom…wiped his face with a warm wet towel. After he brushed his teeth, I helped him change to pajamas and tucked him in bed. He looked tired. When I said, "Goodnight," he smiled and thanked me.

Alice was drinking a cup of tea quietly at the dining table. I put some sandwiches on two plates and gave one to Alice. While eating, I told Alice about my mother's condition. She was apologizing for taking me away from my mother, but I told her what her doctor said about her condition, and besides, my father came home to be with her.

TV news announced on the Clubhouse fire, "So far, the police did not find any evidence of arson or foul play on the death of Daniel Thomas. The fire of the Clubhouse seemed to be caused by a false gas connection in the kitchen. The renowned corporate lawyer, Daniel Thomas, was working on the organization's financial records as a volunteer auditor at the time of explosion. The witnesses said they heard two loud explosions. The wife of Mr. Daniel Thomas, however, identified her husband's mutilated body at the medical examiner's office. His funeral would be announced in the newspaper in a few days."

After I heard the news, my suspicion crept up into my mind. Daniel's death in a mysterious fire increasingly troubled my inquisitive mind.

There were no retrievable documents left, including the office computer and Daniel's laptop. I felt some ominous plot or conspiracy involved in this mysterious fire. Someone knew the Thomas family's rituals, such as Alice and Daniel worked in the office every Saturday morning. Gregory could be right. If they were with Daniel, they might have been dead as well.

I could not contain my suspicious thoughts to myself, so I sat beside Alice at the dining table and talked to her.

"Alice, I have been thinking about Daniel's death. I think the explosion was plotted against all of you. Somebody knew you would be in the office this morning, so they installed some explosive devices in the file cabinet in the office and then to the gas line in the kitchen. They said they heard two explosions. One explosion probably occurred in the office first and then in the kitchen. Remember those gangsters put explosives underneath a car to blow up the car in the movies?"

My suspicious and inquisitive thinking came right out of my mouth. I could not stop.

"Those explosive devices were installed inside the file cabinet. When Daniel opened the file cabinet, probably the explosion took place in front of him. That must be the reason his body was mutilated."

I sipped tea and continued. "According to the police, the contents in the cabinet were irretrievably charred. When I think about it more, the explosion was to destroy all the contents in the file cabinet. The file cabinet was supposed to be fireproof, right?"

Alice nodded.

"The charred content proves that the explosive device exploded inside the file cabinet. Somebody knew Daniel would open the file cabinet to do his work this morning. If the explosion occurred by the gas leak in the kitchen, the fireproof cabinet should be intact."

"Do you think Sue Mendosa did that to cover up something?" Alice asked.

"Yes. Sue Mendosa always had the conniving or criminal mind since she was a child. She does not seem to know right from wrong. She is not a normal person like us, very vicious. She probably hired someone to do it for her."

"I don't know about Sue, but Mrs. Mendosa could hire somebody. I was told she hired some underground professionals and sleazy lawyers to get the entire fortune from her husband before he was jailed."

"Who has access to the Clubhouse?"

"Sue Mendosa, Mrs. Lisboa, Daniel, and me."

"Who knew you worked in the office every Saturday morning?"

"Mrs. Lisboa and her husband, few board members, Mrs. Mendosa, and especially Sue Mendosa. Since she became an accountant at the beginning of this year, Daniel as an auditor often asked Sue to come to the office Saturday mornings to explain her accounting book to him so he could help Sue make a better spreadsheet or an accounting report."

"Did you use your key or Daniel's key to open the Clubhouse every Saturday?"

"When we were together, I used my facility key to open the main entrance so Daniel did not have to retrieve his key chain from the safety box. His key chain with four keys was always in the safety box for emergency or for Mr. Lisboa, who took care of the facility and the renters." Alice's explanation was very easy to understand.

"Now, Daniel only kept the safety box key. Correct?"

"Correct."

"What about Mr. Lisboa?"

"He used his wife's safety box key to retrieve Daniel's key chain to open the facility," Alice answered and added. "After Mr. Lisboa inspects the Clubhouse, he gives back the incidental deposit to the renters if they pass the inspection. The renters must clean stove, oven, refrigerator, floors, tables, chairs, and emptying the trash. Mr. Lisboa would use three keys for the renters—to open the entrance door, the kitchen door, and the banquet room door. The fourth key to the office door was never used because the phone in the office was not permitted to be used…always phone in the kitchen for the renters. He keeps Daniel's key chain with four keys until the end of the event. After the inspection…returned the incidental check back…locked all the doors…put back the key chain back to the safety deposit box. He had done this volunteer work for years. Since Mr. and Mrs. Lisboa live near the Clubhouse, he did not mind doing it. His wife, Mrs. Lisboa, is the chairperson of this nonprofit organization board for a long time."

"Does each key have engraved names or something?"

"Yes, the numbers are engraved on each key. Number 1 for the president, Alice; number 2 for the auditor, Daniel; number 3 for the accountant, Sue; and number 4 for the chairperson of the board, Mrs. Lisboa. We four know the owner of the keys by looking at the number. I don't think other people paid attention to the numbers, but we four do."

"So how many keys each have?"

"Well, Sue and Daniel have six keys. Mrs. Lisboa and I have five keys. Daniel and Sue have six because they have the file cabinet key to each."

"So Daniel kept the safety box key and the file cabinet key separately? Right?"

Alice nodded. "Yes. He carried them separately for safety reasons. The file cabinet contains cash or renter's checks along with the documents and accounting books. Sue and Daniel were the only one who used the file cabinet."

"So, Sue had six engraved keys as number 3, and Daniel had six engraved keys as number 2, correct?"

"Correct."

"This morning, Daniel had to retrieve his own key chain from the safety box because you did not go with him. Correct?"

"Correct."

"Alice, I am very suspicious about the explosion."

"Mary, according to Mrs. Lisboa, her husband inspected the gas valve, stove range thoroughly last night after the big event ended. They passed the inspection, so he gave the incidental deposit check back and locked all the doors around 11:00 p.m. He thinks somebody must have tampered the gas line after he left."

Alice paused for a while and sipped some tea. Her pretty eyes were still puffy, and her face looked somewhat pale. She obliviously looked at her teaspoon and whispered, "According to Daniel, those past three weeks, he could not audit the organization's accounting book because Sue had the book, bank statements, renters' checks, and deposit slips. She was supposed to leave them in the file cabinet after recording all the deposits and payments. So Daniel called Sue several days ago to bring everything to meet him this morning."

"Was she supposed to meet Daniel this morning?"

"No, Sue told Daniel that she returned the accounting book and everything in the file cabinet on Thursday. Then she told him she was leaving for a two-week cruise on Friday, which was yesterday."

"A two-week cruise? How convenient! I think she tried to set an alibi. Alice, the explosive device was planted inside the file cabinet to destroy the things Sue put back. I wonder what kind of wrongdoings Sue tried to cover up."

Chapter 22

SUSPICION

Alice looked puzzled and asked, "Mary, do you really believe their cruising is to set up their alibi?"

"Yes."

"Sue Mendosa is capable of killing Daniel?"

"Yes. I think she is capable. Sue had tortured me in her wicked way and intimidated me by her obsessive jealousy when I was a child. Remember she stole someone's purse and put it in my desk and said she saw me steal it. Oh, I had a miserable school life. However, I survived because I acquired a self-defense mechanism to fight Sue back. My self-defense mechanism was to write. It is a long story. I will tell you all about my writing someday. Anyway, I was intimidated, bullied, humiliated every single day."

"Was Sue that bad?"

"Yes. Every time she saw me after school, she used to chant by calling me ugly Jap or ugly hapa haole. She was such bully, I used to have nightmares. In my nightmares, she appeared as Cinderella's ugly stepmother to scare me. I screamed and cried a lot."

"Mary, I did not know about your suffering. What a wicked person Sue had been! I knew she acted psychotic, and her behavior was a teacher's nightmare. Mary, what should I do if Sue plotted Daniel's murder?"

Alice's voice was still quivery. I recalled the intimidated or harassed feeling I used to have when I was a child. Sue's plot was not murderous at the time, but to my young mind, it was worse than a murderous plot. That was how I invented a self-defense mechanism to rebut revengefully out of desperation. She died every night and I buried her before I went to bed.

"Alice, I will help you solve the problem, but we have to find a criminal lawyer first. Do you know any criminal lawyer? I am sure he would investigate this matter fast. I will help you with the expense."

"Yes, I do. Daniel's friend, Troy Maddox. He was a detective in the police department here before he became a criminal lawyer. He is one of the best in Maui. He does not live in this neighborhood, but his office is not that far. Let me call him to see if he can meet us tomorrow. We just talk to him and tell him your suspicion on Daniel's death. Troy was Daniel's first client when we moved here. He had a problem with his partners in his law firm. Daniel won the case for him. They became good friends since. He was divorced several years back. His two boys and ex-wife moved to Florida, but his children come to stay for the summer with Troy every year. Daniel and Troy used to take Gregory and his two boys fishing on the weekends. He is a very nice fellow. So he might take this case."

The next day, even though it was Sunday, Troy Maddox met us in his office. He has a delightful, gentle personality. His expression and gesture are compassionate and genuine. I thought his tall and stout figure should intimidate the criminals in the courtroom to his advantage. He looked about the same age as Daniel.

Troy Maddox was born in Hawaii. His father was stationed in Hawaii for a long time as a military man. His parents were from Florida. After his father's retirement, his parents and younger sister moved back to their hometown in Florida. Troy remained in Hawaii.

He went to college in Honolulu by working in the police department as a part-time clerk. After he finished college, he married his family friend who came to visit him while he was in college.

After his marriage, he worked in the police department in Honolulu for a while before he landed a detective job in Maui.

While working as a detective, he kept pursuing his law degree in criminal justice.

Several years after his criminal law firm was established, his wife became unhappy living in Maui. She had suffered from depression from time to time—she wanted to go back home to Florida by taking their two boys.

Troy did not want them to leave Maui. They talked a lot, but she was determined to leave Maui because she felt as though she was dying from suffocation, as Maui is such a small island. In the end, Troy understood and agreed to a divorce. Their divorce was amicable.

"Alice, I am very sorry about Daniel. You may not know it, but Daniel was my mentor and a good friend. He will be missed by his friends and especially by me. I hope you and Gregory would overcome this tragedy soon. So, Alice, ask me anything. I will be glad to help."

"Yes, thank you for meeting us today. Troy, this is my dear friend, Mary. She works for one of the major airlines as a pilot. We practically grew up together like sisters in Honolulu. Since I have been overwhelmed with my situation, Mary came to help me. She is Gregory's godmother. The reason I asked you to meet us here today is that Mary likes to explain her suspicion on Daniel's death."

I nodded and addressed him as Mr. Maddox. "Mr. Maddox, I think Daniel was murdered. This is just my speculation. So please hear me out. Daniel was murdered by someone who knew he would be in the office every Saturday morning. I think the explosion did not come from the kitchen but came from the file cabinet first. When Daniel opened the file cabinet to retrieve the accounting book and other bank statements, the explosion occurred. The mutilated Daniel Thomas's body and charred documents in the fireproof cabinet prove that the explosion occurred inside the cabinet. The police said that the gas leaks caused the explosion, but I don't agree with them."

I sat up straight and continued. "My suspicion is that this particular family in the organization probably hired someone to plant an explosive device in the file cabinet. Alice had been the president and Daniel had been the accounting auditor for the organization. I suspect this Mendosa family plotted against Alice and Daniel. I don't know what it is or why it is, but my guess is that they tried to cover up their wrongdoings. Sue Mendosa had been the accountant. Her mother, Matilda Mendosa, had been the founder of the Clubhouse."

"Did you say Matilda Mendosa?"

"Yes. Do you know her?"

"Did she live in Honolulu many years ago?"

"Yes. Alice and I went to school with her daughter, Sue Mendosa. Her father, Mr. Leonard Mendosa, was the chairman of the school board and practically owned our private school at that time. They were one of the richest families in Honolulu."

"Leonard Mendosa? I was in college and followed up on his case. I remember he was indicted for embezzling company assets and illegal stock trading."

Troy Maddox added, "I was told Matilda Mendosa got her husband's entire fortune before he was convicted. My friend who worked at the DA's office said that Leonard Mendosa hardly had money left to defend himself. Nevertheless, when he was in jail, he was poisoned and died. The speculation was Mrs. Matilda Mendosa hired somebody to poison him, but they could not prove it."

Alice said, "I did not know he was dead. No wonder Mrs. Mendosa and Sue have been tight-mouthed about it. I always wondered what happened to Mr. Mendosa."

"Do you think the Mendosa family had something to do with Daniel's death? Why?"

Mr. Maddox became very curious. Alice had to answer to make him understand why Daniel was in the office on Saturday morning.

"Sue Mendosa was an accountant for the organization. Daniel was the account auditor. He had some gut feelings about Sue and her mother. He speculated that they were doing something to alter the accounting book since those were in Sue's possession for three weeks. The accounting book was always supposed to be in the file cabinet as well as the monthly bank statements, checks, and deposit slips, but Sue held them all for three weeks. That was why he requested Sue to meet him in the office Saturday morning, which was yesterday, but Sue told him everything including the accounting book was returned to the file cabinet on Thursday, which was two days ago. She also told him that they were leaving for a cruise on Friday. Then a fire occurred on Saturday morning. If we went with Daniel as we had always done Saturday morning, Gregory and I should be dead as well."

Alice's eyes were filled with tears. She gestured me to continue my suspicion further.

"Mr. Maddox, my speculation is that Sue hired a professional killer to plant an explosive device in the file cabinet at night after the Clubhouse was closed. The explosive device in the file cabinet was probably connected to the gas line in the kitchen to make the second explosion."

"Did that file cabinet need a key to open?"

Alice answered, "Yes. That file cabinet was supposed to be fireproof. Daniel and Sue were the only ones who could use the file cabinet. Each had the key. The file cabinet contained all kinds of financial documents for the organization such as the insurance policy, mortgage payment slips, old and new accounting books, bank statements, checks, other financial transactions, receipts, so forth. I was their accountant for many years. That is how I know."

Alice additionally explained to Mr. Maddox that only four people have the sets of keys, and those keys are all engraved with numbers: 1 for the president, 2 for the auditor, 3 for the accountant, and 4 for the chairperson. She also explained that Daniel's key chain with four keys was always in the safety box for emergency.

"So even the safety box key is numbered. Right?"

"Yes."

Mr. Maddox was contemplating for a while and said, "If Sue or Mrs. Mendosa hired a killer to plant the explosive in the file cabinet, that killer must have three keys to reach the file cabinet, right?"

Alice was thinking and answered, "Yes, one to open the entrance door and one to the office door, another one to the file cabinet. Yes, three keys."

"Is there any other way to reach the file cabinet?"

Since Alice told me all about the keys, I did not mind answering, "The killer could need only two keys, safety box key and file cabinet key. One to open the safety box and retrieve Daniel's key chain to open the main entrance and the office door, and then use the file cabinet key. Two keys."

I coughed a little, but repeated what Alice told me about Daniel's keys. "Daniel carried two keys separately—safety box key and file cabinet key. The only people who could open the file cabinet were Daniel and Sue. If the killer need to set the explosive inside the file cabinet, he or she must have Daniel's number 2 key or Sue's number 3 key. The report said that all the contents and documents in the file cabinet were charred and Daniel's body was unrecognizably mutilated. That proves Daniel was too close to the explosive—he was probably opening the file cabinet when it exploded. The second explosion was probably caused by the gas leak in the kitchen."

Alice helped. "If the killer had Sue's safety box key and file cabinet key, yes, he could retrieve Daniel's key chain to open the entrance door and the office door and then use Sue's file cabinet key to install the explosive device in the file cabinet."

Troy Maddox repeated, "Did you say each key had engraved numbers, Alice 1, Daniel 2, Sue 3, Mrs. Lisboa 4. Only Sue and Daniel had the file cabinet key. Correct?"

Alice and I nodded.

Troy Maddox continued. "Well, that means if the killer was hired by Sue, she must have given three keys—for the entrance door, office door, and file cabinet. However, if Sue instructed the killer to retrieve Daniel's key ring, only two keys are needed—safety box key and file cabinet key. Right?"

We nodded.

"Alice, did Daniel use his key chain from the safety box to open the office door yesterday morning because you did not go with him?"

"Yes." Alice nodded.

"Well, if the file cabinet key was used to set up the explosive device inside, the killer must have at least two number 3 keys. Right?"

We nodded.

"If the hired killer retrieved Daniel's key chain to open the office door and used the file cabinet key to set up the explosive device, he had a total of six keys. The key chain with four keys and two keys the killer brought. Right?"

We again nodded.

"After the killer set up the device, he carefully locked the file cabinet, the office door, probably the kitchen door if he tampered the gas line, and then the main entrance door before returning Daniel's key chain to the safety box. If the killer was not instructed what to do with Sue's two keys, he probably put them in the safety deposit box with Daniel's key chain altogether, by thinking Sue could retrieve them later or did not care one way or the other because the building would be blown away anyway. This is just my hunch. What do you think, Mary?"

I nodded several times.

He moved his chair toward us and continued. "Daniel must have seen Sue's two number 3 keys in the safety box when he retrieved his own key chain yesterday. He must have wondered what Sue's keys were doing in the safety box. He thought Sue made a mistake depositing those two keys at the time of returning the accounting books to the file cabinet on Thursday, so he took those two keys with him to the office, intending to keep them for Sue until her return from the cruise."

I totally agreed with his theory. I thought Troy Maddox was a great detective.

"If my hunch is correct, Daniel had his own key chain with four keys, Sue's two keys and his own two keys. Therefore, a total of eight keys when he came to the office."

We nodded without any hesitation.

"I know it could be confusing to other people who do not know the significance of those engraved numbers on those keys, but I understand clearly. I must look for those keys today. If I find Sue's number 3 keys at the crime scene or the fire site, yes, she hired someone to murder Daniel. You both did a great job explaining. I thank both of you for bringing your suspicion to my attention. Well, I had better start looking for those keys at the crime scene."

Alice said, "Troy, we saw yellow tapes around the fire site yesterday."

"Oh, don't worry. I have many friends in the police department. I am sure the fire department will be cleaning up tomorrow. So I must look for those keys today."

"Does this mean you would take this case? I would like to help Alice pay for your fees."

"Mary, you may not know it, but I owe Daniel a lot. He helped me when I had a problem with my law partners. He represented me and won the case for me. After that, I was able to reestablish my own law firm. He also helped me arrange the financial loans from the bank and registered me as a criminal justice lawyer in the state reference book in order to gain future clients. I have been very thankful to Daniel. He has been a legend in this law community here. He was the most decent lawyer I have ever known in this greedy law society. He had been so compassionate and generous to his clients and friends. I was fortunate to know such a decent lawyer. He would be missed by many friends, especially by me. His legacy would stay with me forever. So my service will be my contribution to my friend, Daniel. I will do my best to solve the problem and make the guilty party see justice. Do not worry about the fees."

Alice said in a quivery voice, "Thank you, Troy. I won't forget your kindness."

Alice's eyes were filled with tears again. I was so happy to know what Daniel had done for other people, especially for Mr. Maddox. My father was correct: "What goes around comes around." In this case, it is a positive way. Daniel's decent deeds came back as a decent deed. His legacy would remain forever in the hearts of his friends because of his decent deeds.

I became philosophical about life in general. I was sure Sue's wicked treatments of others and her criminal mind derived from her obsessive jealousy, inferiority complex, greediness, and her mental illness called grandeur delusion would come back to haunt her or punish her in the future.

"By the way, Mary, don't address me as Mr. Maddox. I feel old if you call me Mr. Maddox. I think I am still young. Call me Troy."

"Sorry. Okay, I will call you Troy."

"Alice, I will have the police patrol around your house just in case. If you need my help, do not hesitate to call me. When I find Sue's keys at the fire site, I will explain my theory to my police friends and then we will start investigating. More likely, we will start from the airport to find the hired killer. Right now, I must find Sue's keys first."

Troy stood up, reached his brief case, and gave each of us his business card adding his home phone and cell phone numbers. I also gave my business card with my cell phone number as well.

"Alice, do not contact the Mendosas yourself when they come home. Let the board members work on the finance, bank account, and fire insurance. I am sure they have tons of questions for Sue to answer since she was the accountant. Do not tell any of our suspicions or investigations to anybody. Let's keep it to ourselves until we catch the killer."

Alice and I nodded.

"Alice, when you get scared or feel alone, call me. Mary, it was nice to meet you. I will call you periodically to let you know the progress on the investigation, or you can call me anytime. Thank you for discussing your suspicions. You could be a great detective when you grow up."

Troy winked at me with a beautiful smile and shook my hand. "Mary, is this your cell phone number?"

"Yes. Most of the time, I use my cell only, so use that number to contact me."

"Okay. Well, I must check the fire site with my friends from the police department. Alice, see you soon. Where is Gregory?"

"He is with Mrs. Lisboa and her grandchildren. We will pick him up on the way home."

After Alice and I went outside, Troy locked his office door behind him and drove off by waving at us. Alice looked so relieved as though she gained a strong ally to combat her fear. She did not look alone anymore. I understood exactly how she felt. When I was writing a murder series an ancient time ago, story writing was my strong ally to combat my fear of Sue's intimidation.

Family Secrets

Troy Maddox's hunch was correct. He found a total of eight keys including Sue's two number 3. Additionally, the police department found evidence of the explosive.

Troy took numerous pictures of Sue's keys at the police department and sent them to the police lab. As Troy explained his theory to his friends in the police department, they agreed to start the investigation quickly and quietly.

Troy called to let us know that those numbered keys are the major evidence in the case. He was glad that all the keys had engraved numbers. Alice and I smiled at each other.

I helped Alice arrange the funeral and the obituary in the newspaper. The funeral was held Thursday after the arrival of Daniel's parents and siblings from Chicago. His casket was closed due to his mutilated body. There were many flowers and plants from families and friends. Alice and Gregory sat with Daniel's aged parents. The family seemed to be very close. Alice and Gregory looked comfortable with them. I sat next to Nina and Tom who flew to join me.

Many people came to the funeral service including Daniel's law firm colleagues, Troy Maddox, clients, friends, the society members, and neighbors. One of his colleagues made a eulogy and made Alice cry.

After the funeral service, Nina, Alice, and I huddled together and cried quietly. Gregory held his grandmother's hand and went into a car. Alice looked tired and distraught.

Alice and I were alone in her house on that funeral night. Gregory was spending a night with his grandparents in the hotel. Nina came from the nearby motel to join us to chat. I wanted to tell Nina about Sue, but Alice showed some stern gestures, so I decided not to tell Nina about the investigation…also remembered what Troy said, "Keep it to ourselves until we catch the killer."

We could ask anything to each other and confess anything without hiding…but not this investigation…yet. So I asked Alice about her financial situation.

"Alice, did Daniel leave enough life insurance for you and Gregory?"

"Well, yes. Daniel had $500,000 term life insurance and $250,000 accidental insurance, but I must do the paperwork. It might take for a while, but when we get the insurance money, I would like to pay off the mortgage and save the rest for Gregory's education. Now I am the breadwinner of the house, so I must get a full-time job to earn our living. I may work as an accountant for a while, and later I might join a corporate law firm, probably the law firm Daniel worked, but I don't know if they would hire me or not. I will try."

"I think it is a good idea to be busy at work. You should ask Troy Maddox to see if he needs an accountant? If you get to work in his office, you could be protected by Troy."

"Alice needs to be protected?"

Nina looked puzzled. Alice gave me a stern look.

"Did I say protected? I thought I said Alice could be provided."

"Oh."

Alice's face became gentle. Nina was yawning. She said she and Tom were leaving early in the morning to get to work on time. After Nina left, I apologized to Alice, but Alice had a smile on her face.

On Friday, at the airport, I told Alice that I would call her often. Gregory looked sad, so I told him I would ask Mr. Troy Maddox to help him fly the kite. He nodded. I also told Alice to be careful and let Troy Maddox handle the investigation. I told her to write a novel she used to enjoy writing when she was in high school or play computer games with Gregory to occupy her mind.

At the departure gate, their eyes were moist as though they wanted me to stay longer or wished I lived closer.

Chapter 23

INVESTIGATION

On the commuter flight, I realized I spent almost a week in Maui without thinking about my mother who had been in a coma. I felt guilty. Why didn't I think about her while I was in Maui? Did I trust her doctor too much? Or did I rely on my father too much? In any rate, I just did not think about my beloved mother.

Even though I felt guilty, I felt as though I were a heroic figure, more like a great detective who suspected Daniel's death as foul play. If my suspicion did not get Troy Maddox's attention, Daniel's death could be treated as an accidental death. I was sure my mother would understand, and forgive me, or she might be even proud of me, but I still felt guilty.

It took only thirty minutes to fly between Maui and Oahu. My car was left in the employees' parking lot, so I drove to the hospital. My father was there and glad to see me. He knew I was coming home this afternoon because I called him before I left Maui.

Apparently, my mother's immune system was stabilized. She was moved to a separate ICU room, more like a private ICU room for a coma patient. We were encouraged to hold her hands and talk to her. The doctor thought touching and talking would stimulate the sense of hearing or five senses in general.

Her face was no longer swollen; her bruises on her eyelids were almost gone. Her head and neck were still covered with some bandages, but not bulky anymore. Nevertheless, she was still unconscious.

My father said he had been talking to her for hours every day. He already told her that Mary would be coming to see her today, so I should hold her hands and talk to her for a while. He went out to the hallway to call his office in Los Angeles. He was setting up the retirement date.

I held my mother's hands and told her that I went to see Alice because Daniel died in a fire. I did not tell her anything about the investigation of his death. After that, I did not know what to talk about, so I told her that I met my grandmother in Okinawa for the first time and apologized that I did not tell her much of my recent trip to Okinawa sooner. I also told her about the story of Mr. Okuma and her mother, and her musical talent came from those two of the greatest musicians who have loved each other for all their lives. I held both of her dainty hands tightly and told her those talented fingers are from their forever love.

Finally, I told her that she should consider forgiving her mother for her disownment and reconcile so that she could visit her in Okinawa after her recovery. I thought her fingers moved a little, but it must have been my imagination. I did not think that she was listening. Her pretty face had some color on her cheeks, but she was still asleep.

I met my father at a restaurant and ate dinner with him on the way home. I told him about Daniel's tragic death. I did not go into my suspicion or investigation, but I simply let him know the police department decided to investigate further. He nodded as though he agreed with their decision.

"By the way, Mark is coming to live here in Honolulu soon. He took the offer…Honolulu is his home base to Asia. He found an apartment before he left for San Diego so that he could move in any time. Another thing I forgot to tell you…Mark and Minoru received 2.5 million dollars each from Kim at the time of her passing."

Family Secrets

He never mentioned much of Mark when he was in Los Angeles, except bragging about his flying skills. Now, he is telling me about Mark's inheritance that happened several years back? Is he hinting me that Mark could be a great candidate for my future? Or he found out about our relationship?

Relationship! Whoa! I forgot all about Mark's existence while I was in Maui. My face was blushed by the guilt. Why didn't I think about Mark? My love at first sight! Was I really into the detective job? Did my suspicion of Daniel's death wipe out my reality? What should I tell him when I speak to him? How could I forget all about my gorgeous George Clooney? I hope he would forgive me.

I did not think my father suspected our relationship, such as sleeping on the first night together or love at first sight for each other. It really happened to us in reality, but why didn't I think about him while I was in Maui? I had the cell phone with me, but I did not call him because I forgot all about him. I panicked.

As soon as I walked into my place, I got on the phone to call Mark. From my living room, the ocean at night still looks fabulous. The moon is not full, but the moonlight is generously shining on the earthlings below.

"Hello, Mark, this is Mary. Do you remember me? I just came back from Maui. I am sorry I did not call you."

"Mary? Which Mary? Do I know you?" I heard his laughter at the end of the line. "Of course, I remember you, my princess. I thought my love at first sight was too good to be true. I thought about you every day."

"I thought about you too, but I was so wrapped up with the death of Alice's husband and arranging the funeral with her, I just did not have the time to call you." I lied and hoped he would forgive me. He said he understood how busy I was. My George Clooney is very understanding, and forgiving. Oh, I love him dearly.

"Mark, I would like to see you soon. I am missing you terribly."

I was not lying this time. My heart ached when I said it and felt tears in my eyes. It was genuine.

"I have missed you a lot every day. Mary…I am heading toward the airport right now. I will be back tomorrow night. Is it all right to call you tomorrow night around nine? By the way, I will be moving to Honolulu as soon as I get the transfer paper. I can hardly wait to see you. I will call you tomorrow night and every night, if it is all right with you."

"Yes, of course. Call me every night. Mark, fly safely. I will be home for a while, so call me anytime. Talk to you soon."

Troy Maddox explained his theory to his detective friends in the police department by showing the pictures of Sue's two number 3 keys that were found at the crime scene, or rather at the fire site. That proved the killer was hired by Sue Mendosa. The significance of the engraved number 3 was explained to his detective friends.

Troy also explained the probability: a hired killer probably came by airplane from Honolulu to Maui Friday and planted the explosive device in the file cabinet after the Clubhouse was closed and flew back to Honolulu Saturday. The police began the investigation according to the probability. They searched for a suspect who came to Maui Friday and left Saturday.

Their finding was fast, three suspects, one female and two males. Their names, addresses, and phone numbers were found from the computer record—Melissa Silva, Joe Paolini, and Andre Hannemann.

They checked the rental car record at the airport because the killer must have rented a car to reach the Clubhouse that is far from the airport. Joe Paolini was the only one who rented a car. However, the reservation was made by a local person.

The clerk at the rental car company remembered that a woman who wore dark sunglasses came Thursday to make the one-day-rent reservation for Joe Paolini and paid cash.

The woman also gave the clerk a white envelope. It contained two metal objects inside. She told the clerk that the envelope contained two keys to her house. Her brother, Joe Paolini, must have those keys because she and her family would be out of town before

Family Secrets

his arrival. She repeatedly said to put the envelope in Joe Paolini's reservation folder and paid cash.

After she left, the clerk accidentally dropped the envelope on the cement floor; the envelope was torn open. She took out the contents…two keys with a written message…more like an underlined instruction that was written in red pen. She could not help but to read the instruction:

1. <u>the first key</u> to open <u>the safety box</u> in front
2. retrieve a key chain to open <u>the entrance door</u> and <u>the office door</u>
3. <u>the second key</u> to open <u>the file cabinet</u> in the office
4. do not forget to put the key chain back to <u>the safety box</u> after finishing

The clerk put the message and the keys into a new envelope and sealed. She did not pay much attention to the message at that time, but later, she thought that her brother just came to his sister's house to retrieve some important documents from her file cabinet.

Later, Troy and his detective friend went back to show the picture of Sue Mendosa that was generated from her driver's license. The clerk could not identify her because the woman who paid for the reservation had long blonde hair with dark sunglasses. The driver's license picture showed the woman with dark short hair and brown eyes, but she said the age was about the same.

Troy also showed the pictures of two number 3 keys. The clerk said the keys looked similar, but she did not think that the keys had the engraved number. Troy Maddox was confident that the killer used Sue's number 3 keys to install an explosive device in the file cabinet even though the clerk could not identify the engraved numbers. The fact was those keys were found at the crime scene and belonged to Sue Mendosa as number 3.

The police found the data on Joe Paolini in the FBI's records. He was arrested once in New York for suspicion of bombing a car—no one was killed. He was working as an electrician for an appliance company in New York. An eyewitness who happened to know Joe

Paolini said that Joe was at the car a few minutes before the explosion. The police arrested him as a suspect, but Joe profusely denied. As they did not have any evidence against Joe, he was released.

Nevertheless, Troy Maddox found more facts on Joe Paolini: the car explosion in New York was supposed to kill the husband of the wife who hired Joe Paolini.

The half of the contract money was paid, but he did not kill the husband, so the wife wanted the money back. The husband who was almost killed suspected his wife's doing and told the police about it. So they started questioning the wife and looked for Joe Paolini.

Therefore, Joe Paolini panicked and hastily quit his job and disappeared. He lived somewhere in the remote countryside for a year. After the dust settled, he moved to Honolulu, far away from the mainland USA and opened his own electronic repair shop in Honolulu…he used his store as the facade of his underground contact.

Troy called me periodically and informed me about Joe Paolini. "Mary, we got the hired killer, Joe Paolini. He was arrested yesterday in Honolulu and will be extradited to Maui tomorrow. Joe Paolini said he was not even in Maui on that day, so we faxed the rental car and airline receipts. Now he refused to talk to the police and hired a lawyer. We have already given him a deal. If he named a person or persons who hired him to set the explosive device to kill Daniel Thomas, we would give him a deal of reduced sentence. Right now, his lawyer is recommending him to take the deal."

"Did Sue and her family come home?"

"Alice said they should be arriving today or tomorrow. However, since Joe Paolini has not named anyone yet, we won't be able to arrest Sue Mendosa. Now the investigation is out in the open and the media is broadcasting Daniel's death as foul play. I hope Joe Paolini will name Sue Mendosa soon. By the way, Alice is working for me now as an accountant. She likes it and seems to be happy." Troy also mentioned that Mrs. Lisboa hired a lawyer and they are waiting for Sue Mendosa.

After two weeks of time off from work, I had to fly irregular routes to make up my flying time for the month. My father was taking care of my mother. I, too, stopped at the hospital to see her on the way home. Mark and I have been talking every night on the phone, but I have not talked to Troy or Alice for several days.

After I changed my uniform, I was determined to call Alice.

"Hello, Alice."

"Hi, Mary."

"Alice, you sound normal and much better. Troy told me you are working for him. Is everything working out all right with you?"

"Yes, much better than staying home. After I send Gregory to school, I work for Troy Monday through Friday. Mrs. Lisboa keeps Gregory after school. Troy and his young law partner are very busy every day. I keep their accounting book and also help them with legal papers. You know I am a licensed corporate lawyer. Anyway, I enjoy working again. I left a message on your cell because I did not hear from you."

Alice probably thought my call was to return her call, but I was too busy to retrieve her message. "I am sorry. I have been very busy making up my flying time for the month."

"Mary, Sue Mendosa and Matilda Mendosa were arrested on the same day they arrived. At their arrival, Joe Paolini told the police that Matilda Mendosa hired him to plant an explosive device in the file cabinet. Yes, he also confessed he was indeed hired to kill the entire Thomas family. He received half of the contract money from Matilda Mendosa and the other half was supposed to come from Sue Mendosa after completing his work. The mother and daughter stayed in jail for several days after the cruise. Yesterday, their lawyer arranged their release on a $100,000 bond each. Natalie was sent to the foster care center, but now they all are at home."

Alice stopped for few seconds and continued. "Can you imagine how cruel Sue and Mrs. Mendosa are? So inhumane! I never hated anyone before, but I really hate them. They killed my beloved husband, Daniel, and almost killed Gregory and me. What a criminal-minded family they are! Mary, because of your suspicion, they were arrested. You are the greatest detective! I owe you a lot. Thank you."

"You are quite welcome. I think they both are mentally ill and do not know right from wrong. They are despicable, deplorable, vindictive, hideous, delusional, conniving, greedy, murderous, psychotic, and…" I heard Alice's laughter when I described the killers with the numerous repulsive adjectives. "By the way, Alice, how is the committee's investigation going?"

"Well, Sue is not cooperating with the committee. She keeps saying all the financial records were left in the file cabinet for Daniel Thomas to audit, so she should not be accountable."

"Who are the bank signature authorities?"

"Daniel and Sue. Now Sue only."

"Well, Sue can explain to the bank about the fire—losing all checks and account book, so they need new checks and the account summary."

"Mrs. Lisboa said Sue refused to do it. So she and the lawyer went to see the bank manager this morning and explained everything what happened in the fire…losing all the documents, accounting book, and checks."

Alice coughed, but continued. "According to Ms. Lisboa, the bank manager was very helpful. He located the organization's account and brought a printout to explain what had happened to the account. Mrs. Lisboa was shocked to hear his explanation—the organization's bank account was closed two weeks prior to the fire. The Clubhouse property was sold to a foreign company, and a check of $850,000 was deposited three weeks prior to the fire."

Alice again stopped for a moment.

"Alice, are you okay?"

"Yes. Something got in my throat. I am okay now. Let me go back to Sue. Since Sue came to close the account as the accountant and the signature authority, the bank did not have any choice but to close it. However, they issued two certified checks, $250,900 as bank balance and $850,000 as the newly deposited check amount. Those checks were issued to the name of the organization. They told Sue that those checks must be deposited in the same name account of the nonprofit organization."

"Did she open the same name account?"

"I don't know. When Mrs. Lisboa told the bank manager that Sue closed the account without notifying the committee, so he voided the certified checks as a fraud transaction."

Alice wanted to explain more.

"Opening the nonprofit organization's bank account needs the proof of nonprofit status from the IRS. Without it, a new account cannot be opened. However, the accountant can change the account number to open a new account and transfer the balance by closing the old account. Then she can write new checks to embezzle. As a corporate lawyer, I have experienced that kind of embezzlement by some clients. Anyway, Sue just closed the organization's account hoping she could get the balance to her name as the accountant. I am sure she was very disappointed."

"By the way, how does the organization get the property deed back?" I asked.

"Well, in order to get the deed back, the lawyer has to provide a legal verdict on the property by stating the property sale was fraudulent. That legal statement and the check of $850,000 must be returned to the buyer in order to annul the sale, then the property deed should be reverted back to the organization. I heard that the lawyer and bank manager are working together on that matter."

"Does the organization have the home insurance?"

"Yes. As soon as we get the property deed back, I will help Ms. Lisboa because I happen to have a copy of the home insurance policy here. This year's home insurance was paid before I transferred the accounting book to Sue. The insurance is intact. We lost all the documents, but not the insurance paper. It might take for a while for the insurance company to reconstruct the Clubhouse, but we are hopeful. Mary, Gregory wants to eat dinner at the new restaurant tonight, so I must go. Call me again."

"I will. Bye." I tried to hang up.

"Wait, Mary. Wait. Nina said all the committee members are to meet at the hotel the day before the class reunion. You and I must do the reception and putting all the printing materials in the envelopes including alumni books and alphabetize all the name tags. Please make sure to take several days off for the reunion so we can help Nina. She has been working too hard. I will be staying in the hotel for a couple of days. I will call you when I check in."

"Okay."

"Oh, I forgot to tell you one more thing. Eric Johnson and his girlfriend, Nancy, will be coming to Maui soon. They will be staying here for a week before the reunion. I wrote him everything about Sue and her mother who hired a killer to kill Daniel and that your suspicion led to their arrest. He now knows Sue was released on bond. So he is determined to get his parental rights before the state takes Natalie away since she is a minor. Mary, I must go. Talk to you soon."

The following day, Troy Maddox called to inform me of his further investigation. He asked me if I heard anything about the Clubhouse's financial investigation. I told him that Alice had informed me most of the details. In any rate, he thanked me again for being suspicious about Daniel's death. He told me if my suspicion were not there to open the investigation, Daniel's death could be treated as an accidental death.

Additionally, he told me that he took Gregory to the beach and flew his kite successfully. I thanked him. I knew I had asked him to help Gregory with his kite whenever he had the time. He said his children should be arriving soon for the summer. I was very sure Gregory would be very excited about fishing with his children during the summer. I pictured Gregory's beautiful smile.

Chapter 24

Reconciliation

While I was making up my flying time for the month, my mother was still in the same status. My father was faithfully visiting her in the hospital. I did the same on my way home from the airport.

One day, I was scheduled to stay overnight in Los Angeles. Instead of going to my father's condominium, I stayed in one of the airport hotels.

Mr. Nakaya visited me after his work at the airport, and we ate dinner together at the hotel restaurant. I told him about my mother's condition, but I did not tell him about Mark. Nevertheless, he seemed to know we were in love, and we have been talking to each other every night.

"Mark told me you both are madly in love. I am very happy for both of you, especially for Mark. His mother really wanted to introduce Mark to you so he could wake up and see the other world. You may not know about Mark's personal history with his longtime girlfriend. Mark wasted a chunk of his life with her. His mother and I were worried about it, but we concluded that we could not live Mark's life, so we did not do anything about it."

He stopped and sipped some coffee. "When I heard about you from Mark, I wish Kim were here to rejoice this happy news."

I thought I saw some tears in his eyes. He mentioned all about Mark's longtime girlfriend who lived with him for ten years. He also said Kim died worrying about her son. Mr. Nakaya emphasized not to mention our conversation to Mark. If Mark wants to tell me all about his longtime girlfriend, let him do it on his term. In the meantime, he wanted me to forgive him and love him.

He also said, "Mark has been a wonderful son to us for all his life. He came to the house every Sunday to see us and cooked for his music friends, mowed the lawn, cleaned the gutter, and helped his mother with her account book."

I felt very close to Mr. Nakaya for the first time after the conversation. Now I understood how my father felt about Mark and Mr. Nakaya. They have been my father's family all along.

He also told me what he has been doing for my father recently. He found someone who might buy his condominium and his Cessna. He said my father decided to retire and live with his wife again. He would miss John, but John would be happier in Honolulu. I nodded.

He jokingly said aloud, "If Mark and you get married and have some of my grandkids, I might retire in Honolulu too. John and I can see our grandkids every day and play gold together. I can hardly wait to see you both marry."

My face blushed.

Mark had been calling me almost every night. I did not mind staying on the phone with him for a long time, asking each other many questions. Some people might say we had a phone date every day.

Mark and I only met once, well…more like a one-night stand, but we have bonded through our numerous phone conversations. Now we both feel as though we have known each other for many years.

On the phone, we talk about what we like to do, what kind of food we like to eat, which countries we have visited, what we have learned from our own experiences, what kind of people we like to be friends with, what kind of bad habits we have, and discuss some philosophical and political issues. At the end, we become very romantic and kiss each other on the phone.

Family Secrets

Because of Alice's tragedy and my busy flight schedule, the thought of Mr. Okuma and my grandmother did not come to my mind. I totally forgot about them. I decided to call Mr. Okuma and let him know my mother had a car accident and had been in the hospital unconscious. I did not want him to be worried or upset about my mother's condition, but I thought they should know about it.

When I told Mr. Okuma about my mother's condition, he was almost shouting on the phone, being shocked, I thought he was in tears. I told him what her doctor said about her vital organs, having some color on her face, and might be coming out of the coma in any minute. Finally, he calmed down.

"I will talk to your grandmother so we can visit your mother in the hospital soon. I hope it won't be too late. After you left, your grandmother kept saying that she must see Keiko soon and reconcile. So I must bring her to Honolulu. I hope your mother will wake up while we are there."

"Yes. I think my mother will wake up if she hears her mother's voice. It has been too long. After I came back from Okinawa, I meant to tell my mother about you, but I did not. Now I must wait until she comes out of the coma. My father knows about you, and he is very happy about it."

I also told Mr. Okuma that I held my mother's hands in the hospital and told her about her real father, but I did not think she heard me. He said it was all right; he would tell her when the time would be right.

"Does your father still live in Los Angeles?"

"Oh, no. He stays in my mother's house. He goes to the hospital every day and talk to her. He is planning to come back to Honolulu and retire. Although they have lived separately, their commitment is stronger than a couple who have lived together for years. So we should not worry about them. Please bring Grandma and let her talk to her daughter. Who knows, she might wake up."

"Okay. I will let you know as soon as we arrange the trip. By the way, is it all right for us to stay for a month?"

"Oh, yes. Of course. Can't you stay longer? In any rate, please visit us in a hurry. Hope to see you soon. Please let me know your arrival time. We will pick you up at the airport."

"Okay, my Little Cute Mary. I will call you."

On the following day, when I flew back from Los Angeles, I had a phone call from Mr. Okuma. He told me they would be arriving the next day around noon in Hawaiian time. I was so glad that they managed to find a flight so soon. The reunion of my mother and my grandmother should be something I could hardly wait to see. I thought to myself, my mother should be so surprised that she may not have any choice but to wake up.

My father and I went to the airport the next day and welcomed Mr. Okuma and Grandma. It was Grandmother's first time to visit Hawaii. My father embraced my grandmother and shook Mr. Okuma's hand.

She was sobbing. I wiped her tears with my handkerchief and embraced her. I held her hand all the way to the parking lot just as she held my hand when I was in Okinawa. She looked so happy being with me again.

We drove them straight to my mother's house. I gave my room to Grandma and the guest room to Mr. Okuma. I was very sure they were used to having their own rooms. After they changed their clothes, we visited my mother in the hospital.

When my grandmother saw her daughter, she started sobbing uncontrollably. This time my tears were streaming down as though both of my tear ducts were reactivated. My father and Mr. Okuma had some tears in their eyes as well.

My grandmother stood beside my mother's bed and held both of her hands, wept. She did not know what to say, so she kept kissing her hands. She wanted to stay with my mother for a while alone. We did not mind it at all.

At the cafeteria, we ordered a cup of coffee for each. Since Mr. Okuma and my father were talking nonstop in Japanese, I stepped out to make a phone call to Alice, but her phone was busy, so I joined Mr. Okuma and my father again. "How was your trip?"

"The trip was very smooth. Your grandmother slept soundly. When she woke up, she thought our airplane was returning to Okinawa because she saw the same color ocean down below."

"When I have the time, I will show Grandma the entire Oahu island."

"She would like that. I don't think she had traveled much in the past, except being in Paris. I think she would also enjoy the view from your house…the ocean and the perfect sunset."

My father nodded.

When we went back to my mother's room, we could not believe our eyes. My mother was awake and looking at Grandma inquisitively and tried to recall who she was. Grandma was just sobbing. A nurse was standing beside my mother, disconnecting some of the inserted tubes, and raised her head higher so she could see everybody. The nurse said that the doctor was already contacted and would be arriving soon.

When we lined up at the side of the bed, she was pryingly looking at us, seemingly could not grasp what happened to her or where she was, why we were lining up in front of her. No words came out of her mouth as though she forgot how to speak. My father went to her and kissed her forehead and said, "Keiko, I love you."

She repeated after my father. "Keiko, I love you."

My father said with a smile, "No. You are supposed to say, 'John, I love you.' Say, 'I love you, John.'"

"I love you, John."

We applauded.

"Mom, do you know who I am?"

She did not react but staring at me.

My father said, "This is your daughter, Mary."

She repeated. "This is your daughter, Mary."

"No. You are supposed to say, 'Hello, Mary.'"

"Hello, Mary."

I went closer to her and kissed her cheek.

She held my teary face with both of her hands for a while and called me, "Mary."

"Yes, Mom. I am Mary." I kissed her again.

My tears gushed out; my voice got quivery. "Yes. I am your daughter, Mary."

Her eyes were sparkling and repeated, "Mary."

I nodded several times. My mother was looking at my father and said, "John."

My father nodded several times with his wet eyes as well.

Now she was looking at my grandmother and Mr. Okuma, trying to recall who they were.

I told her, "This is your mother, and this is Mr. Okuma."

My grandmother went closer and held my mother's hands without saying a word with tearful eyes.

Suddenly, my mother started crying and said, "I missed you, Mom."

My grandmother nodded several times, and her face was flooded with tears as well. They embraced each other.

"I missed you, Keiko. I missed you a whole lot for all these years."

"I missed you a whole lot too, Mom."

My grandmother was wiping her daughter's tears with her fingers. I saw tears streaming down on Mr. Okuma's face too.

My father brought one large hospital towel from the bathroom and motioned them to use it for their tears. I was sure he meant it as a joke to cheer them up. My grandmother simply thanked him and wiped off her daughter's tears and her own tears with the oversized towel.

The doctor walked in cheerfully because his comatose patient came out of the coma. He was so happy that he did not notice our red eyes. He patted my mother on the back of her hands.

"Welcome home, Mrs. Richardson. You rested for a long time. Can you hear me and understand me?"

His voice was loud. My mother nodded.

"Well, I am very elated because you came back from your hibernation."

My mother repeated, "Hibernation?"

"Don't worry. All the big words will come back to you soon. I will ask you some simple questions. If you cannot answer it, don't worry. First, do you remember all these people in front of you?"

The doctor's voice was still loud. My mother nodded.

"Good. If you know your name, say it."

"Keiko Richardson."

"What is your husband's name?"

She looked at my father and said, "John Richardson."

"What is your daughter's name?"

"Mary Richardson."

"Congratulations! You passed all the tests."

The doctor patted my mother on the back of her hands again and called a nurse to tidy up her bandage around her ear and be ready to move her to a private room. While the nurse worked on my mother, we, including grandmother and Mr. Okuma, were called to his office.

"I am very elated. Congratulations!"

"We really thank you for the medical care you have given to my wife. You are such a great doctor…very positive with an excellent bedside manner."

"Thank you. I am glad you trusted me. Well, finally Mrs. Richardson will be in a nice private room. Let me tell you what we are going to do for her with your help. First, we will immediately begin a physical therapy twice a day. All the coma patients tend to forget how to walk, so we must help her. We need someone to watch out for her during the physical therapy. They tend to fall and fracture their bones, especially at the beginning. If one of you can come twice a day to help her walk, her recovery would be faster."

The doctor took out a pen and wrote something on a sheet of paper. My grandmother spoke in English, "Do you allow someone to stay twenty-four hours a day in the private room?"

"Oh, yes. We can arrange a bed in the room free of charge. If somebody can stay every day with Mrs. Richardson, it would be very convenient for us because we don't have to call you on the phone each time when we give her a physical therapy or whenever we encounter a problem with Mrs. Richardson. In any rate, the more you help her walk each day, the faster she recovers."

"I am her mother. I would be glad to stay with her here until she gets better."

"Wonderful. Can you start tomorrow?"

"Yes, but I don't mind starting today."

"Well, you could come back early in the morning tomorrow, but if you insist starting today, I would be glad to arrange it."

"Yes, I would like to start today."

"Okay. I will notify the nurse. By the way, we don't have meal services for the family, so you must eat at the cafeteria. They open from 8:00 a.m. to 8:00 p.m. Well, let's go see Mrs. Richardson in the private room."

We followed the doctor. My mother was sitting up on the fresh bed. When we entered, we saw the nurse instructing my mother how to use a straw to drink water. Apparently, she forgot how to swallow water. We watched her practice. She looked fragile, but her eyes were sparkling. She did not say much to anybody, but her smile revealed she was happy.

After my father brought a dinner box for my grandmother, we kissed my mother goodnight and left her with my grandmother. She could borrow a hospital gown for her sleep tonight and use a disposable toothbrush to brush her teeth. The next day, we would bring her toothbrush, pajamas, and some clothes she might need.

On the way home in my father's car, I had to use my imagination to imagine how my mother woke up. When my grandmother held my mother's hands, talked to her in a quivery voice, my mother probably thought the voice was so familiar, and so was the touch of her soft and warm dainty hands. She could not recall who possessed that familiar voice, and that touch. She probably tried and tried to recall, but she could not because her eyes were closed. So she used her all mighty power to open her eyes to find out who was holding her hands. That was probably how she woke herself up just out of curiosity.

I could tell my mother was longing to see her mother for all those years by saying, "I missed you, Mom." She forgave her mother instantly. Therefore, they reconciled. It was a happy and unexpected reconciliation.

Now they could restore their lost relationship while being together in the hospital. They could talk and talk without stopping. They could reacquaint to make up the forty years' lost.

I could picture my mother holding on to her mother's arm, strolling together in the hallway or on the hospital corridor twice a day or many times a day. I was sure they were glad to be alone so they could talk without any interruption. In the meantime, my mother would be stronger and stronger.

I also imagined grandmother's efforts to reconcile with her daughter after Ambassador Itoh's passing ten years ago. My grandmother probably wrote many letters to her daughter, pleading for her forgiveness, but my mother probably did not reply because she had resented her parents for a long time. My grandmother probably kept her sadness to herself and waited for a chance of reconciliation.

My grandmother stayed in the hospital without coming back to my mother's house. I visited them in the hospital after work. My mother was getting stronger. Sometimes my grandmother and I went to the cafeteria and ate dinner.

Mr. Okuma and my father visited the hospital every morning and fished in the afternoon. They caught a lot of fish. Mr. Okuma cleaned them, and my father fried them. They both seemed to enjoy each other's company.

They made a temporary ramp for a wheelchair from the garage to the kitchen upstairs for my mother. She was ready to come home, according to her doctor's prognosis.

I told everybody including Alice, Nina, and Mark that my grandmother came all the way from Okinawa just to wake my mother up. They thought I was joking, but they were happy about my mother's miraculous recovery from a coma.

However, they did not know that I had a grandmother in Japan for all these years because I did not talk about her in the past. When I added that Mr. Okuma, whom they met before when we were young, became my biological grandfather, they were more surprised but very happy for me.

Chapter 25

CONFRONTATION

Eric Johnson learned that Sue and Matilda Mendosa hired a professional killer to kill Alice's husband, Daniel Thomas. His heart was torn for Alice as well as for his child, Natalie. Natalie's future welfare as a minor would be at risk when Sue Mendosa was to be imprisoned soon. Eric had to do something fast for Natalie.

Therefore, he wrote to Alice that he really wanted to talk to Natalie. He wanted his daughter to hear his side of the story and convince Natalie to get her DNA tested, and then he would hire a lawyer to obtain his parental rights.

His parental rights would save Natalie from the upcoming state custody case. Alice wrote him that obtaining his parental rights would be a great idea for Natalie's welfare, but it had to be done fast before Sue and Matilda Mendosa were to be sentenced soon.

Eric Johnson and his girlfriend, Nancy, hurriedly came to Maui a week prior to the reunion. Alice arranged a rental condominium unit on the beach for them to stay.

On their arrival, Eric got a rental car and met Alice. She gave Eric the schedule sheet of Natalie's tennis practice. Natalie had to practice tennis at least three hours a day with her tennis team. Spectators could sit on the bleachers along the fence to see their practices.

Alice gave the address of the school as well as Sue Mendosa's home address. She also gave the description of Natalie, with dark long hair and thick eyebrow, fair skin, medium height, looks somewhat Sue, but prettier. Alice warned Eric that Sue and Matilda Mendosa were released on bond, so Sue might be coming to see Natalie's practice.

If Sue found out that Eric Johnson was snooping around to locate his child, Eric might be harmed. If Sue found out Alice was the culprit of giving information on Sue's whereabouts, Alice might be harmed as well. Eric must disguise himself so Sue could not recognize him.

Eric wore a pair of dark sunglasses. Nancy held Eric's hand and sat on the bleachers together. Eric did not see Sue on the bleachers, but spotted Natalie on the tennis court. Her hair was ponytailed; her toned body was in good shape and very swift. She seemed to be a good tennis player.

Nancy did not see much resemblance of Eric in Natalie, but the way Natalie raised her hand with her open palm to the opponent, she thought that was Eric's palm.

On the second day, Sue was sitting at the end of the bleachers. She gained a lot of weight since Eric saw her. Wearing a bulky top made her look old and unattractive. Sue was watching her daughter's game obliviously. She was probably thinking about how her supposed-to-be perfect crime went sour.

After the practice, Natalie just disappeared in Sue's Mercedes quietly. She acted as though she did not appreciate for Sue to sit on the bleachers to watch her game. She rather wanted Sue to stay inside of her car to wait. She seemed to be very ashamed of her mother because everybody knew she hired a killer to kill Daniel Thomas and destroyed the Clubhouse by a fire because of her greed.

On the third day, Natalie noticed that the same man and woman sat on the bleachers. Whenever Natalie glanced at them, they both smiled at her. It happened every time she glanced at them. Natalie was contemplating…those people were probably from the police department or from the newspapers to observe her as a child of the criminal-minded family. Or they probably wanted to be her foster parents since they heard about her becoming a recipient of the state foster care services. Or they could be her relatives from Seattle where her rich father and her wealthy grandparents used to live?

Before Sue Mendosa and Matilda Mendosa were arrested, Natalie really thought she was the luckiest child in the world having such a rich grandmother and traveling around the world in such a luxurious way. Before the trip, the school principal gave her two weeks off from school and gave her some social science credits for exploring the foreign countries.

When her grandmother and her mother were arrested at the cruise port, Natalie thought the police made a mistake. She was separated from them and taken to a hospital-like facility and slept there several nights.

When she read the newspaper, she was appalled to learn all about her family's hiring a killer to kill Daniel Thomas, whom she knew at the Clubhouse. He was always kind to her. That killing was beyond her comprehension.

Now all the community people, neighbors, as well as her classmates were avoiding Natalie. She was thinking about running away to somewhere. She wished she knew some relatives of her deceased father in Seattle or somebody who could rescue her from this miserable situation. She was helpless as a minor without any money or without having any relatives.

Natalie was not sure about her trust fund that her mother was bragging about; she understood her paternal grandparents in Seattle set a trust fund for Natalie before their passing, but her mother had never shown her the evidence or document of her trust fund.

Natalie was worried because her mother had always borrowed money from her grandmother, Mrs. Mendosa, to pay Natalie's school expenses and other expenses. Sue was supposed to have her own money because her husband was rich and gave her a large diamond wedding ring when they were married in Las Vegas. Additionally, she heard he left his fortune to Sue and Natalie when he died, but her mother seemed to depend on Mrs. Matilda Mendosa's wealth.

If she knew where her trust fund was saved, at least she could visit the bank to discuss about the release of her fund early or borrowing money against the fund and run away somewhere.

Natalie understood her grandmother's beach mansion would be confiscated and sold by the state or by the bank. They would use the sale assets for their legal fees, their debts, or fines. Even though Natalie was emotionally torn for not knowing her future, she did not want to stay home moping around with her mother and grandmother until their court day. Therefore, she was determined to spend her time playing tennis as much as she could.

The lawyer whom they hired from Honolulu was not concerned of Natalie's welfare; he was simply working on the legal defense for Sue and Matilda Mendosa, or he might be involved in their wrongdoings as well. She wished she had a father or someone whom she could consult with.

Natalie wanted to know why those man and woman were on the bleachers every day to watch her play. On her break, she went up to the bleachers and asked some questions.

"I have noticed you both come to watch me play. Do I know you? Do you know me?"

"Are you Natalie Mendosa?"

"Yes."

"I am Eric Johnson. This is Nancy."

"How do you know my name?"

"Natalie, is there any way we can take you out for lunch after the game. I will explain everything."

Natalie called Sue from the office and told her that she had to each lunch with some friends. She asked her mother to pick her up around 3:00 p.m. at school.

Natalie felt very comfortable with Eric and Nancy because of their gentle smiles. They went to a nearby hotel restaurant, which was quieter than the regular restaurants.

Eric Johnson explained everything to Natalie—his encounter with her mother seventeen years ago in Seattle, how Eric found out Sue was carrying Eric's child after her disappearance. Sue might deny the fact of her pregnancy, but he was sure Natalie was his daughter despite of Sue's story about marrying a wealthy man in Seattle and dying before Natalie was born. Eric told Natalie that Sue had rather lied than marrying Eric who was merely a poor factory worker at that time. Sue was afraid of her mother's rejection of marrying such a poor man.

Therefore, Sue hid her pregnancy from Eric and lied to her mother to be accepted. Sue had lived in her lies and believed in her lies by wearing an expensive wedding ring for years. Eric told Natalie that he had been looking for their whereabouts for years and finally found them from a friend in Maui. He was just elated to see Natalie who was kind enough to hear him out without any objection.

Natalie was crying. Nancy was holding her and letting her cry on her shoulder.

She said in a quivery voice, "How can you prove I am your daughter? I am sure my mother would deny the whole thing. She would be shocked to learn that I know about the secret of my birth."

"If your mother really loves you and cares for your welfare, she might tell you the fact of your birth without hiding it. She might tell you to look for your father, Eric Johnson. However, if she denies everything about your birth, we still could have our DNA tested in the hospital. When the test proves I am your father, I would be hiring a lawyer to obtain my parental rights to take you away from the state's custody because you are a minor. If your mother acknowledges I am your father, things could be much easier. So ask your mother first."

"If she would not admit anything, what should I do?"

"If she stubbornly believes your father was a wealthy guy she met in Seattle, ask her to show you her marriage certificate."

"Is it all right to ask her for my trust fund as well?"

"What trust fund?"

"My mother said my deceased grandparents in Seattle left a trust fund for me, but I have not seen the document at all."

"I think she might be lying unless she set a trust fund herself for you. Your mother might be a psychotic liar or suffering from a mental illness. If she gets angry and denies everything, it could be a dangerous sign. Just be careful and be gentle with her."

"I will. I will be careful, but I hope she will tell me the truth."

"You may ask her if she knew Eric Johnson. Ask her if Eric Johnson could be your father. Don't forget…Eric Johnson's name can be a taboo for her. So be careful. If she gets upset, stop everything, call me. Here is my cell phone number. Don't lose it. Remember, we will pick you up very quickly. We know where you live. After we pick you up, we go straight to the hospital. Our next step will be to get our DNA tested. Remember, I will be waiting for your call."

"Thank you. Right now, I dislike myself for living with them under the same roof. I know I love them, but I am utterly ashamed of them for murdering Daniel Thomas because of their greed. I was told my mother withdrew all the organization's assets and killed Daniel Thomas. I also know that my grandmother hired someone to poison my grandfather in jail because she wanted his entire fortune to herself. It happened long before I was born. I will call you, so pick me up and take me away. If they prove I am your child, is it okay to call you Dad?"

Eric's eyes were moist and nodded several times with a smile.

"I really do not want to go home. I'd rather stay with you."

Eric did not respond but said, "Nancy and I have a nice four-bedroom house in Seattle. Nancy's son, Jeff is in fifth grade. Nancy started decorating your room before we came here. We are thinking about getting married soon and would like to be your parents officially as well as for Jeff."

"Why didn't you find me sooner?"

Eric explained he had been looking for Sue's whereabouts for many years. Recently he found Sue's whereabouts from his classmate. At the same time, he learned that Sue was arrested for a murder charge and facing imprisonment. Therefore, they came quickly to rescue her from the state's custody before it's too late. He promised Natalie that he would obtain parental rights as soon as possible to take her away from this mess.

"Thank you. I am so glad you came to rescue me. I can hardly wait to be with you and live in Seattle. My teacher said I could be somebody if I keep up with my studies. She thinks I am a nice and smart young lady. I hope you would be happy with me. Nancy, thank you. You both are very nice people. Thank you for lunch."

Eric stood at the car door and embraced Natalie for a while. "You have my cell phone number. Call me. If you feel danger, do not confront your mother, just call me. We will pick you up immediately. Please be careful. I will be waiting for your call." He embraced her again as though he were sending his daughter to an unknown danger.

Natalie's hazel eyes looked just like Eric's. Nancy embraced Natalie with a gentle smile.

When Eric and Nancy dropped Natalie off at school, Sue's Mercedes was waiting. Eric stopped at a half block away from Sue's car because he did not want Sue to recognize him. Natalie waved to him and ran to her mother's car.

Eric had a premonition that this was the first and the last time he would see his daughter. He gazed at Sue's car obliviously until it drove off.

While Nancy was taking a bath, Eric was moping around in the living room impatiently. TV was on, but he was not watching. He was just waiting for a phone call from Natalie. She said she would call him as soon as she talked to her mother. It had been quite a while since they dropped her off.

On TV, special news came on: Natalie Mendosa, sixteen, was shot to death by her mother, Sue Mendosa. The neighbor who saw Sue Mendosa wandering around on the beach with a gun, called 911. She was delusional according to the arresting police officer; she did not seem to remember where she was and what she had done. The body of Natalie Mendosa was sent to the hospital morgue. Sue Mendosa was cuffed and sent to a mental hospital for further examination. This killing occurred while Sue Mendosa was released on bond from a previous arrest; she was arrested two weeks ago for hiring a killer to kill the renowned lawyer Daniel Thomas. Her mother, Matilda Mendosa, was also arrested for conspiring to murder Daniel Thomas. Additionally, they are now sued by a nonprofit organization in Maui for selling the organization's property without the board's permission and attempting to embezzle by closing the bank account.

Eric Johnson hollered loudly like a person who was physically tortured. When Nancy heard Eric's holler, she came out of the bathroom in a robe in a hurry. She thought Eric fell and hurt himself, but on TV, she saw a gruesome scene of Natalie's body, lying on a pool of blood before the stretcher arrived. She became horrified and speechless. Eric was hollering and pounding on the sofa. Nancy sat beside him, held him tightly. Eric buried his head on her lap, wailed like a child, and kept saying that was his fault.

"Honey, it was not your fault. That was Natalie's fate. You did not kill her. Her mother killed her. Remember we came here to rescue her. Do not blame yourself. It was not your fault. No. It was not your fault."

She had to repeat her words for Eric's sake, but Eric shook his head, kept weeping on her lap. The only thing Nancy could do was to smoothen his hair gently and let him wail.

Nancy phoned Alice what happened to Natalie, but she already heard about the news. Alice had tears in her eye as though she were recalling her husband's recent death. She asked Nancy if Eric had a chance to talk to Natalie. Nancy did not go into details but told her they managed to eat lunch together. Alice was happy because Eric was able to see his child at last but empathized with Eric for his loss of Natalie, just as her own loss of Daniel.

Eric and Nancy decided to go home instead of attending the reunion in Honolulu. However, Eric had to do one thing with Sue Mendosa. He wanted to confront Sue himself to see if Natalie were indeed his child. Troy Maddox arranged a meeting for Eric.

The psychiatric ward nurse released Sue with her watchful eyes at the interrogation room. When Sue saw Eric, she could not recognize him first. It had been too long to see each other. Sue looked ten years older than her actual age with wrinkles. Eric thought all the mental illness finally surfaced on her face. They diagnosed that Sue had suffered from an untreated bipolar disorder and a combination of some other psychotic disorders. The doctors would be evaluating her illness further before her court appearance.

Eric sat in front of her. "Sue, I am Eric Johnson from Seattle. I hope you remember me. I would like to ask you just one question. Was Natalie my child?"

Now, she remembered him and started crying without answering.

Eric patiently waited and asked her again, "Sue, was Natalie a daughter of Eric Johnson?" Eric had to repeat loudly.

Sue finally nodded and said in a quivery voice, "Yes."

"Thank you. That is all I want to hear."

"I am very sorry. I really loved Natalie. I did not know what I was doing. I just remember what Natalie said—I was a psychotic liar all my life, lying about her father and lying about her trust fund. When she asked if Eric Johnson was her real father, I could not remember why I was holding a gun and why Natalie was lying on the floor. I am so…"

Eric did not want to hear Sue's apology. He stood up and kicked the chair back and left the room. He was crying, did not care what kind of punishment Sue would receive for killing his child. Nancy was waiting outside the room. Both just held each other's hands and left the psychiatric ward quietly.

The next day, Nancy left a message on Alice's cell…they decided to go home to Seattle.

Chapter 26

CLASS REUNION

The day before the class reunion, Alice arrived and stayed in the same hotel where the reception was to be held. All the committee members met Nina at the banquet hall and listened to the hotel manager's welcoming speech.

The diagram of the banquet hall with the guest tables and the position of the reception tables was shown on the TV screen on the stage. The stage for the live band music was already set by the hotel staff. Some committee members were helping the hotel workers by putting tablecloths and table numbers on each table.

Alice and I squatted down on the floor to open several boxes of printed materials and alumni books. Putting the printed materials and alumni books in each envelope was time-consuming.

All the filled envelops Alice and I worked on were stacked up behind the reception table neatly. Nametags were displayed alphabetically on the table. On the reunion day, Alice would help find the person's nametag, and I would be giving a filled envelope to each alumnus at the same time, and then other committee members would escort them to the numbered tables.

After finishing the setup for the class reunion, all the committee members said good night to each other and left. Nina and the committee accountant were still with the hotel manager. Alice and I waited for Nina in the hall. We were going to eat dinner together.

While we were waiting, Alice told me all about Eric and Natalie. I felt very sad for Eric. Nina finally finished and came to where we were. Now we were heading toward the restaurant.

After ordering the dinner, Nina said, "As soon as I finish this responsibility, I am thinking about secluding myself in a room for a couple of days. I hope Tom can take care the children and all the household tasks. I think I deserve at least two days' rest. I hope everything will be all right tomorrow." Nina looked doubtful.

"Nina, you did a beautiful job. Without you, we don't think this class reunion could be possible. Yes, you deserve to have a vacation. If you want to stay in a hotel to relax, Mary and I can arrange it for you—free of charge. Do you want that?"

"Oh, no. I was just kidding. It was just hectic to organize the class reunion as a chairperson, but I really enjoyed it. I felt although I had accomplished something great, it is quite a job to have so many participants including their spouses and partners from all over mainland USA. Ordering alumni books was time-consuming too."

"We, the committee members, know your hard work. Oh, I forgot to tell you…I canceled Eric's hotel reservation directly with the hotel. They had to go back to Seattle."

"I thought Eric and his girlfriend were excited about attending the class reunion. What happened?"

"Eric and Nancy came to Maui a week ago to work on Eric's parental rights for his child, but his daughter, Natalie, was murdered."

"Oh my god! Who murdered his daughter? Tell me what happened."

"Well, it is a long story."

Alice and I had never told Nina about Eric's letter. We were afraid of revealing Sue's lies because it was dangerous. Daniel's death was nothing to do with Eric's letter, but we did not tell Nina anything about that, either.

Alice continued, "Remember I told you about Sue's marriage to a son of a wealthy family in Seattle? That was Sue's grandeur delusion. No such husband existed in her life. Actually, she had a child with Eric. Remember Eric Johnson, Mary's high school sweetheart? However, Sue seduced Eric to take revenge on Mary—she thought they were still in love. Anyway, she got pregnant with Eric, but lied to her mother that she married a wealthy husband, but he passed, so she came back to Maui and had a baby. Eric had been looking for Sue's whereabouts because he believed Sue bore his child. That was the reason Eric wrote to Mary to find out Sue's whereabouts, but Mary did not know. Because of our class reunion, I used his old address that Mary had to contact him and also gave him Sue's address."

"Who murdered his daughter?"

"Sue did."

"Oh my god! Sue killed her own child? Is she crazy?"

"Yes. She is mentally ill. Mary and I did not tell you much about Daniel's death, but Sue and her mother, Mrs. Mendosa, hired a killer to murder Daniel as well. Since the investigation was secretly conducted, we decided to wait to tell you. Sorry."

Nina nodded as though she was saying it was all right.

Alice put some food in her mouth and finished chewing. "Anyway, let's me go back to Eric. After Sue and her mother were arrested for Daniel's murder charge, Eric had to act fast to obtain his parental rights because Natalie was a minor. Otherwise, his child would become a recipient of the state foster care services after their imprisonment."

Alice cut the vegetables in small pieces on her plate and continued. "Eric met Natalie and told her he might be her father, so Natalie confronted Sue to get the truth, but something went wrong. Sue killed Natalie. After the killing, Eric confronted Sue. Indeed, Natalie was his child. He was heartbroken and went back home. The doctor said Sue's mental illness had never been treated in the past—she seemed to have suffered from the mental illness for all her life."

Nina looked speechless, as though she missed all the news while she was working for the class reunion. So Alice apologized to her again.

"I am sorry Mary and I kept Eric's letter and the investigation to ourselves because we were afraid Sue might harm us if she found out her secrets were unveiled by us."

"That is all right, but I am sorry about Daniel. I did not know Sue hired a killer to murder him."

"If Mary's suspicion were not there to open the investigation, they would have declared that Daniel's death was accidental. I am very thankful to Mary. Nina, I am also thankful to you because of your phone call on the day of Daniel's death."

"Why is that?"

"If you did not call me that morning, Gregory and I could be dead by the explosion too. Your phone call stopped us from going to the office with Daniel. The hired killer confessed that that explosion was supposed to kill the entire Thomas family. Your phone call saved my life and Gregory's life. Thank you. It must be my fate, but I strongly want to believe your friendship protected us."

Again, Nina was speechless. Now Alice told Nina everything. With Nina's smile, we have bonded just as before. While ordering dessert and coffee, Nina asked, "Alice, do you think Mrs. Mendosa has the same kind of mental illness as Sue?"

"I think so. The time of Sue's shooting Natalie, Mrs. Mendosa was at home and the police found her in the closet. She was talking to herself like a crazy person. The police had to put her in the mental hospital too."

I was listening to the conversation of Alice and Nina. Sue's murdering of Natalie reminded me of the recent college campus massacres. Most of the campus shootings were committed by mentally ill students who were untreated or refused to take medications. There were thought to be many untreated mentally ill people in this world. It is indeed scary. The number of mental patients is on the rise due to the stressful circumstances in modern society.

The insane people's behaviors are caused by some chemical imbalance in their brains—medication is the only solution to balance the chemicals. The illness could not be cured but could be controlled according to the medical specialist. Daniel and Natalie were victims of the mental illness; so were the college students.

Alice told us that her work in Troy Maddox's office has kept her mind busy—no more fear of Sue. Gregory was staying with Troy and his children during the class reunion. Alice's weight loss revealed her suffering from the death of Daniel, but her eyes were sparkling. I hoped it was something to do with Troy Maddox.

Alice gave the updated information on the organization. Those voided two checks were deposited in the organization's new bank account. The bank helped their lawyer to retrieve the organization's property deed by returning the payment of $850,000.

Now the insurance company is working with a builder to build the Clubhouse. The bank foreclosed Mrs. Mendosa's mansion to pay her loan from the bank, and some other debts. She apparently borrowed a lot of money against her mansion. Her fortune was probably depleting over the years. I thought the idea of having a mansion on the beach probably originated in her grandeur delusion, or her mental illness, or something to do with her inflated ego.

In any rate, Mrs. Lisboa and the board members asked Alice to remain as president to help reorganize the nonprofit organization all over again. Alice agreed.

On the class reunion day, Alice and I kept standing up behind the reception table instead of sitting down because we were continuously busy. We greeted each alumnus and gave a large envelop with a nametag. Other committee members were busy escorting the alumni and guests to the tables.

Nina made an excellent speech as the chairperson as well as representing the committee members. Our retired high school teachers were invited. Nina humorously introduced some notable alumni who became doctors, movie stars, authors, musicians, professors, company presidents, and lawyers including Alice, even I as a rare species of female pilot.

At the end of her speech, she asked us for a moment of silence by naming three deceased classmates who died young and did not make it to the twentieth class reunion.

The dinner was excellent, and the performance of Hawaiian dance gave everybody some nostalgic feeling of being Hawaiians. At the end, everybody mingled around with old pals instead of dancing with the live band music. Some were dancing, but most of them were busy rekindling friendships with their old friends by introducing their spouses.

I wished Mark were with me so I could introduce him as my date because most of them were with their spouses or dates. Alice and I did not have any date with us, so we just sat at the table and watched the others. Some of the classmates who knew Alice came and gave her their condolences on the death of Daniel.

When I heard Eric and his girlfriend, Nancy, went home, I felt somewhat relieved. I was nervous about meeting Eric and Nancy because I did not bring my date. Mark was still in San Diego. Eric might have felt awkward because I was still single, or without any prospect.

Next time when we have the thirtieth class reunion, I hope I would be able to introduce my Prince Charming. By then Eric would be married to Nancy, should have another child. Who knows I would be married to Mark and should have my children as well? If that would happen, Eric and I would shake our hands, rejoice our reunion, and might reminisce about our wonderful past and smile at each other without any regrets.

Our twentieth high school reunion was a success. Nina closed the class reunion by saying to be healthy and live well until we meet again ten years later. She asked everybody to embrace each other and say "Aloha." We gave an accolade to Nina by giving her a standing ovation.

My father was pushing my mother's wheelchair on the ramp that he and Grandpa Okuma built. He helped her sit on a lounge chair at the terrace. My mother looked very happy seeing the ocean view again. My father knew the terrace was her favorite place to relax. She probably missed the scene just as I had always missed my own sunset when I was away.

She did not wear any bandage around her head anymore. My grandmother rolled my mother's hair nicely around her left ear to cover some scars.

Mrs. Kitano brought some food including my mother's favorite dessert to welcome her home. Some of the neighbors and Mr. and Mrs. Yamagata came to see my mother as well. Mr.

Yamagata seemed to be taking care of the garden even though my mother was not home.

The doctor said my mother was not strong enough to walk by herself. For a while, she would need a wheelchair for shopping or any outings. She was told not to use the steps. She must use a walker around the house and then a cane. She must take high dose of various vitamins, especially vitamin B12 every day to regain her stamina.

My grandmother was glad to prepare balanced meals for her daughter just as she used to do when my mother was growing up. I could tell my mother was very grateful having her mother around while recuperating.

On my grandmother's mind, my mother was still her young child—helpless young child who could not do much around the house. So she always had her watchful eyes on my mother.

Several days after my mother came home from the hospital, I was overjoyed to learn that Mark vacated his apartment in San Diego and shipped all his furniture to his apartment in Honolulu. After spending several days with his father in Los Angeles, he would be moving to Hawaii for good.

The night before Mark's arrival, I could not sleep well because I was so excited about meeting Mark for the second time. In reality, I only saw him once. Even though we talked every night after that, I felt awkward. My gorgeous George Clooney might have changed—probably became ugly and old. I tried to picture him, but George Clooney's face appeared. I felt guilty.

When Mark called me from the airport, my father and I went to meet Mark at his apartment. He had a rental car to bring the two suitcases full of clothes. Mark had not changed at all—still gorgeous. Mark hugged me, but no kiss in front of my father. Apparently, Mark did not tell my father about our relationship. Of course, I had not told him either.

His apartment had two bedrooms with a kitchen and a large living room on the second floor. Some furniture were already delivered. The landlord probably allowed the delivery company to place the furniture in appropriate places such as a bed and a dresser in the bedroom, bookshelves and TV in the living room, so forth.

I helped clean the bedroom while my father and Mark were moving TV, computer, bookshelves, and some other furniture. His books and personal items were in a large box. I put away some of his clothes in the dresser.

My father and Mark were talking constantly, not their personal things…only sports, politics, other men stuff. I did not think my father suspected our relationship.

On the other hand, it was possible that Mark's father, Mr. Nakaya, might have been talking to my father about us. In this case, he might be pretending or just waiting to hear from us.

My mother called my father on the cell asking him to pick up some groceries for my grandmother on the way home. He had to leave, so he asked Mark to bring me home and eat dinner with them. Mark thanked my father for helping him move and inviting him to dinner.

As soon as my father left, Mark started acting as George Clooney in a romantic movie. He scooped me up with my waist. His sexy lips were approaching mine as though he heard the director's call, "And action!" After our many kissing scenes were rehearsed, we were on his uncovered bed, and the camera was rolling to take our erotic scenes from different angles.

Two sexually deprived lovebirds were tangling. We heard our own moanings as a final take. We both felt relaxed and snuggled against each other like puppy dogs. We fell asleep until my cell phone rang. That was my father.

It was the first time Mark met my mother in person as well as meeting my grandparents. I remembered he saw my mother at ICU, but not in person. My mother probably heard about Mark favorably from my father, and she knew Mark was the son of Minoru.

My grandmother's fried fish dish was excellent with plenty of fresh vegetables. Her homemade Japanese green tea ice cream was superb.

After our dinner, Mark made a surprising announcement without consulting me. He was asking my father in Japanese if it is all right to propose to his daughter to be his wife. My father was positively nodding. Then he turned to my mother and grandparents and asked them to witness his proposal.

He knelt on the floor in front of me and took out an engagement ring. "Mary, would you please marry me? I love you very much. I would be the best husband and make you the happiest person in this world, and I would like to be your Prince Charming forever. Please marry me."

I was blushed and flabbergasted since I did not think we were ready for this advanced stage. I looked at my parents. My parents were nodding several times as though Mark was already certified as their son-in-law. My mother's eyes were sparkling. Perhaps, she was already told we were madly in love.

My grandmother and Mr. Okuma looked delighted, and they were applauding aloud out of joy. They looked as though Mark's proposal was the most romantic proposal they had ever heard in their lives.

"Mark, are you sure you want to marry me?"

"Yes, Mary. I love you very much. Say yes."

My audience was holding their breaths.

"Yes, I will marry you."

Suddenly, I heard loud applauds from the audience.

Mark put the diamond engagement ring on my finger and kissed my palm. The audience applauded again and looked relieved.

My grandparents probably thought Mark and I had dated for many years and finally Mark decided to propose to me. If they knew that we just met several months ago for the first time and then he proposed on the second meet, they might have had second thoughts about us.

I was very sure my father would not say anything to my grandparents how long Mark and I have known each other. If they would ask him, he would probably say he has known Mark since he was a child, Mark would make a fine husband for Mary. That would probably satisfy my grandparents.

Mark also told the audience the wedding ceremony would take place before my grandparents' return to Okinawa. My grandparents were very much impressed by Mark's kind gesture. I was glad too because I wanted my grandparents to witness their only descendant's marriage.

Mark said our wedding would be very simple, but a happy one. My father volunteered to secure a nice place with a chapel. He was very enthusiastic about being in-charge of his daughter's wedding… in a traditional American way. My mother said she would ask Mrs. Kitano to help make my wedding dress in a hurry. She would probably know a priest or a minister to marry us as well.

Mark looked so brightly handsome when he was discussing our wedding plans with my family. For some reason, my father looked so proud of Mark as though Mark was his own son.

Mark wanted to spend a night with me in my place instead of going back to his apartment. I did not mind it at all. I felt so loved and comfortable sleeping with my George Clooney. I thought we were becoming soul mates.

Mrs. Kitano was elated to hear our wedding plan from my mother. She knew someone who could make my wedding dress in a hurry. I was called to meet a seamstress at my mother's house the next day. Mrs. Kitano also found a minister who would be glad to marry us.

I saw my grandmother and Mr. Okuma practicing several pieces from classical music for my wedding, my grandmother with violin, and Grandpa Okuma on my mother's grand piano. When I heard their music practice, I was overwhelmed with the thought of their forever love, and brought some tears to my eyes. Their forever love was never materialized as a marriage, yet their forever love remained in their hearts for all their lives.

Mrs. Kitano was busy instructing the seamstress how to sew certain parts of the dress. She drew the style of the dress on a sheet of paper. I liked it very much, so did my mother.

Mrs. Kitano was a professional dress designer for many years. She and her husband once owned a very successful clothing store on Waikiki Beach. After her husband died, Mrs. Kitano sold their clothing business and retired.

As her two married daughters lived in New York, not visiting Mrs. Kitano much, she was alone and lonely. As my mother did not have any relatives, except us, they both bonded just as sisters. Their relationship was similar to my relationship with Alice. As my mother was much younger than Mrs. Kitano, she always looked after my mother.

As our wedding would take place in ten days, we did not have time to send invitations. Therefore, Mrs. Kitano volunteered to call the people whom we wanted to invite to the wedding. There would not be many guests, just my dear friends and their family members, our family friends, Mark's father, his high school classmates from Los Angeles, and pilot friends from San Diego.

According to Mrs. Kitano, when she called Alice and Nina, they were flabbergasted and almost hysterical. Nina called me first, and then Alice. They both said they felt neglected not knowing about my wedding.

I had to tell them that I was surprised myself since Mark and I met several months ago. However, I explained Mark is a son of my father's dear friend in Los Angeles. I knew of Mark through my father, but never met until several months ago. We became love at first sight to each other, and we fell madly in love instantly.

I also told them that I did my detective work asking many blunt questions…he was clean. They laughed aloud with a relief. They repeatedly congratulated me and said they could hardly wait to see Mark at the wedding. I did not describe how Mark looked. Well, they might be thinking Mark might be fat, short, and unattractive that was why he wanted to marry beautiful Mary in a hurry, just as Beauty and the Beast.

Chapter 27

THE LAST SECRET

Mark and I had to decide where we should live after the wedding. If we lived in his apartment, it would be too far away from my parents. So I suggested him to move into my place and later we could look for a house somewhere on the hill. In the meantime, my condominium could be our palace. He agreed.

My mother started walking without a cane. Whenever she wanted to walk in the neighborhood, my grandmother went with her. Mr. Okuma and my father kept fishing every day. My grandmother fried fish whenever they caught fish. She was told eating fried small fish with the fine bones would be good for my mother's bones, so she often fried, especially small fish.

Mark flew one round trip by staying in Asia for one night each week. I flew two turnaround trips between Honolulu and Los Angeles each week. Therefore, I was home every day.

I was happy thinking about my being a married woman. I recalled I was another woman to someone in the past. That was forgotten and buried, but the odd feeling stayed in my heart even to this date. I was very sure Mark would be a faithful husband forever, unlike Bruce Hudson.

As I was so caught up with my wedding plan or other personal things, I almost forgot about unveiling the secret of my mother's birth to her. Did my father tell her that Mr. Okuma is her biological

Family Secrets

father? I asked my father if he told Mom about Mr. Okuma, but he said no.

He thought I had already told her. I panicked. My mother must know before my grandparents' return to Okinawa. It would be soon. I realized my mission was still incomplete. I was a little nervous about how she would react to the truth of her birth, but I was determined to unveil the secret.

Several days before my wedding, my father planned a trip for Mr. Okuma and my grandmother to sightsee the entire Oahu island. He wanted me to stay with my mother and have a heart-to-heart conversation. I knew what he meant—he wanted me to unveil the secret of my mother's birth.

Before he left, he patted on my shoulder as though he was saying, "Good luck!"

I made some green tea and asked my mother to sit with me to chat. I was nervous, but I was determined to complete my mission. I approached her in a direct manner. "Mom, do you know Mr. Okuma is your biological father?"

She was not startled, but her eyes widened. "No, but I suspected he might be my biological father for a long time."

"How did you suspect he might be your biological father?"

"Because we looked alike. When I was in Paris, I found Mr. Okuma's picture from my mother's wallet. It was scotch-taped to the back of my picture. I asked her who the man was. She gave me his name as Mr. Masao Okuma, and she said he would be the most important person in my life. I did not understand what she meant, but I remembered his name."

I poured some more green tea into her cup.

"When we came back to Japan, Ambassador Itoh went off on business trips quite often. Sometimes he stayed away for many days. I was already in high school. Ambassador Itoh had a bad habit when he had too much alcohol, he used to hit my mother for no reason. I hated him for that."

My mother sipped green tea and continued. "I used to use a frying pan to hit him to stop. He probably had a grudge against my mother because she did not give him a son. He had kept a mistress somewhere in the countryside. Then we heard his mistress had a son. That made him very happy, and he stayed with them days and days. Ambassador Itoh built a house for them. He was spending my mother's inheritance money to build their house."

"Mom, how old were you?"

"Probably, eighteen, I was about to finish high school. Anyway, he spent more time there than he spent in his own house. Nevertheless, whenever he came back home, he invited the government officials or his friends as though nothing had changed in his family life. He had kept his secret double life for years. However, Mom was relaxed and peaceful whenever he went away to his mistress. Let me tell you something. One day while Ambassador Itoh was away to his mistress, my mother took me to a concert for the first time. The concert flyer had a big picture of the symphony conductor, Mr. Masao Okuma."

My mother had a sip of tea and continued.

"My mother did not think I remembered his name, but I did. His picture was just like the picture I found from her wallet. After the concert, Mr. Okuma came to see us, and my mother introduced Mr. Okuma to me as her childhood friend. I was startled because I resembled him so much, like our smiles, our eyes, our long fingers."

My mother was looking at her dainty hands and long fingers while she was rubbing both hands together.

"I was sure my mother had not seen Mr. Okuma for a long time, but I thought they had been writing to each other, so they knew what was going on in their lives. Their eyes, however, revealed as though they had longed to see each other for many years. Mr. Okuma took us to a restaurant and asked me many questions about my piano practices and my future. I told him I wanted to go back to Paris to study music. I still remember his big smile with his teary eyes. I thought about his teary eyes often and wished he were my father who would appreciate music and did not mind for me to be a musician."

She sipped more tea and continued. "At that time, Ambassador Itoh stubbornly rejected my plan to study music in Paris. He said it would be a waste of money. A girl should get married and have many children instead. My mother literally fought Ambassador Itoh to accept my plan to study music in Paris. I was already accepted by Sorbonne University by then. My mother threatened him if he did not release some of her inheritance money, she would expose his secret double life—having an illegitimate son and a mistress to the government officials. He reluctantly released some of her inheritance money that was given to her by her father before his passing, but Ambassador Itoh kept it in his bank. Anyway, that was how my mother was able to send me to Paris."

"Did you ever ask your mother about Mr. Okuma possibly being your biological father?"

"At that time, as a teenager, I did not have any doubt that I was Ambassador Itoh's daughter, even though I resembled Mr. Okuma a lot. I thought the resemblance was just coincidental. I did not question my mother at all. However, I had already built a great rapport with Mr. Okuma by seeing him at the concert. He was my make-believe father who understood me as a musician. After I was disowned by my parents, Mr. Okuma was the only one who supported me and visited me in Honolulu. Whenever he visited us in Honolulu, I always saw him as my make-believe or possible biological father because I saw some resemblance between you and Mr. Okuma such as your cowlicks and texture of your hair. I also thought about what my mother said years back about Mr. Okuma as the most important person in my life."

I told my mother how my grandmother spent the last night with Mr. Okuma before she left for Paris. Several years later, she wrote a letter to assure Mr. Okuma that her daughter, Keiko, was indeed his daughter. She also assured him she would love her, nurture her, and look after her, so he should not be worried. However, it was kept secret between them for many decades until I visited Mr. Okuma. I was the first one whom Mr. Okuma had ever confessed to. My mother intently listened to me with tears.

"Thank you, Mary. If you did not visit Mr. Okuma, the fact of my birth would be buried forever between them."

"Probably so."

"When I was working for Mr. Okuma, he taught me his advanced skills as a pianist. He showed me the difficult finger movements, scheduled me for many solo piano concerts, other than his symphony concerts. That was why people thought I was a promising pianist. He has been my inspiration as a musician since I have known him."

"Mom, you may not know, but the first time Mr. Okuma came to visit us years back, Grandma wanted him to find out if we lived in poverty since you married a poor American soldier. If we lived in poverty, she was going to help us financially. Remember Mr. Okuma kept buying stuff for me, like Barbie dolls? That was all Grandma's idea for years. Mr. Okuma was a secret messenger, or a guardian sent by Grandma."

When I laughed, Mom started laughing and said, "I remember Mr. Okuma was very surprised when he came to stay with us in this house for the first time. He thought we lived in a small apartment just as we did in Tachikawa. He wanted to know how we could afford the house this big. I explained to him about John's inheritance from his deceased parents. I, too, thought I married a poor American soldier until he bought this house."

We both laughed again.

"Does your Dad know about my birth secret?"

"Yes, I told him. He is very happy about the whole thing. I was supposed to take Grandpa Okuma and Grandma for sightseeing today, but somehow he wanted me to do the honor of unveiling your birth secret. Yes, he knows it. Did you know Ambassador Itoh passed away ten years ago?"

She nodded and said, "My mother wrote me. She wrote me many letters to apologize to me for the disownment, but I did not write her back. I missed her a lot, but I could not forgive her."

Her eyes were moist, so I had to cheer her up.

"Mom, let's surprise Mr. Okuma by calling *Otoosan* and *Ojiisan* in Japanese."

"Okay. I'll also tell him I am very proud to be his daughter. I am going to tell both of them how proud I am to be a child of the greatest musicians."

"Oh, I can hardly wait to see them. Mom, I will prepare some dinner tonight for a change. Mark is away today, so I will eat with you."

"Mary, I am very happy that you are getting married to a person you love. Mark and you are a very good match. You will have a beautiful life with Mark. Congratulations."

"I am glad I found myself a Prince Charming. I thought I would be single for the rest of my life. Do you think I may become a mother?"

"Oh, yes. You are still young. Some woman can have children until fifty. So concentrate on having my grandkid soon."

"Okay, I hope my children would be musically talented like you." I smiled at my mother. I stood up and started working at the kitchen. My mother wanted to help me, but I told her to sit at the terrace and enjoy the view.

When Mr. Okuma appeared at the door, my mother called him Otoosan and I called him Ojiisan in Japanese, and we embraced him at the same time. His eyes were so wide and sparkling just as my mother's eyes and nodded several times with moist eyes. My grandmother and my father were watching us with a big smile.

At a small chapel, the wedding ceremony was held with a minister. The photographer whom my father hired was taking many pictures. Gregory carried our wedding rings on a tray. My father gave me away. Mr. Nakaya was standing beside Mark. We exchanged our vows. I was so nervous that my wedding dress was trembling and my hands were ice-cold. I could not remember what the minister said, but finally we were announced as man and wife in front of our guests.

I saw Alice, Troy Maddox, his two children, Gregory, Nina and Tom, their three children, Mrs. Kitano, Mr. and Mrs. Yamagata, about seven of Mark's high school friends from Los Angeles, and five pilot friends from San Diego. After the ceremony, we moved to a restaurant-like banquet room with a raised open stage that had a piano.

The table of the groom and bride was in front of the guests near the stage. The wedding cake stood at the corner. Two long tables were facing each other just like a conference room setting. My parents, grandparents, and my friends sat at my side. Mr. Nakaya and Mark's friends sat at Mark's side. All the tables were draped elegantly with white cloth. All invited guests were there. The atmosphere was filled with much love, smiles, and everybody looked very happy to witness our wedding.

Because of Mrs. Kitano, I was able to wear a custom-made wedding dress. She and my mother chose a combination of lobster and steak dinner for the guests. They together ordered a tall wedding cake for us. The flower arrangements were tastefully done by both.

My father stood up and made everybody toast champagne before his speech. He thanked everybody to witness his only child's wedding. He emphasized Mary and Mark are skillful pilots and they both share a common destiny. He jokingly said he has known Mark since he was a child, therefore, today Mark officially became his adopted son, not son-in-law. Everybody laughed.

He also introduced my grandparents as Mary's grandfather, the famous symphony conductor, and grandmother, the talented violinist…they would like to play a piece from Chopin's piano concerto for Mark and Mary.

Mr. Okuma wore a tuxedo, and Grandmother wore a black long dress. They both looked very young and handsome. They started playing. The room was very quiet. The waiters quietly brought the dinner plate to each guest.

After their performance, everybody, even the young children, applauded loudly. I thought Mark applauded louder than everybody else did. I did not think Mark was a music lover, but he seemed to be impressed by their performance.

While eating, Alice and Nina were smiling at me whenever our eyes met. They signaled me how handsome Mark is by touching their faces and placed their fists on their chests with a saluting gesture and threw some congratulation kisses at me with their biggest smiles. They looked awfully relieved because the wedding was not for Beauty and the Beast.

After dinner, we cut our wedding cake. Mark and I fed each other a piece. The cake was specially made by a French chef whom my mother knew. It was just delicious.

By then, the music with trumpet, guitar, drum, and piano was played by Mark's high school classmates from Los Angeles. They played familiar tunes from a big band. One of his classmates brought a saxophone to Mark and took him to the stage.

Everybody was flabbergasted because the groom was a talented saxophone player. I was stunned because I did not know this part of Mark. He had never told me anything about his saxophone.

In his tuxedo and the way he held the saxophone, his sex appeal was much more than George Clooney—just out of this world. I saw Alice and Nina who looked mesmerized by and drooled on my George Clooney.

My grandparents looked stunned when Mark played saxophone. They were probably thinking about their musically talented future descendants. Mr. Nakaya looked very happy knowing that Mark's music friends came to entertain the guests. He knew all of Mark's friends who frequented his house and practically grew up together with his son, Mark.

Mr. and Mrs. Yamagata looked so handsome. Mrs. Yamagata was quiet but smiled a lot. Mr. Yamagata was talkative in his broken English and looked very happy; the champagne probably made him talkative.

When Mark's friends started playing slow music, we were told to dance on the floor. Mark held my waist, and we danced around. Everybody started joining us. Nina's daughters were dancing with Troy's boys. Troy was dancing with Alice and Gregory.

My father came and danced with me. Mark danced with my mother slowly because of her condition. Mr. Okuma was dancing with Grandma. I went to Mr. Nakaya and danced with him. While we were dancing, he thanked me and said I was the best thing that happened to Mark. I told him Mark was the best thing that happened to me as well. He smiled with his moist eyes.

Mark and I left for our honeymoon trip to Isle of Capri, Italy for a week. I visited there several times before and always thought that the place has the most romantic atmosphere on earth. Mark had never visited there, so he was hesitant first, but when I showed some pictures of the island, he became enthusiastic.

We took a ferry from Sorrento to Isle of Capri and a funicular to our hotel on the hilltop. The town is built on the hill. As the island is surrounded by the eroded rock walls, the only place people can dwell…is on the hilltop. The beautiful Tyrrhenian Sea surrounds Isle of Capri.

Our hotel room was on the highest floor with a large bedroom and a sitting area with a huge window; unbelievably magnificent sights could be seen from our room, the sunrise from the bedroom and the sunset from the sitting area.

All the narrow streets in the town are neatly paved, and car driving seems to be prohibited…just bicycles. Nevertheless, there are scheduled buses between the towns. The church bell would give some nostalgic sounds to the indigenous islanders. Every house is neatly kept with flowers. All the shops and restaurants are filled with people, probably tourists, but in an orderly manner.

Mark could not take his eyes off from the magnificent sights around the island. One day, we rode the open sky lift to the very top of the mountain and enjoyed the view of the ocean and the town below.

We ate delicious Italian cuisine every night with wine. Sometimes, a group of musicians came and sang familiar Italian songs. Mark was very happy with the choice of our honeymoon place and said, "Mary, when we need to recuperate from the hectic schedule, let's come back here. This island could be our retreating place, soul healing or soul-searching place…stress free, no traffic, no pollution…that is what we need from time to time. I really love this place."

While we were on the honeymoon trip, my grandparents went home. My mother probably told them at the airport that as soon as her doctor would permit her to travel, she and my father would be visiting them in Okinawa. My mother probably embraced her mother for the longest time.

When we came back home from the honeymoon trip, my parents were gone to Okinawa for a month. They left a message saying if we would like to stay in their house, we were welcome to do so.

As we were in the transition of everything such as Mark moving his stuff to my place and store some of his furniture in the rental storage, my place was in a mess, so we took up my parents' offer to live in their house to continue our honeymoon until their return.

I knew I was an average cook, but I tried my best to make decent dinner. Surprisingly, Mark was a very good cook, so most of the time he was in charge of our dinner. Yes, I helped him in the kitchen as his assistant.

Mark's playfulness often got out of hand. He purposely aroused me in the kitchen, and eventually we stopped whatever we were doing and made love.

Epilogue

My mother was holding Nichole, and my father was with Steven. Mark and I stood behind them. The photographer took a family portrait with the background of the ocean at the terrace. The picture was for my grandparents in Okinawa and Mr. Nakaya in Gardena. They had not seen the picture of the twins. Our children are fraternal twins. Nichole was born five minutes earlier than Steven.

When I found out I was carrying twins, I took a maternity leave from work for a year. Alice and Nina did not know much about twins but gave me tons of their advices on my pregnancy. I read many books about babies as well.

My mother and Mrs. Kitano come to my place to cook healthy meals for me to eat and took me out for shopping so I would not be a couch potato.

Mark and I attended some meetings for new parents-to-be. My mother was so excited that she bought two sets of nightwear, socks, blankets, including paper diapers to be ready. She acted as though she would be the mother.

Mark and I had to clear the second room in my condominium to make room for the babies. Two cribs, two sets of everything filled the entire room. We had to store unnecessary furniture including my elaborate language lab in the rental storage.

When the babies and I came home from the hospital, I really felt our place was too small for the four of us. Mark and my father often went out to look for a house but could not find a house in the desirable neighborhood.

After a year of maternity leave, I went back to work. My parents volunteered to take care of the twins while I flew twice a week for turnaround schedule. I was home every day except two afternoons. Mark had to overnight in Asia once a week, and for the rest of the week, he was home.

Mrs. Kitano's health was declining because of her old age. She was not sickly, but her big house was too much for her to maintain. She told my mother about selling her house and buying a condominium unit.

My mother wondered if Mark was interested in buying her big house. When we heard about it, Mark and I did not hesitate. Yes, we were ready to buy her house because it is on the hill, and still in the desirable neighborhood for the twins, most importantly, it is right next to my parents' house.

As she wanted to buy a condominium unit, we told her about exchanging our condominium unit with her house. We knew a mortgage banker who could find the market value of each property and calculate the difference.

Her house with the yard would be more expensive than my condominium, but Mark could afford to pay the difference.

The exchange without any commission satisfied Mrs. Kitano. When Mark wrote a check of the substantial difference on her house, she was very happy. We signed and exchanged the property deeds.

Mark hired a group of professional movers to move Mrs. Kitano's furniture to the condominium and then moved our furniture to Mrs. Kitano's house. Mark was going to do the major overhaul on the house by hiring some professional builders. In the meantime, we four were to live with my parents.

Each room needed to be painted. The new carpet was installed throughout the house. The new kitchen cabinets and the utility units such as new dishwasher, new refrigerator, and new stove range were installed.

The house had four bedrooms: three upstairs, one downstairs with a two-car garage. The stone and granite facade outside was jet washed and waxed professionally, and a new roof and guarded gutters were installed. The entire house was remade and looked brand-new.

It took almost two months. Mark was so elated to live in his own house for the first time. He said he had never lived in a house after he left his parents' house.

My parents were thrilled to have us next door. The neighborhood is still considered a great neighborhood for the children to grow up. Mark and I finally felt as though we made a nest for our children.

Our terrace and the master bedroom faced the ocean from high above just as my mother's house, but the view was obstructed by a tree and its branches. Mrs. Kitano probably did not experience viewing the beautiful sunset. She probably took the view for granted and missed out the daily majestic Hawaiian sunset.

Anyhow, we hired a tree surgeon to take down the tree. I hated to do that, but I had to see the sunset that was my source of inspiration since I was a child.

After the tree was gone, the view of the horizon, ocean, and most importantly my perfect sunset looked just as a scene from a movie. I felt nostalgically happy. Moreover, my George Clooney was mesmerized by my sunset and decided to rehearse some kissing scenes with the actress named Mary in front of the toddlers.

After living in the condominium for several years, Mrs. Kitano decided to live in a retirement home for the elders near the beach. Mark insisted his retired father to buy her place and moved to Honolulu, but Mr. Nakaya was hesitant because he had never lived in anywhere else. He was born in the same house, had believed he would die there just as his parents and his wife, Kim, did.

Mark persistently persuaded him to buy the condominium so he could see his grandchildren whenever he wanted. Therefore, Mr. Nakaya sold his house and bought Mrs. Kitano's condominium without paying the realtor's commission.

My parents, especially my father, was ecstatic about Mr. Nakaya's move. He helped him settle in his condominium, took him around the neighborhood to show grocery stores, parks, good restaurants, and also drove him around the island so that he could familiarize with his new retirement place or paradise.

Now, his daily ritual is to walk on the beach in the morning and visit his grandkids who usually stay with their grandparents. He watches them eat breakfast and talk to them a lot, and when John gets ready, they are off to fishing or playing golf. They usually stop for breakfast at their favorite restaurant before their next activity.

Minoru Nakaya is very happy living in Honolulu, so is John Richardson who came back to live with his wife. They both often say, "We brothers are happily retired in paradise."

Mr. Nakaya, Mark, and my father often meet for lunch on the beach. They are planning to buy a Cessna soon by putting money together so that they could fly to outer islands to play golf or fishing. I just hope they would include me when it comes to flying the airplane. If they don't, I might call them "male chauvinistic pigs" aloud.

Nina's oldest child would be going to college. Alice and Troy Maddox seem to be getting along well, but no hint of marriage. Gregory and Troy's children want them to get married so they don't have to drive the long distance to each other's houses. Troy's boys came to live with Troy several years back because their mother married someone who did not care for the children.

According to Troy Maddox, Sue and Matilda Mendosa were imprisoned in different locations; Sue was sent to Big Island, and Mrs. Mendosa was imprisoned in Oahu. They do not seem to know each other's whereabouts because the police somehow blocked their communications. Sue tried to kill herself several times in her cell, but now the medication seems to be helping her combat her mental illness and depression.

Eric and Nancy got married and had a girl. They seem to be very happy together and still live in Seattle.

Mrs. Lisboa and the board members have been managing the organization without any problems since the reconstruction of the Clubhouse. Alice Thomas had helped Mrs. Lisboa with their legal issues including the IRS nonprofit status. According to Alice, all the members seem to be enjoying the new Clubhouse facility, such as using the exercise room, the tennis court, and the playground. The Clubhouse's rental business is thriving as well.

My grandmother finally moved into Grandpa Okuma's condominium. According to Grandpa, they both stroll along the beach path early in the morning to be young again. They reminisce about their past and talk up a storm as they used to do; they never forget to practice music together after dinner. He said the perfect sunset visits them once a day without failing. My grandmother no longer works at the restaurant; her niece and her husband bought the restaurant from her. I call them often on the phone; so does my mother. My mother sends pictures of Nichole and Steven periodically. Grandpa Okuma thinks the twins look handsome just like him with their cowlicks.

By the way, Nichole's middle name is Keiko, and Steven's middle name is Taro. My father said we finally completed the two countries' textbook names in our family. I smiled, but my mother pretended she did not know what he was talking about. Mark had no clue.

When we celebrated my children's fifth-year birthdays at my parents' house, my mother had Nichole play piano first and Steven next. I was flabbergasted by their talented performances. I thought I saw Grandpa Okuma and Grandma Itoh in them. My eyes were filled with tears when I thought about my grandparents' forever love.

My mother has been giving piano lessons since they were three. She thinks both are definitely gifted. My father told my mother, when Steven and Nichole get older, he would give them flying lessons just to see if they have his genes. Mr. Nakaya and Mark shook their heads with a smile.

Whenever I look at my twins, I become somewhat philosophical. I feel as though my obligation to my ancestors was completed by bearing the twins, just as completing a life cycle of the human species. I realized all living things must be perpetuated by repeating the life cycles. Nevertheless, unlike other species, a human life cycle always comes with the history or the storybook of their ancestors.

For my children's storybook, I would tell them all about my side of ancestors and how musically gifted and decent people they all were. Mark would tell them his side of ancestors as well so that they can fill every page of the storybook without leaving any blank.

I would also tell my children their musical gifts are from their ancestors' forever love. Because of their forever love, their grandmother was born, their mother was born, and then they were born. Therefore, I want them to understand life in general.

The half of my storybook was blank for a long time until the family secrets were unveiled. I believe, however, my children's storybook will be filled with many happy and decent episodes of their ancestors without any family secrets.

Milton Keynes UK
Ingram Content Group UK Ltd.
UKHW021828190124
436347UK00011B/754